Accolades for
America's greatest hero
Mack Bolan

"Very, very action-oriented.... Highly successful, today's hottest books for men."
—*The New York Times*

"Anyone who stands against the civilized forces of truth and justice will sooner or later have to face the piercing blue eyes and cold Beretta steel of Mack Bolan, the lean, mean nightstalker, civilization's avenging angel."
—*San Francisco Examiner*

"Mack Bolan is a star. The Executioner is a beacon of hope for people with a sense of American justice."
—*Las Vegas Review Journal*

"In the beginning there was the Executioner—a publishing phenomenon. Mack Bolan remains a spiritual godfather to those who have followed."
—*San Jose Mercury News*

PARTY LINE

Mack Bolan had heard the rumors, too. Peace was breaking out all over the world. And whoever believed that was a fool. Sure, a few walls had come tumbling down, but others were being built overnight. The reason was simple, Bolan knew. Man's base instincts remained unchanged. So did his dreams. The drug trade meant money and power, and you could never have too much—in the U.S. or the U.S.S.R.

The Executioner's Everlasting War was raging on.

"Mack Bolan stabs right through the heart of the frustration and hopelessness the average person feels about crime running rampant in the streets."
—*Dallas Times Herald*

DON PENDLETON's

MACK BOLAN®

COUNTERBLOW

A GOLD EAGLE BOOK FROM
WORLDWIDE®

TORONTO • NEW YORK • LONDON • PARIS
AMSTERDAM • STOCKHOLM • HAMBURG
ATHENS • MILAN • TOKYO • SYDNEY

First edition August 1991

ISBN 0-373-61424-1

Special thanks and acknowledgment to
Charlie McDade for his contribution to this work.

COUNTERBLOW

When you are occupying a position which the enemy threatens to surround, collect all your force immediately, and menace *him* with an offensive movement.

—Napoleon 1: *Maxims of War,* 1831

The enemy is all around, threatening to devour innocent lives. The message, delivered by my opening guns so many lifetimes ago, is clear. The enemy knows precisely what he's facing.

—Mack Bolan

CHAPTER ONE

The van wobbled from side to side as it struggled up the narrow, rutted Mexican road. Down below, and behind it, the Pacific Ocean started to shrink, as if it were evaporating. By the time the van reached the top of mountain, the huge waves looked like ripples. The driver, wiping sweat from his forehead with a dirty rag, cursed as the van lurched, then listed dangerously. The squeak of its ancient springs was drowned out now by the thump of a flat tire.

He braked, shut the engine off and stepped out of the vehicle. Walking to the rear, he looked down at the ocean for a long time. The sun hammered at him until sweat beaded on his neck and soaked his collar.

This was the kind of work he hated, in a country he didn't understand at all. Finally, realizing he couldn't postpone it any longer, Johnny Rivera walked back past the van and up toward the crown of the ridge. Changing a flat on the old van was iffy in the best of circumstances. There was no way in hell he would even try, sitting on the side of a mountain, unless he could find a flat spot big enough to accommodate the battered old crate.

He still had three hundred yards to go to reach the top, but even there it was too steep to trust the cumbersome jack. As he stepped over the line, a hot wind ripped at his clothes. The flapping of his sleeves made him nervous. The thought of changing a tire up here made him nervous. Hell, lately everything made him nervous.

On the far side of the mountain, on the descent, he spotted a slight leveling-off about five hundred yards below him. He wasn't sure whether it would work, but he couldn't risk pushing the van too far on the crumbling tire. If he screwed up the wheel, it was over. Somebody—he didn't know who— would come looking for him, and he would surely end up with his ass in a sling or, more accurately, his head on a stake. He wasn't sure who he was working for, and he didn't really want to know. That was the best way to stay alive.

Rivera was conscious suddenly of the weight on his hip. He wondered if that meant he was going to need the gun. He drew the pistol from its holster and flicked off the safety. Try as he might, he couldn't shake the feeling that he was being watched. Christ, his nerves were shot. Way the hell up here, who could sneak up on him, anyway? He could see all the way back to the Pacific on the ocean side, and about three miles down and across the valley on the interior side.

He put the pistol back in its holster, then walked back to the van. Kicking it once, he made a dent just behind the driver's door, then climbed in. Cursing, he turned the engine on and slowly edged the vehicle toward the ridge line. When he reached the top, he backed off the gas and let the groaning van coast the rest of the way.

At the flat spot he braked hard, and the van stopped. He shut the engine down and set the emergency brake before climbing out again. Walking to the rear of the vehicle, he fished in his pants pocket for the padlock key. When he got the door open, he cursed. The spare was buried under a dozen crates. He'd have to unload most of the damn rust bucket to get the jack and the spare tire out.

Rivera wrestled the heavy crates to the edge of the van, then levered them out. When he uncovered the spare enough to remove it, he sat on the rear bumper and wiped his face again. The sweat was burning his eyes.

With the spare tire free, he tugged the jack loose and removed the folding crank, then lay on the hard-baked dirt at the edge of the road. Sliding the jack in as far as he could, he positioned the crank, got it to click home and started turning.

The jack kept wiggling until it was flush against the van's frame. It was rough going, trying to lift the van and its remaining cargo. He wished to hell he knew what was in the crates, but at this point it didn't matter. Knowing wouldn't make the damn vehicle any lighter.

As he cranked, he could see the tire beginning to resume its normal shape. But every crank hurt his arms. His fingers were getting cramped, and he started to curse Tony with every half turn. Finally the van was high enough for him to get the bad tire off. He loosened the lugs and spun the tire with the T-shaped wrench. When the last nut came free, the tire tilted, and he got to his knees to pull it off.

His shirt was caked with mud now, where the sweat had mixed with the baked clay. He rubbed his fingers through the doughy paste, then scraped the clay off with the edge of the fender. Leaning into the front of the van, he grabbed a thermos containing Scotch whiskey and water. He shook it twice, but the ice had long since melted. The highball tasted bitter going down, but at least it was wet.

After he finished half the thermos, he walked back to the rear of the van. Squatting, he felt a cramp at the back of his thighs. He straightened again and walked away from the vehicle, trying to work the cramp out.

Rivera looked at his watch and shook his head. He was already more than two hours late. Tony was going to be pissed, but it couldn't be helped. If the man didn't like it, he could get better equipment.

The damn van looked as if it had been through a war.

Glancing at his watch again, he walked back to the van. This time, instead of squatting, he got down on his knees to relax his legs. Then he muscled the spare into place, strained to lift the heavy wheel, caught it on the bolts and rammed it home.

He heard the noise as he tightened the last lug. At first he thought it was a bug circling his sweaty back. But as he finished with the wrench, he realized the noise was much more distant than that, and made by something much larger than a bug.

Rivera straightened and walked to the front of the van. The noise came from somewhere in the valley. Squinting against the bright sun, he traced the road all the way to the point where it disappeared into the trees, nearly two miles away.

The road was empty.

But the noise got louder. He watched for several minutes but saw nothing out of the ordinary. The sound rose and fell, an angry, snarling buzz, like a distant power tool. It seemed to be coming closer, but he couldn't be sure.

Rivera shrugged and went back to the van. He tossed the tools inside, then started on the stack of crates. When he had most of the crates back in, he noticed the sound was getting progressively louder. He jumped down to the roadway and pulled the pistol out of its holster. Moving to the cab, he reached under the seat for the MAC-10, snared it by its sling and tugged it out.

He checked the road again and saw three small dust clouds, which plumed out behind three fast-moving vehicles. They were small, and it took him a moment to realize they were ATVs.

Trouble was on its way, and he didn't know what to do. He couldn't leave the rest of the crates, but he'd never be able to outrun the ATVs. Not on this terrain, where they had the edge in maneuverability. Even if they were slower than the van, and he wasn't sure they were, they could cut corners.

Rivera sprinted back to the crates and tipped over a pair of them. He hoisted one on top of the other, then tilted a second pair.

The ATVs were less than a mile away now, and they were charging straight up the side of the mountain toward him. They seemed to know exactly what they wanted. That could only mean they knew he was coming. But how?

The more he thought about it, the more confused he got. It occurred to him that the ATVs had probably been waiting for him below, and when he hadn't shown, they'd started looking for him.

Who the hell were these guys? he wondered. They were close enough for him to see the drivers now, but that didn't help. They weren't wearing uniforms, so it was unlikely they were *federales*. Unless they were moonlighting. But then that wasn't outside the realm of possibility. Mexico was famous for its unpredictability.

A quarter mile away the ATVs fanned out. The drivers worked well together, and Rivera realized they were communicating with one another. All three wore helmets with tinted visors. He couldn't see their faces, but he couldn't afford to waste any more time.

Rivera opened up with the MAC-10. He nailed a rear tire on one of the ATVs, but it was too late. They were close enough to return fire, even on the move. Without thinking, he threw up his hands.

The driver of the middle ATV raised a bullhorn to his face and shouted, "Drop your weapon!"

Rivera waved the MAC-10, let it dangle from one finger, then tossed it out in front of the crates. Next, waving a hand to indicate he wasn't through, he lifted the pistol at his hip, tossed it out and held both hands over his head.

Two of the ATVs snarled, kicking up clods of dirt, then sped toward him, braking on either side of his pathetic barricade. The drivers dismounted and stepped toward him with drawn weapons. The taller of the two reached into his pocket, pulled out a small leather case and flipped it open. "DEA, Rivera. And your ass is ours."

CHAPTER TWO

Viktor Sharkov stood at the window and looked down into the teeming street. Damn, he thought, how I hate these malarial backwaters. The streets were full of brown people in exotic garb, and it made him miss Moscow. Not that he would ever see it again, but that was a choice he'd made. Besides, there was still Berlin and Paris, maybe even London, if he played his cards right.

There was nothing to stop him, really, if he was careful, and Viktor Sharkov was nothing if not careful.

He was a throwback in that respect. Nothing was wasted. Everything was remembered. They had drilled that into him for years under Andropov. But that was in the old days when the KGB had meant something. That was in the days when the organization was feared. Now it was a joke. The KGB was no better than a nursery school these days.

Glasnost. Perestroika. That was what they called it. The Soviet Union was nothing now. He should know. He had been there in the old days when the mere mention of the KGB could cause heart attacks. The next thing on the reformers' agenda would be guided tours of Lubyanka Prison. Maybe Disneyland could run the show. Charge a few rubles and bail out the Soviet economy. The British did it with their Tower of London. The Americans did it with Alcatraz. Why not, indeed?

Sharkov let the curtain fall, shutting out the sight of Peshawar, but not the sound. Or the smell. It was no better than Kabul, really. The Third World cities all pretended to be something they couldn't be for a hundred years—civilized. How could any city clog its arteries with beggars and pushcarts and call itself modern?

There had been a setback, so he would try again. He wasn't infallible, just determined. They were looking for him. He knew they were. And he didn't blame them. Had the shoe been on the other foot he, too, would be looking. They were even right. No organization could survive if it permitted a member to walk out unopposed. He knew too much, and they knew what he knew. They always did.

What he knew involved them, and they didn't want to be involved. It was some kind of Olympian complex. Maybe it was how they lived with themselves. Power was often its own justification. And its own reward. But not for him, not anymore. He wanted his rewards bankable, preferably Swiss bankable. And that was why he'd left.

They probably knew that, too, because, after all, he'd been one of them. Surely they must have had the same urges. Perhaps that was why they wanted him so badly—because he'd had the courage to do what they could only dream of doing. He'd been smart enough to plan it, and brave enough to try. And they wanted to bring him down to justify their own cowardice.

Only nobody was really looking at themselves. They were seeing their own reflections in funhouse mirrors, and they didn't like what they saw. So they looked at him, pointed the finger and everything was set right again. *If* they could catch him.

And he'd make damn sure they didn't.

The room was beginning to get hot. He thought at first the weather had changed, but then he realized he always felt this way when he thought about the possibility of failure. It was a stifling thought, one calculated to make his hair stand on end, his breathing turn shallow, his heart beat a little bit faster.

But he was ready for the challenge. So what if he'd had a setback. That wasn't uncommon. You had to try something, after all, to become a failure.

Sharkov kept watching the window, as if he expected someone to step through it. It was, he knew, because the world out there was alien territory for the moment. In the past, secure in his position, if not satisfied with it, he had always known that he was in charge of things. He had been the hunter.

Now he was the prey.

He knew all the tricks. A car on the corner, its engine suddenly racing as he stepped off the curb, was a prelude to murder. A strange envelope, no return address, posted from some exotic corner of the world, might blow him to pieces when he opened it.

Even his food might kill him. If he wasn't careful, there were a hundred ways to bring him down. But he *was* careful, and he'd remain so. Too much was at stake. Too many wheels were already turning, and he couldn't stop one of them without destroying them all. They were interconnected in one giant, complex machine whose sole purpose was to make him wealthy.

And then he heard the knock he'd been waiting for. Finally. So clearly had he imagined it that he thought he could even recognize the knuckles on the flimsy wood.

Still, he couldn't be too careful. Not now. He took the Makarov out of his pocket and held it by his thigh as he walked to the door. The rapping sounded again, the short, complex pattern that only four men knew, and he quickened his step. He looked through the peephole for a second, relaxed not at all when he recognized Chebrikov, then undid the latch.

Stepping away from the door, he said, "Come in."

The knob rattled softly, and Chebrikov ducked inside as soon as he could fit between door and frame. He replaced the latch and looked at Sharkov.

"Well?" the KGB rogue asked impatiently.

"Not good."

"Why not? What happened?"

"They got him alive."

"He doesn't know anything."

"He knows enough."

"Then take care of it."

"Not so easily done."

Sharkov waved a hand in exasperation, then walked to the window. Looking down without pulling the curtain aside, he asked, "And why is that?"

"Because you no longer have the apparatus behind you. You keep forgetting that."

"Apparatus? That was nothing. It was only men. We have money. What else does it take to buy men?"

"You know it's not that easy."

"But I know no such thing. You're being paid, Vasily, paid very well. I think you should get used to this new way of doing things."

"The Americans have him."

"Of course they do. You don't think the Mexicans have any use for him, do you? It's the Americans, after all, who view us as a problem. They're the market we wish to tap. But they're also the ones who have the most to lose if we succeed."

"I wish I saw everything as simply as you do, Viktor. It all sounds so easy when you put it that way. But it's not that easy. Not really."

"Then find a way to make it that easy, Vasily."

Chebrikov sat down heavily. He tapped one foot on the gritty floor. He found the texture of the sand under his sole somehow interesting and began to scrape across it rhythmically.

The sound annoyed Sharkov, but he said nothing. One had to be flexible, to learn to tolerate the petty annoyances of one's underlings. In that way, at least, things were as they had always been.

He turned from the window and watched Chebrikov without speaking. The scrutiny made the younger man nervous, but he tried not to show it. Sharkov had always made him nervous. Now, with so much more riding on every move and therefore on every possible mistake, he knew he had to be extremely careful. Sharkov tried to pretend that he was comfortable, but Chebrikov knew better. Neither of them was comfortable. Chebrikov half believed he would never be comfortable again, no matter how successful their little experiment in capitalism might prove.

"What are you thinking, Vasily?" Sharkov asked, dropping into a chair opposite his associate.

"I was just wondering how the DEA knew the courier was coming. That's all."

"A very interesting question. What do you think the answer is?"

"It seems to me there's only one answer."

"And what might that be?"

"Somewhere along the lines of communication there's a breach in security."

"Any idea who that might be?"

"None."

"Find out."

"I don't know if I can."

"Of course you can. You're an intelligence officer, after all. Use your skills. They were provided to you at great expense by our beloved country. The least you can do is see to it that someone receives the benefit of that training. And who better than you and me, eh?" Sharkov laughed, but the sound was brittle, almost hollow in the small room.

"And how do you propose I do that?"

"Simple. You go to Los Angeles. That's where the leak must be. Find it and seal it. Whatever it takes."

"And if I can't find it?"

"You must, Vasily. Everything depends on it. Everything."

Chebrikov didn't want an exhaustive inventory. He knew that at the very least his freedom would be on the line, and possibly his very life. He was prepared to part with neither.

"I'll need help, Viktor. I can't do this by myself."

"Get what you need. Men, materials, whatever. Just do it."

"And where will you be while I'm chasing my tail?"

"I have to go back to Kabul. I'm leaving in the morning."

"Is that wise?"

"It's necessary. That's the only question that matters. I've asked myself several times whether it's necessary, and it is."

"It's not safe, Viktor. You know that."

"Life isn't safe, Vasily. And, besides, Kabul is no more dangerous for me now than Kiev or Minsk. Probably safer."

"I hope you know what you're doing."

"We'll see, Vasily, won't we?"

Chebrikov stared at the window. There was nothing to say. He nodded vaguely. "Yes, I suppose we will."

CHAPTER THREE

Johnny Rivera fidgeted as he sat at the long gray table. His hands were like balls of worms, his fingers twisting and turning on the wood. One foot tapped the floor, less in time to some internal rhythm than in response to unpredictable nervous tremors.

He looked at a large mirror that took up almost an entire wall. He was no fool. He assumed he was staring at one of those trick mirrors. Somebody was watching him. That was how they did it. He'd seen it in a hundred movies.

The room itself had only the table and four folding metal chairs for furniture. It was brightly lit, almost too brightly. The glare hurt his eyes, and he kept blinking. He wanted to look around the room, but there was nothing to look at, nothing to take his mind off things. And that was on purpose, too. They didn't want him to have anything to occupy his attention. They would come in soon and start asking him questions. And that was all they wanted him to think about—that and what would happen to him if he refused.

Behind the glass, Dalton Hatch fidgeted with his tie. He turned to the big man standing beside him. "That's him. That's Johnny boy."

"What have you got on him?"

"Oh, the usual. In and out of detention homes when he was a kid. Street gangs from the time he was thirteen. A rap sheet as long as my right arm. Nothing ever stuck, though. It rarely does."

The big man walked closer to the glass. "How long's he been in there?"

"Two days. You know the story, right? Brognola filled you in?"

"Refresh my memory if you don't mind."

"Picked him up in Baja. Driving a decrepit old van. Son of a bitch had a flat. Can you believe it? We waited five hours for the bastard. Finally had to go looking for him. The van was full of weapons—sixteen crates of automatic rifles plus ammo. And the pièce de résistance—five kilos of grade A heroin. Turkish stuff."

"How did you get onto him in the first place?"

"The usual. Street talk, that sort of thing. Plus we'd been watching his gang for about a year. The Mambo Mothers, no less. Cute."

"You followed him everywhere?"

"Sure."

"Come on, Hatch. You don't expect me to believe that, do you?"

"Look, Belasko," Hatch said, using Mack Bolan's current cover name. "I can't tell you any more than that. We have to protect our sources. You can understand that, can't you?"

"Sure. Why didn't you just say that?"

"What difference does it make?"

"Maybe none."

"There, see? What are you bitching about, then?"

Bolan didn't answer. The question was obviously rhetorical.

"You want to go inside and ask a few questions?" the DEA man asked.

"I'll just watch."

"Suit yourself."

Hatch left the observation room to step out into the narrow hallway. A moment later he was back with two men in tow. Bolan watched Hatch carefully. There was something about the guy he didn't like. DEA types ranged from street smart to corporate climber. Hatch, unless Bolan missed his guess, was one of the latter. He was a player, adept at the bureaucratic games that made law enforcement tougher than it had to be. Turf rats, some people called them, guys who cared more about credits, building a résumé, than their alleged purpose. Their allegiance was to their agency rather than the law.

That was Hatch. In spades.

Bolan looked at the two newcomers. In the dim room everybody looked like everybody else. He wondered if that was by design, or just an accident of the lighting.

Hatch introduced him to the two men. One of them, a big kid named Brian Mahoney, was almost as tall as Bolan. He had thick wrists and hands that would do nicely as Ping-Pong paddles. The kid had a tangle of red hair, and a liberal sprinkling of freckles was visible above a ginger beard that needed a trim. He wore biker's denim and a studded jacket, with a bandanna tied around one knee and another knotted around his forehead.

The other, a small terrier of a man, was called Tony Salvato. He looked like every Italian mother's nightmare, the kind of guy she would rather die than see come to the door for her daughter. In the cutoff sweatshirt he looked almost like a barrel with arms. Two tattoos, one on either forearm, sported writhing snakes, each featuring a flicking tongue. His dark hair was a mass of tight curls, and his mustache was a straight line over a thin-lipped mouth.

Both men were a stark contrast to the *GQ* style of Dalton Hatch, whose own thinning, limp blond hair was close-cropped on the sides and modishly long on top. Hatch looked out of place alongside his two agents—like an accountant at a longshoremen's convention.

"You here for the show?" Mahoney asked Bolan when the introductions were finished.

"Sort of."

Mahoney nodded. "Sorry. I should save my questions for the scuzzball."

"Right," Bolan agreed. But he smiled.

"All right, guys, let's get it in gear," Hatch said. He walked out into the hall, and the other two followed him. The door closed, and Bolan was alone in the room. A moment later Hatch materialized in the fishbowl. He waved in Mahoney and Salvato, then pulled the door shut, tugging the knob once to make sure the latch clicked.

Bolan walked over to the control panel and turned off the sound. He wanted to watch for a minute. Words could be misleading. Sometimes it was more useful to watch. Besides, the interrogation would be taped and he could always listen to a playback. Watch it, too, for that matter. It was, after all, the age of video.

He studied Rivera. The kid seemed less nervous now for some reason. Maybe because he was finally able to do something, to talk to somebody besides himself. Or maybe there was another reason. Bolan watched the preliminaries, then clicked the sound back on.

"Okay, Johnny," Hatch said, "you know the drill."

"Yeah, I know the drill, man. Why don't you save all this garbage? I don't know nothin'. I don't know nothin' and I ain't gonna tell you nothin' because I can't, all right? That it? Can I go now?"

"Not very cooperative, Johnny. We take points off, you know. You get enough points off, we throw you in the shark tank at the aquarium. In the middle of the night. You want that?"

Rivera waved a hand in disgust. "Man, don't try to give me bullshit like that. You think I'm a jerk? You think I believe that kind of crap?"

"Yeah, I think you're a jerk, Johnny. How'd you know? And you know why I think you're a jerk?"

"Why don't you tell me, man?"

Rivera kept looking at the mirror. Bolan wondered why. Maybe the kid was just distracted, but it seemed more than that. Almost as if he were worried about who might be behind the glass.

When Mahoney took over the questioning, he concentrated on the nitty-gritty details. The mechanics of the operation emerged in bits and pieces for Bolan, not from Rivera's answers, but from Mahoney's questions. The kid fielded the questions well, and Mahoney was good. But after an hour Rivera had told the DEA agent virtually nothing they couldn't have guessed for themselves.

Salvato seemed more like an observer than an interrogator. The men were wasting no time on games—good cop, bad cop—and the rest of it. Instead, they hammered away incessantly, but with little result.

After two hours Hatch stormed out. Bolan waited for him to come into the observation room, but he didn't. Fifteen minutes later Salvato took Rivera by the arm, handcuffed him and led him away.

Mahoney sat at the table for a few minutes, deep in thought. Then, as if suddenly inspired, he asked, "Belasko, you in there?"

Bolan was taken by surprise. He clicked on the audio. "Yeah, still here."

"Wait a minute. I'll be right over." Mahoney got up, turned off the lights and closed the door. Two minutes later he stood in the observation room doorway. "You feel like a cup of coffee?"

"Why not?"

"There's a greasy spoon about fifteen miles from here. It's open all night, so we can get a bite, too, if you're hungry. The food's pretty good, and it's cheap."

Bolan nodded. He let Mahoney lead the way outside. It was a beautiful Southern California night. They were about a hundred miles southeast of Los Angeles. The house was isolated, nestled in a narrow valley. Bolan stood back and looked at the place thoughtfully.

"Doesn't look like much, does it?" Mahoney said.

"Nope. It sure doesn't."

"It's secure, though, if that's what you're wondering. The night crew features four of the baddest mothers on the planet. Guys who've been out in the woods so long they think like the guys we're trying to bust."

"What do you make of Rivera?"

"Small-time. Not too bright. A mule, if you ask me. I don't think he knows much about anything."

"I'm not so sure."

Mahoney seemed interested. "Why's that?"

"I'm not sure. Just something about the way he acted in there, like maybe he'd slip and say the wrong thing. I don't think he minded that part, but he kept looking at the mirror. As if he were worried about who might be on the other side."

"That's pretty normal, really. These guys are certified paranoids. The way they live, they don't trust anyone. Can't afford to."

"Even at Rivera's level? I mean, you're not talking about a Colombian drug lord here, just a poor, dumb grunt."

"I don't know," Mahoney said. "Maybe you're onto something. Let me think about it. We'll talk it over at the diner."

CHAPTER FOUR

Maxim Goncharov punched the heavy bag as hard as he could. The inertia of the bag seemed to infuriate him. The harder he punched, the more inert it seemed to be. He threw himself into a quick flurry, putting his weight behind every punch, and the bag wavered a little on its chain. But not much.

Peter Grebnov watched him quietly, standing in the doorway to the gym. Goncharov didn't realize he was there, and that was the way Grebnov wanted it. There were rumors about Goncharov, and he'd heard them from too many sources to discount them.

Goncharov was one of the best, and he'd taken top grades every step of the way. On the surface he seemed ideal, the perfect Soviet man. Bright, an excellent physical specimen, and unbearably honest, almost to the point of tactlessness. So what was wrong?

Grebnov meant to find out, and he had the perfect excuse. He watched another flurry, this time budging the bag half a meter off dead center. It swung away and seemed to hang as Goncharov bore in, landing punch after punch, grunting with every blow, until the gym seemed full of the sound of leather on leather and the straining of the solitary man in single combat with immovable reality.

When the flurry was over, Goncharov seemed to sag a little. He wiped at his brow with the back of one glove, then pushed his hair up and away with the tip of the other.

"Bravo!" Grebnov shouted.

Goncharov shook his head slightly and smiled. "It wasn't that good, Peter."

"I know. But it was spirited. I see you're regaining your energy and health."

"Slowly. But I'm a patient man."

"Good. The one thing you'll need is patience."

"Need? For what?"

"Your leave is about to expire."

"Not for a month yet."

"That was yesterday."

"And today?"

"And today I have a very ticklish affair to discuss. Even old gymnasiums have ears, my friend. Let's find someplace we can talk."

"Let me shower. I'll be with you in ten minutes."

"Make it five, Maxim."

Goncharov stared at the older man for a long moment, then nodded. "Very well."

Grebnov waited for him, amusing himself by taking a few swipes at the heavy bag. His wrists were frail, and he was no match for the weight. He teased the speed bag for a moment, remembering when he was capable of serious work with the leather. But those days were behind him. Now he was confined to memory, and the inevitable regret that life was ebbing away. Every day he felt a little older. Every day, too, everyone else seemed just a little younger than he, and a little more graceful, a little more energetic.

It was the conceit of an old man, he knew. But it was no less painful for being only a partial truth.

He envied Goncharov his youth. For that matter, he envied the youth of anyone who had enough of it to squander a little without ill effect, which was almost everyone he knew except for those who were even older than he. But their numbers were dwindling, falling like birch leaves ahead of winter winds.

He must have looked solemn, because Goncharov startled him by asking, ''Is it that serious, Peter?''

''What? Oh, no, I was just thinking.''

''Thinking can be bad for your health.''

''Even when you're thinking about your health?''

''Especially then, Peter. Where shall we go?''

''My dacha, if you have no objection.''

''Why should I? It's my favorite place in the world.''

"I know. And I had hoped one day to will it to you, since I have no children of my own. But these days who knows what one will have to leave behind. Things are changing so fast."

"And you're not sure it's for the better."

"No, I'm not sure. But I'm wise enough—at my age that's unavoidable—to know something had to change. I just don't know how much is enough."

"Neither does the president."

"You're probably right. But I give him credit. Why let the tiger eat you if you can climb on and ride him, eh?"

"Is that what he's doing?"

"I certainly hope so. Or else the tiger will eat all of us, Maxim. And spit out the bones."

"Something *is* bothering you."

Grebnov nodded, then held a finger to his lips. He wasn't worried about being overheard, but he wanted to think for a bit before broaching his subject. "Let's go to my car."

Goncharov nodded. "As you wish."

They walked in silence out through the gymnasium doors and past the registration office. Goncharov nodded to the young woman behind the glass window, and she waved a hand without really looking at him. She was new and probably had no idea who he was. That was all right. There was a certain comfort in anonymity. It was one of the things that had first attracted him to his present career.

Outside, the weather was turning sour. It was only late October, but the rising wind carried the chill of Siberia. In another month Moscow, too, would feel and look like the vast tundra to the northeast.

Grebnov led the way to a gleaming new Volvo and opened the passenger door for his protégé. "You like it?" he asked as Goncharov stopped long enough to run his fingertips over the smooth metal of the rear fender.

"Very much."

"We can learn a few things from the West, yes?"

"Not this. The man who conceived the ZIL will never be able to imagine something like this, even if one runs him down."

"We should live so long."

Goncharov patted the old man on the arm and slipped into the seat. Grebnov closed the door for him, then passed in front of the car and opened his own door as Goncharov leaned over to release the latch. When Grebnov was seated, he started the engine, let it purr for a few moments, then shifted into gear.

"Automatic," Goncharov observed. "You're being rather good to yourself in your old age."

"I woke up one morning and realized I didn't have much time. I thought I might as well."

"What is it you want to talk about?"

"Not now, Maxim. Just relax and enjoy the ride."

Grebnov backed out of his parking space and plunged into the heavy traffic. It was beginning to get dark, so he clicked on the headlights as they moved toward the northern edge of the city. "Moscow," he said, "such a beautiful city. If you can forget about her history, you could almost fall in love with her."

"I already have."

"Don't be blinded by that love, Maxim. These are perilous times. And Moscow is like any other woman. She can turn her back on you without warning."

Grebnov lapsed into silence again, and this time Goncharov sensed that it would last for the rest of the trip. The city fell away, the traffic thinned, and soon they were pulling into the driveway of Grebnov's dacha.

Modest by upper-echelon Party standards, Grebnov's dacha was still impressive, largely thanks to its idyllic, tranquil setting. Goncharov had always felt at peace here. But he sensed the dacha was doomed. Not so much the building, but the way of life it represented. Marx and Party privilege were under siege these days. The people, particularly, aimed their burgeoning democratic spleen at such symbols of the old order. Communism had become a dirty word in the Soviet Union.

When they got out of the car, Grebnov didn't open the house immediately. Instead, he led the way through the winding hedgerow into the rose garden, which had noticeably gone to seed.

"The garden looks somewhat forlorn, doesn't it, Maxim?" the old man said, breaking the silence.

"Yes, it does," Goncharov replied.

"I always tell myself it's just the season. Winter is so close now, and the roses will be back next year. But I don't know whether I believe it. Sonya kept such good care of the flowers."

"She's been dead a long time, Peter."

Grebnov nodded as he thought about his dead wife for a painful moment. When he finally spoke, he changed the subject. "You know, in a way, this garden is a good symbol for what's happening all over the globe. The gardener is away and the weeds are taking over."

"What's on your mind, Peter? You didn't haul me all the way out here to talk about horticulture."

"Not 'what,' Maxim. 'Who' is on my mind."

"Then, who?"

"You worked with Viktor Sharkov once, didn't you?"

"Yes, in London many years ago. He was the resident in charge of clandestine activities."

"When was the last time you saw him?"

"Oh, a dozen years ago, maybe even longer. In Hanoi, I think."

"Have you kept up with his career?"

"Not really."

"He was in Kabul, you know. For a long time."

"No, I didn't know. It must not have been when I was there, or I'd have known about it. But what's the point? What are you leading up to?"

"You were always impatient, Maxim. You never let me lead up to anything. It was always 'Now, Peter!' 'Spit it out, Peter.' It's a wonder you've managed to live as long as you have."

"You'll get to the point eventually, won't you?"

Grebnov smiled. "All right. I see I can't avoid it any longer. The point is that Viktor has gone off the deep end."

"That doesn't surprise me."

"Nor me."

"But . . . ?"

"But someone has to do something about it."

"Me, I suppose?"

"Yes, Maxim, you. And no one must know. Only you and I, and two other men, neither of whom you know, and with whom you will, in any case, have no contact."

"What do you want me to do?"

"Before I tell you that I want you to know that I don't ask this of you lightly. It's too dangerous for me to be casual. I don't know where he is, or what he's up to. But I have an idea, and he has to be stopped. Whatever it takes."

"I understand."

"Do you?"

Goncharov nodded.

"Good. Let's go inside. I have a great deal to tell you."

CHAPTER FIVE

"You want to see what it's really like out there, Belasko?" Mahoney asked.

"I know what it's like."

"You want a refresher?"

"What's on your mind?"

"That punk we saw earlier? He's nothing. A damn cog in a machine, that's all. But the thing of it is, we're looking at a new machine. This stuff is Turkish. That isn't new. But there's something happening out there that we don't know about."

"And you have a lead, is that it? You think you've got a line on this new source?"

"Not on the source, no. But on this end of the supply chain. There's a load coming in tonight supposedly. We've got two guys making the buy. I'm one of them. And you met Tony Salvato. He's the other."

Bolan thought about it for a while. He sipped his coffee and looked out of the diner's greasy window. The upsurge in heroin on the West Coast was ringing alarm bells all over Washington. It wasn't getting much press because of the high profile cocaine and crack currently enjoyed. But it was growing, and people who ought to know were getting worried. He was supposed to do something about it. The sooner the better.

He had his instructions from Hal Brognola, and they were as loose as usual. Find the pipeline and shut it down. Whatever it took. That was about as close to carte blanche as he ever got.

Mahoney hailed the waitress for another jelly doughnut and a second coffee. When he was finished placing his order, Bolan said, "Okay, I'll go. Maybe I'll learn something."

"You're not like the usual geeks they send out here," Mahoney commented with a lopsided grin.

When Bolan didn't say anything, he went on. "No, I mean it. Usually some geek comes out here, looks around, makes notes in a little book, then goes back east and writes a position paper or something. Most of the time it's just garbage, and that's okay, because garbage we can live with. But sometimes they get ideas, bad ideas. They pull some strings, push some buttons, and all of a sudden there's some policy implementation directive or some such bullshit, and then somebody gets killed."

Bolan smiled faintly. "They're not all bad."

"Not all, no, but the good ones don't last."

The Executioner shook his head. "I've been there, Mahoney. I know what you're saying. Just don't judge them all by the worst."

"Hey, the worst? I'd just like to see a good one so I can die happy." Mahoney swallowed the doughnut in three bites, licked the powdered sugar from his fingers and took a long sip of coffee. "Okay, let's go."

They took Mahoney's car, a souped-up Camaro, and the kid drove like Steve McQueen in *Bullitt*. He clicked on a tape player and filled the small car with music. "You like jazz? Or would you prefer some blues?"

"It's your car."

"That's what I hoped you'd say." He turned up the volume, and over the soaring alto of Charlie Parker, conversation became impossible.

That was fine with Bolan. He didn't really want to talk, anyway. He was still trying to figure out Johnny Rivera. There was a lot more to the guy than met the eye, and Bolan wanted to know what it was.

Out on the deserted highway Mahoney opened it up a little more. They were cruising at eighty, and the rumble of the big engine made the floorboards tremble. The DEA man turned up the music a little louder to compensate for the thunder, glancing at Bolan to make sure he didn't object.

When the tape ran out, Mahoney said, "We're going to coyote country. The damn border down here is like a sieve. A sieve without a screen. Hell, you could bring an elephant caravan full of grand pianos across here, and the chances are nobody'd even notice. A few pounds of high-grade heroin is nothing."

"You have any idea who the supplier is?"

"Nope. Just that it's nobody who's been around. See, all this shit has a signature. The packaging, for instance. Everybody has a different way of doing it. Or the process. Hell, when they run this stuff through the lab, they can tell you if the chemist's a Libra. But this new stuff is just that—new. We're dealing with a new player here. He's moving the stuff in large volume all of a sudden. Six months ago he wasn't on the scene, not even a bit player. Now he's Mr. Heroin. I can't figure it."

"Anything else change?"

"What do you mean?"

"I'm not sure. The mules, for instance, on your end. Anybody new?"

"By name, yeah. By type, no. Same sort of losers."

"Anything else going on?"

"Officially?"

"Not if unofficially is more interesting."

"It is, Belasko, it is. I'll tell you about it later."

Mahoney pulled the car off the road, then turned off the lights and let the engine idle. He opened the car door and got out. Bolan heard him tap the roof of the car as he walked to the rear. A moment later he was back. He dropped into the driver's seat again and closed the door.

"What was that all about?" Bolan asked.

"It's so damn dark out here in the desert that you can see headlights for miles in either direction. The road's empty. I just wanted to make sure. We have another three miles before we reach an old gas station that nobody uses much anymore. I don't know why the old geezer who runs it stays in business, let alone how. But it's a convenient drop."

"Unusual, isn't it? Usually the buyer takes no risk. He hands over some money and walks away with the buy. The dealer handles all the transportation."

"I told you there were some unusual things about this new pipe. That's one of them. It's almost like whoever it is is washing his hands of the stuff as soon as he can."

"You pick the station or the seller?"

"The seller." He jammed the car into gear and eased back onto the asphalt, leaving the headlights off as he crept along the road carefully.

When they got to the gas station, the whole place was dark. The concrete pad by the pumps was cracked and chunks were missing near the edges. The Camaro rumbled around to the rear of the building, and Mahoney killed the engine. "Here goes nothing."

"Where's Salvato?"

"He's bringing his own car. He should be here any minute." Mahoney checked his watch. "We still got fifteen minutes. You better get out of sight. Tony'll go bananas if he sees you. He doesn't like any wrinkles."

Bolan glanced at the building. "How about the roof of the garage?"

"Fine. Whatever. Just stay out of sight until the deal goes down."

"You have any backup?"

"You kidding? A Stealth bomber costs half a billion dollars. You think there's money in the budget for backup?" He laughed, but there was an edge of bitterness to it.

Bolan hauled himself onto a window ledge, then swung up to the roof. A moment later the sound of another car drifted across the desert floor.

"Sounds like Tony's car," Mahoney said. "See you later."

He drifted away from the building and leaned against the trunk of the Camaro. The second car also had its lights out, and judging by the sound of its engine, Bolan figured the car couldn't be more than a half mile away, if that.

It took three minutes for the vehicle to roll into the parking lot and come to a dead stop. The driver got out and, despite the darkness, Bolan immediately recognized the squat body and curly hair of Tony Salvato.

Mahoney said hello, then lapsed into silence. Salvato leaned against the car with him, but didn't say anything. The relationship between the two men seemed strained. It might have been the tension of the situation, but Bolan was curious. He made a mental note to ask Mahoney about it later.

Headlights sliced into the gloom from the south at the same time the sound of an engine rolled down the sloping desert floor toward them. Bolan had a good vantage point to watch the other vehicle approach. The driver was casual, not worrying about light or noise. Then a beat-up van appeared on the last hill and coasted toward the garage.

The driver pulled up and parked, then climbed out. He waited as Mahoney and Salvato walked toward him. "You got the money?" he asked.

"Let's see the goods," Mahoney said.

"Hey, what do I look like, some kind of crook?" He laughed, but no one joined him. "Okay, okay, time to rock and roll. He walked to the rear of the van, Salvato following him. The driver opened the rear door, and Salvato had to move away as it swung back. In a flash four men jumped out of the vehicle as the driver reached for a gun in his waistband.

All four men were armed with automatic weapons. Bolan yanked out his Beretta and shouted as Salvato started to turn to see what was happening.

Mahoney started forward as Bolan fired the first shot.

The Executioner nailed the driver, who squeezed his own trigger as he went down. His gun went off, and the slug caught Salvato in the back of the leg. The pudgy agent fell to the ground, which probably saved his life. A burst of automatic gunfire sailed harmlessly past his head and shoulder as he fell.

Mahoney opened up with his own weapon, but Bolan and the agent were heavily outgunned. The warrior fired again as Salvato tried to scramble toward Mahoney's car. The four hardguys sprayed fire indiscriminately. Mahoney dived behind Salvato's vehicle, and Bolan watched helplessly as one of the gunners walked a spray of lead across the ground, almost teasing Salvato before slicing the muzzle in a vicious arc. The agent's body jumped and bounced as the slugs ripped through him.

Bolan returned fire, but it was too late to save Salvato. The 9-mm slug slammed into the gunner's head, killing him instantly. The three remaining gunmen realized they were being fired on by a hidden party and they jostled one another as they dived behind the van. Bolan's suppressed Beretta spit again, but this time he missed. The slug pinged off the bumper, scattering sparks and fragments but doing no damage.

As long as the gunmen had the van for cover, he and Mahoney were trapped. If they worked it out, the bad guys could flush Mahoney and then come looking for him. Bolan couldn't let that happen.

He spotted the gas tank cap on the side of the van, and it gave him an idea. Reholstering the Beretta, he pulled out his Desert Eagle. The big Magnum felt cold in his hand, its weight comforting.

He fired three times, working his way across the bottom of the van. With any luck he'd punch a hole in the gas tank. The third shot did the trick. He could hear liquid gushing out.

Opening up with the Desert Eagle again, he managed to strike a few sparks with his first shot, but nothing happened. The warrior fired again with the same result. On the third try, though, he hit pay dirt.

The gas on the ground caught fire, and Bolan saw the flames leap toward the tank. One of the gunmen shouted, and two of them sprinted away from the van, angling out toward the road. The Executioner was ready.

He dropped the first guy with a single shot from the Beretta. The second man stopped in his tracks, then turned back toward the van and dived to the ground as the vehicle exploded.

A huge ball of flame mushroomed into the desert sky. The right rear door slammed into the prostrate gunner. A quick flurry of gunshots from the left told Bolan that Mahoney's man was in the open. He looked just as the DEA agent's final shot hit home. The gunner fell back as if he'd tripped over something, then lay still. In the bright orange glare Bolan could now see everything.

The warrior climbed off the roof, landing lightly on the balls of his feet. He walked toward Salvato and knelt. He felt for a pulse, but there was none, then looked up at Mahoney and shook his head.

CHAPTER SIX

Maxim Goncharov was nervous. He worshiped Peter Grebnov, but he couldn't help wondering whether the old man had given him something too big to handle. Grebnov always thought more highly of his abilities than he did. And Viktor Sharkov wasn't some maladjusted physicist champing at the bit. He was a seasoned professional, one of the KGB's most dangerous operatives.

And now Maxim was about to go into Afghanistan, a country the Red Army had failed miserably in. It had been dangerous enough then. Now it was all but impossible. The Soviet presence was gone, and the country was a chaotic nightmare.

Even so he had no choice. Grebnov hadn't exactly given him a direct order, but then the old man seldom gave anyone an order. He relied on the keen understanding of reality that he drilled into every one of his prized pupils. Goncharov was one of the elite, but only one. Should he refuse to go, Grebnov wouldn't force him, but the old man would never forgive him, either.

Grebnov was the closest thing he had to family. He couldn't turn his back on his mentor, not now, not when so much was at stake. So he had packed and flown to Peshawar in northern Pakistan, then moved on to the border.

The insertion would be simple, or so Grebnov had told him. He would meet a detachment of Afghan regulars, who would get him to Kabul. After that he was on his own.

He stood on the mountainside and watched the sun rise. It was already cold, and snow flurries had gusted around him for nearly an hour. The white stuff didn't stick, but it didn't have to. He understood what it meant. The snow was just a harbinger of things to come.

When the sun had fully risen, he shrugged into his pack and started for the border. Five kilometers. Not much. He'd walked much farther in his time, even if the terrain hadn't been quite so brutal, and the circumstances more comprehensible. Grebnov hadn't told him much about this mission, and he didn't like operating in the dark.

His clothing felt odd to him. Six months out of the field and he was already turning soft. He could feel the slackness in his legs as he half walked, half slid down the rocky mountainside. The ground seemed to shift under him by design. He knew he was reading too much into things, but it was an old habit. There were clues out there, waiting for the perceptive eye. But one had to be alert to read them.

A kilometer from the border he heard the whine of a helicopter climbing over one of the steep, rocky walls that riddled the border country. He had been here once before, for a year, and it was a sound he'd never forget.

The sound of the helicopter faded away, and then a dull roar rolled across the valley, as if someone had suddenly turned on a giant loudspeaker. Only it wasn't a recording; it was real. There was no doubt in his mind that the helicopter had just blown up. That could only mean one thing—mujahadeen.

Since the Soviet withdrawal, they had gotten bolder, and the Americans had continued to supply them with everything but toilet paper to wipe their asses. If they were in the area—and he was convinced they were—his life wouldn't be worth a mouthful of warm spit when they got their hands on him. Russians weren't too popular with Afghan dissidents.

He was about a half kilometer away now, and he was getting worried. He should have seen some sign of the Afghan government detachment. If they failed to show, he might as well sit on a rock and cut his own throat. Going ahead would be worse than suicide.

He mounted a low rise and shaded his eyes with a hand. The orange light reflecting off the barren terrain hurt his eyes and made it all but impossible to see anything clearly. He caught a glimpse of something off to the left, nearly two kilometers across the border. If it was the detachment, he was way off course. He broke into a slow trot, trying to keep his balance by skating over the loose scree and angling toward the apparent motion.

A faint droning sound drifted to him on the cold wind as the ground leveled off and he was about to pick up his pace. He hadn't worked this hard since his training days at the school outside Samarkand. It almost felt good to be testing himself again.

The droning grew louder, and he stopped again to take a look. Fishing field glasses out of his pack, he pulled them from their case and scanned the rolling floor of the valley. Twirling the focus, he could gradually see a motorized column. A small convoy, consisting of two APCs, two battle tanks and a truckload of infantrymen, was wending its way toward him, keeping to the center of the valley to deprive the mujahadeen of any high ground suitable for an ambush. If the rebels wanted to confront the column, they'd have to expose themselves to counterattack to do it. Unless they had American missiles. Stingers and Redeyes were all over Afghanistan, and they were deadly.

The tanks had their guns ready, and a helmeted man sat behind a machine gun in the turret of each. Goncharov changed direction, heading for a spot where he could intersect with the convoy's route. It would save time, and it shortened the remaining hike considerably.

He was about to put the glasses back in their case when something else caught his attention. Behind the convoy, approaching at a sharp angle, a small cloud of dust balled up and seemed to bounce over the rocky ground like a heavy balloon.

Adjusting the glasses, he resolved the fuzzy cloud into a single horseman, but that didn't make sense. No horse could throw up that much dust. The tank radar was unreliable, and Goncharov knew that cavalry attacks, adapted by the mujahadeen from tactics hundreds of years old, had worked very well, almost neutralizing the technological advantage in some situations.

Then he realized what was happening. The lead horseman was dragging something behind his mount, deliberately kicking up a cloud. Somewhere behind him, others, maybe a dozen, maybe even two dozen, concealed themselves in the choking dust. Goncharov had seen the tactic before. It only worked once, because once it happened to your unit, you never forgot it, but there had been such a massive turnover in the ranks that the mujahadeen had gotten a lot of mileage out of a simple ploy.

The trailing horsemen were probably armed to the teeth, possibly even with missiles, but certainly with automatic rifles and grenades. They wouldn't take on the column unless they had some fire-power. In a war that had seen the Stone Age come alive again, the boulder ambush had been raised to a high art.

Goncharov knew what was coming. He could have walked away, forgotten all about it. But he wasn't made that way. He quickened his pace, cursing Grebnov for insisting he not bring a radio. He started waving his arms overhead on alternate steps, even though he was still more than a kilo-meter away from the column. The charging horse-men were little more than twice that distance.

He stopped long enough to strip the cover off his aluminum canteen and started waving it overhead. He thought for a second that one of the turret gun-ners had seen the flash, but the tanks continued to roll on. He could hear the big diesel engines clearly now, and the occasional clanking of a tread as it struck a rock.

At five hundred meters one of the gunners fi-nally spotted him. The tank changed direction, and he thought they were going to stop, but it pressed on. He jumped in place now, waving his arms and gesturing. The turret gunner waved back, still oblivious to the danger behind him.

The billowing cloud of dust was just eight hundred meters behind the infantry transport. It was still closing rapidly, and it was still impossible to see more than one horseman. Goncharov started to shout now as he charged toward the lead tank. But the jarring of his steps and the rumbling diesels made his words unintelligible.

Then the cloud changed direction slightly, driving straight for the infantry transport, homing in on it like a missile. At three hundred meters the cloud veered to the left, and then to the right, like a soccer player weaving downfield toward the goal.

Then, suddenly, the hollow thump of a tube-launched missile rolled across the valley floor. Goncharov saw a white blur for a fraction of a second, followed by a terrific explosion and a gigantic fireball.

The turret gunners both heard the roar at the same instant. The turrets swiveled, and both men opened up, but they were too late. The mujahadeen thundered past, laying down a murderous fire. First one gunner then the other slumped over his weapon. A black dot arced through the air, bounced off one turret and landed on the ground just as a second slammed into the gunner's shoulder and dropped straight down.

Both grenades went off at the same time. A brilliant flash, followed by a plume of black smoke, belched out of the open turret of the lead tank. The smoke fanned into a perfect ring as Goncharov dropped to his knees. He swung his rifle around and took aim on the charging horsemen, but he didn't have a prayer at that range, and he knew it.

The second tank went the way of the first as someone struggled to get the dead gunner out of the way to close the hatch. But another grenade arced through the air. It tumbled end over end, and Goncharov recognized it as an East Bloc variant of the old Nazi potato masher. The grenade dropped neatly into the turret and went off almost at the same instant.

The APCs seemed out of control as they churned the earth with their half-tracks, throwing up rooster combs of dirt and dust behind them. One of them bolted, and charged straight for the regrouping mujahadeen.

Goncharov charged forward, shouting at the top of his lungs. All he had was a rifle, but he couldn't sit there and watch.

Not now.

CHAPTER SEVEN

Mahoney shook uncontrollably. He tried to speak, but all he could say was "Jesus Christ, Jesus Christ." Bolan wasn't sure whether the kid was in shock, or if he was reacting to the grisly sight of Salvato's corpse sprawled in the dirt.

"How the fuck could this happen?" the DEA agent asked, finally able to articulate the question on Bolan's own mind.

"Anybody else know about the meet?" the Executioner asked.

"How the hell do I know? I didn't tell anybody. I doubt if Tony would. That leaves them." Mahoney took in the carnage with a sweep of his hand. "But they were in this together."

"You sure?"

"What do you mean?"

"You recognize anybody here? Anybody at all?"

Mahoney looked at the driver of the van. He stuck out an accusatory finger. "Him. I recognize him. He brought the others. What's to recognize? Jesus Christ, why are you asking me such stupid questions?"

"What the hell do you think this was all about, Mahoney?" Bolan snapped. "You think this was just a simple burn?"

"What else could it be?"

"I'm not sure, but I think we better find out. The sooner the better."

Mahoney shook his head. "I don't know, Belasko. I think maybe you're reading too much into this." He knelt beside Salvato's body. Reaching out with one trembling hand, he closed the dead man's staring eyes, then looked up at Bolan. "I have to get a crew out here. Can you find your way back to the safehouse?"

"Yeah, I think so."

Mahoney straightened, fished the keys out of his pocket and tossed them to Bolan. "Here. I'll be back as soon as I can. The man in charge of the night crew is Ron Hansen."

"No way he'll let me inside."

"I'll call him after I call my boss."

"You sure you don't want me to stay?"

"Yes."

Bolan jiggled the keys as he walked to the car. He opened the door and climbed in. "Anything you want me to do?"

Mahoney shook his head. "Nothing you can do. But thanks."

Bolan cranked up the engine, flipped on the headlights and threw the Camaro into gear. Backing up, he turned the car so that the headlights swept over the bloody scene. Mahoney was still standing there, looking down at his partner. One by one the twin beams picked up the bodies as the car rolled out toward the highway, rocking in the potholes and grumbling a bit as the strain on the engine varied.

Bolan cruised out onto the highway, then gunned the engine a bit. The Camaro zipped up to sixty without a hint of acceleration. He ran through the gears, settled down at seventy-five and rolled down the side window. The cold night air whipping in through the opening cleared his head.

He was still troubled by Johnny Rivera's behavior in the interrogation room. He was troubled, too, by the motive for the slaughter he'd just witnessed. Recreating the events in his mind, step by step, it seemed apparent that the gunmen had meant to kill both Salvato and Mahoney, and would have pulled it off if he hadn't been there.

But what was the point of the double cross? That, he supposed, was obvious. The dealer, whoever he might be, had somehow learned that either Mahoney or Salvato—or maybe even both—was a DEA agent. But how?

That was a question that deserved an answer, even required one, before he got involved much further. Life was too short, and time too precious, to waste his time bumbling around a blind alley with any conceivable cover already blown. He tapped the steering wheel rhythmically as he drove, as if he were trying to jar something loose, maybe an answer, maybe another, more subtle question.

As he pulled into the rutted lane leading to the farmhouse, something seemed wrong, but he couldn't put his finger on it. Halfway to the house, he heard a hollow booming, which seemed to shake the ground. At the same instant a bright flash of orange touched the tall shrubbery, drenching the leaves with its color for a moment, then winked out.

He stepped on the gas and dropped a gear, taking the winding turns as close to full throttle as he could. The Camaro burst into the open as flames began to lick the front of the farmhouse. Half of the shake-covered facade was a sheet of flickering orange, and plumes of black smoke rose forty feet into the air.

Bolan slammed on the brakes as he spotted shadows flitting across the orange background. A car and a van sat with their parking lights on. The front door of the farmhouse was open. One of the shadows spotted him and sprinted toward the rear of the van.

The warrior threw the Camaro into reverse as a hail of gunfire ripped at the windshield. He skidded backward twenty yards or so, turning the car broadside and ducking below the window level. Several slugs slammed into the passenger door, and at least one punched right through and buried itself in the seat behind him.

He shoved his door open and rolled out onto the rutted lane, crawling into the shrubbery as another burst of autofire ripped at the Camaro. The remaining windows shattered, and the car jerked convulsively as first the front and then the rear tire on the right side blew out.

Bolan crawled on his belly, fighting off a tangle of branches and dead vines. Worming through the dense undergrowth, he slipped into an open field, got to his feet and sprinted along the hedgerow as the car blew up behind him. He'd bought time by blocking the lane with the Camaro, and the gunners continued to chew it to pieces. Either they didn't realize or didn't care that they'd have to move the car to get their own vehicles out.

He could see the roof of the farmhouse now. Its asphalt shingles had started to burn, thickening the pall of smoke that hung overhead. Dropping to the ground again, he spread some of the brush aside to see where the gunmen were. The firing had stopped, and two men, automatic weapons in hand, cautiously approached the Camaro. They were halfway between the van and Mahoney's car, and the nearest cover was twenty yards across the open yard.

Bolan brought up the Desert Eagle and braced his wrist. Propping himself on his elbows, he waited until he had a clear shot. The lead gunman was drawing farther ahead of his companion. Backlit by the flames, they were little more than black shadows on tiptoe. As soon as there was a slice of light between the two, Bolan fired.

The .44 Magnum bucked, and he resighted quickly, snapping off his second shot even before the first target hit the ground. Both bullets found their marks. One of the wounded men squirmed toward a stand of trees on the far side of the yard. The second hardguy had already bought it. Bolan fired again at the crawling man, saw his target buck once before lying still.

"Over there," someone shouted, "in the bushes!"

The warrior crawled away as the branches overhead were chewed to pieces. Sharp splinters rained down on him as he rolled to the right, closer to the house.

"Get him!" another voice shouted.

"Fuck that, man. You get him."

The firing stopped and Bolan lay still. He wasn't sure how many gunmen there were, but he'd counted at least five. He was bothered by the absence of gunfire from the house, but he didn't want to think about what that probably meant.

He heard footsteps pound past him, and the steps continued on, heading toward the Camaro. "Bastard's not here!" a voice shouted.

"Find him! Now!" That was a new voice, tinged by an accent of some kind, but faint. Listening in the dark, Bolan wondered whether he'd imagined it, but he could have sworn the new voice had a Slavic inflection. Yet it wasn't Slavic.

Getting to his feet, the warrior sprinted toward the back of the house. He was close enough now to hear the crackle of dry wood as the flames continued to engulf the house. Enough light filtered through the hedgerow to pattern the ground with a network of shadows in close where the roots of the shrubs let it through. Higher up, the leaves were too thick for any light at all to penetrate.

He turned the corner at a dead run and nearly tripped over a low stone wall. He took it with an abrupt leap, almost lost his balance, then staggered a couple of steps before skidding to a stop. The rear of the house was just twenty yards away. It was open to the fields, a broad patio running its full width and extending fifteen or eighteen feet out into a scraggly lawn.

The flames were already licking up and over the roof. The fire would be slow going downhill on this side of the house, but the way the front was raging, the whole place would be an inferno before long. Bolan sprinted across the patio. Getting in would be a nightmare, but the alarm system was worthless now, probably already disabled, either by the attackers or by the fire itself.

According to Mahoney, the night crew consisted of four men. Johnny Rivera made five. If they were alive, and if he could get in, he might still learn why Rivera had been antsy during his interrogation. Bolan fired a single shot into the rear door. The bullet tore through the wood, and he placed a foot just below the lock, putting all his weight into the push, but the door didn't give. It didn't even creak.

Stepping back, he looked up at the second floor. There was a small window, a semicircle, more for ornament than anything else. If he could get up to the roof, he might be able to get in that way. Holstering the Desert Eagle, he launched himself up and grabbed the eaves trough. It started to pull away from the building, but he managed to swing one leg up and over. The eaves trough gave way completely as he rolled up and lay flat. It was a steep angle and he had to be careful.

Rolling onto his stomach, Bolan managed to claw his way up a few feet, enough to risk standing upright. He had to lean forward to keep his footing, but he managed to get near the peak. A wave of heat licked down at him, but the thrust of the fire was upward, and he could bear the high temperature for a couple of minutes. At the window he kicked the glass in, prepared to leap back if super-heated air poured out. But nothing happened.

He slid through the window and dropped to the floor below, a good twelve feet. Moving quickly through the upper story, he found two dead men, one of whom still clutched an Uzi. He grabbed the machine pistol and checked the magazine. It was full. The man had never gotten off a shot. Bolan snagged a couple of spare clips and moved on.

Moving from room to room, he checked every one quickly but thoroughly. The place was empty. Back at the stairs, he started down to the first floor. Still no sign of intense heat. He worked rapidly through the rear of the farmhouse, conscious that any moment the inferno might force him to leave.

Two more dead men were sprawled on the kitchen floor. Like the man on the second floor, they had been taken by surprise. Their weapons were unfired.

The Executioner couldn't get closer to the front. A closed door was already beginning to lose its paint on his side. He couldn't touch the wood for more than a fraction of a second.

Moving toward the rear, he found another door, this one half-open. He pulled it wide and stared down into the brightly lit basement. With the Uzi ready, Bolan started down the steps. At the bottom of the stairway he found himself staring at three cells. All three were locked. Two were empty.

The third held the bloody mess that had once been Johnny Rivera.

CHAPTER EIGHT

Bolan cursed and grabbed the bars of the holding cell. Whatever Rivera had been afraid of, it couldn't hurt him now. The fear had paid a visit and had left a bloody calling card.

Sprinting back up the stairs, Bolan vaulted for the back door just as the fire burst through from the front. A searing tongue of flame licked at the door panel, and hot air geysered through. He could feel its heat on his back as he raced for the rear door.

Once outside again, he circled the house and approached the far side. At the front corner of the building the flames had already begun to work their way down the side wall. Bolan had to give the corner a wide berth. He slipped into the brush just past the outermost reaches of withered leaves. Some of the scrub oak was already burning, and the hedge itself wasn't going to last long.

In the yard three men made a hasty search of the hedgerow. Their backs were to him, and to a fourth man who stood at the rear of the van and watched them. As one of the men reached the end of the hedge, the watcher, a tall, thin man in a gray suit, ran a hand through his graying hair. He shouted to be heard above the crackling of the flames, "Never mind, never mind. We have to get out of here. Hurry up."

Again Bolan heard the faint hint of an accent. But he still couldn't pinpoint the man's native tongue.

He had the Uzi now, and the odds were a little more to his liking. He poked the Israeli machine pistol through the hedge just as the man in the gray suit climbed into the rear of the van. Bolan cut loose at the nearest of the three searchers. The Uzi bucked, and he swept the muzzle through his rather limited field of fire. The tangled branches only let him cover one man.

The searcher went down as four or five 9 mm slugs ripped into him with sickening splats. Small geysers of blood spurted for a second as the man fell. The other two heard the firing and turned as Bolan backed through the hedge, hit the deck and crawled for all he was worth. Behind him a hail of autofire ripped through the tangled but frail vegetation. He lay still for a moment, trying to figure out his next move. He couldn't afford to cut through the hedge. Not yet, anyway. There wasn't enough cover in the yard.

While he debated what to do, Bolan heard an engine spring to life. He was pretty certain it was the van. Creeping as close as he dared to the hedge to peer through the roots, he saw the two gunmen race toward the van. Bolan opened up as the vehicle lurched backward. The lead gunman shouted as the van swerved, momentarily sweeping across Bolan's position with its headlights. The glare blinded him for a second, and he couldn't see the gunmen behind the lights. As the vehicle continued its turn, the lights passed by but the gunmen were now behind the van.

Bolan raked the side of the vehicle with his Uzi. The 9 mm slugs slammed against the metal panels, but couldn't penetrate them. The rear doors waved drunkenly as the van lurched toward the ruined Camaro. A hand reached out to grab one of the doors, and Bolan sprayed the Uzi across the open mouth.

A cry of pain, almost inaudible under the roaring of the van's engine, was followed by one of the men tumbling out of the vehicle. Bolan emptied his magazine through the rear doors, but the van never slowed down. Its engine racing, it slewed across the barren yard. With a horrendous squeal of metal on metal, the van tried to bull its way between the Camaro and the end of the hedge. The engine groaned and the tires spun, kicking up a great deal of dust. The squealing grew even more tortured as the Camaro refused to budge.

Bolan broke through the hedge and started toward the trapped van. The driver knew his business. He hooked his bumper into the Camaro's fender and reversed. The engine roared again, and this time the Camaro began to move. With a loud snap the van's bumper pulled free, but there was enough room now for it to squeeze through.

The Executioner jammed a second clip into the Uzi as he sprinted across the yard. This time he ripped a burst low, ricocheting off the rear bumper and blowing both rear tires. He cut loose with another short burst, and the slugs bounced around the interior of the van.

The passenger door opened, and the tall man in the gray suit leaped out. The driver gunned the engine, sending the van careering straight back. Over the thunder of the engine Bolan heard the thump of both blown tires.

The van roared past, narrowly missing the Executioner as he dived to one side. Again racing the engine, the driver swerved the van and headed straight for Bolan, who scrambled to get out of its way. Slipping in his haste, he was forced to roll as the vehicle rocketed past, narrowly missing him.

This time he didn't wait to see what the driver was going to do. He ran straight at the front of the van, emptying his second magazine. The windshield starred, then collapsed, as if it were a sheet of water cascading over a cliff. Then the horn blared as the driver slumped forward, his foot still on the gas. The van raced headlong into a hedge and stalled.

Smoke started to billow around the stricken vehicle's roof. The horn continued to wail, and Bolan stepped forward to reach through the window and shove the driver away from the wheel. The horn stopped, but continued to ring in his ears.

Now, he thought, where was the man in the gray flannel suit?

He moved toward the Camaro stealthily. As he stepped past the car, he heard a rustle in the thicket nearly a hundred yards ahead. The man was a third of the way back toward the highway and blundering dead ahead without regard to silence.

Bolan sprinted past the Camaro and down the lane. He no longer heard the man charging through the thicket and wondered whether the guy had decided to lie in wait or had broken through and either taken to the lane itself or to the open field behind the hedge. Either way Bolan knew he had to find him soon. If the man got too far ahead, he could hole up until morning. And Bolan had to have the guy alive, had to have some answers to this ever-expanding puzzle.

On a hunch the warrior bulled his way through the hedge and out into the open field. Dropping to one knee, he scanned the meadow just above the tips of the waving grass, but there was no sign of the man.

The Executioner plunged into the tall grass, knowing he could pass within a few feet of his quarry and never even realize the man was there. But he had no choice, so he pushed ahead slowly, his ear cocked for the slightest sound. Twenty yards out into the field, he dropped to his stomach and lay still. He could hear the wind whispering through the grass, but nothing else.

He remained motionless for what seemed like an hour. Twice, he thought about giving up, convinced the gray-haired man had made good his escape. Finally he got to his knees and was just starting to stand when a tremendous roar came from the house. He glanced back to see a shower of sparks swirling on the rush of superheated air. The roof had just caved in.

And then, taking advantage of Bolan's distraction, the gray-haired man made his move. The warrior heard a rustling, then a footstep. He turned as the man tripped over something and disappeared into the grass. Bolan charged toward the spot, but two quick shots ripped through the grass about waist high, and he was forced to dive out of the way. He heard a third shot, but this time the bullet seemed to fly off into the air and vanish.

He paused, holding his breath. He could feel the strain in his neck and shoulders as he waited for another sound, but there was none. Slowly he started to crawl through the grass. Still nothing from the hidden man.

Keeping the Uzi handy, ready to cut loose with a warning burst to keep the man pinned, he wriggled through the grass. And then, just ahead, he saw a gap in the blades, a hollow space where something had pressed them down. Cautiously he brushed the grass aside with one outstretched hand.

The man lay there, looking at him, but not moving.

"Don't move," Bolan ordered, waving the Uzi so the man could see it. But the guy didn't even blink. He just lay there, eyes staring. "Get up slowly," Bolan growled.

Nothing.

Then it hit him. The guy was dead.

There was no sign of a gunshot wound, no trace of blood. Bolan was baffled. Then, as he bent closer, something caught his eye. It glittered on the man's lips. He pressed a thumb against the shiny place and felt the glass against his skin.

"Damn," Bolan muttered. "Suicide."

CHAPTER NINE

Viktor Sharkov watched the sunrise with satisfaction. He stood in the center of the ruined village, oblivious to the roofless shells of stone buildings, the heaps of ashes where wooden huts had been just weeks before. He felt secure here, the destruction around him a perfect cover.

He wasn't a happy man, but he was about to change all that. He expected losses. They were, after all, part of doing business. But that didn't make them any easier to take.

He almost smiled, thinking about how close his new line of work was to the thing he had done so well for so long. It was all about appearances. There were risks, of course, but none that a prudent man couldn't safely negotiate. The risks even added an element of pleasure for him, the satisfaction of having gambled and won, of having outwitted the other side. It didn't really matter whether the other side was the CIA or the DEA. All that really mattered was maintaining control. Decide which risks to take, read the opposition and make your move.

And this morning he was making the biggest move yet. If it worked, and he had no doubt that it would, he would make more than enough to wipe out the memory of recent miscalculations. And he was uncompromising enough to admit that he had miscalculated. He had seen too many men refuse to admit they'd been wrong, and it had cost them. But his mistakes weren't going to destroy him. Instead of pretending he was infallible, he was determined to learn from his mistakes.

Turning on the narrow wall to look toward Iran and, beyond it, Turkey, the source of his brilliant new future, he shielded his eyes against the red glare of the newly risen sun. Kemal was due by noon, and Sharkov was getting impatient, even though he still had six hours. He had never really liked Turks, particularly brutal, unpredictable ones like Kemal.

He climbed back down the ladder, still spry for a fifty-year-old man. He prided himself on maintaining his physical condition. Some of the younger men didn't understand the connection between physical fitness and mental acuity, but he did. He knew you had to be sound of body to make intelligent decisions, to think clearly and quickly under pressure.

Dropping to the ground, he walked toward the angular building he used as his temporary headquarters. Chebrikov was inside, and he didn't feel like talking to him just yet. Sharkov ran through a brisk series of calisthenics. He heard his heart pounding in his ears, and pushed himself just a little harder, enough to take him one level higher, give him that little extra jolt.

Then Chebrikov came out of the building. "Viktor, you're up early this morning. Nervous?"

"Why should I be nervous?"

"It's a big day, eh? It would be natural to be nervous."

"If you're prepared, you don't have to be nervous. Better to be smart."

"I suppose you're right."

"That's why I give orders and you take them. I *am* right, Vasily."

Chebrikov smiled. "So you keep reminding me." He lit a cigarette, then talked around it, his words spewing out puffs of smoke. "What time do you expect Kemal?"

"By noon."

"And you're sure you can trust this Afghan, Hikmal?"

"No, I'm not sure I can trust him. But I have something he wants. He's willing to do what I want to get what he wants. We have an understanding."

"That's a little like having an understanding with a hungry lion, isn't it?"

"That's what lion tamers are for."

"Too bad this isn't a circus."

"Look, Vasily, if you're nervous, you can leave. I won't hold it against you. Better to go now than change your mind when it's too late."

"I'm a bit of a lion tamer myself, Viktor. I don't mind. I just wish you were a little more forthcoming."

"Need-to-know, Vasily. That was always the way. This is no different. Our motives may have changed, but the business is the same. The principles are the same. So are the procedures. I thought you understood that."

"I do, but I thought we were a little more equal this time, colleagues, so to speak."

"That can be pushed too far, Vasily."

Chebrikov didn't respond, but Sharkov could see that his argument hadn't convinced him. But he was used to that, too. Choosing people of talent was only part of the problem. You had to know just how far to go with them. Every man was different. You didn't want someone so docile that he needed orders to blow his nose. But you didn't want somebody thinking too much for himself, either.

Sharkov stepped into the building to snatch a pair of binoculars from a wooden peg on the wall. He wasn't used to something so primitive as simple lenses. His was a world of sophisticated electronics: sensors, bugs, radios, radar. He had them, of course, but the Turk didn't, and had been adamant in his refusal when Sharkov had pressed him on the point. So he had to do without, at least in this phase of the operation.

It was almost refreshing to be reduced to such fundamentals as field glasses and signal flags. It was good for the soul, he thought, to be thrown back onto one's own resources and a handful of simple tools.

He swept the glasses across the valley. He was looking for something even more fundamental: a camel train, a few dozen surly dromedaries carrying a few dozen surly men. And a few hundred pounds of Turkish opium. Nothing was more fundamental than that. It was trade in its most elementary form. The Turk was only too happy to find a buyer.

Off toward the horizon he found what he was looking for. First one dot, then another and a third. They materialized on a ridge as if from thin air. He recognized the peculiar rocking motion of the camels, so different from the fluidity of Hikmal's horses. He held the glasses steady until he'd counted twenty-nine. That was probably all. It was more than enough to carry what he was expecting.

He let the glasses fall, trying to pick out the caravan with the naked eye, but the glare was too harsh. He walked back inside and looped the leather sling of the glasses over the peg. "They're coming. We'll have to meet him below. I don't want him stepping on one of the mines."

"You want me to get the men ready?"

"Not yet. We have at least three hours. But make sure they know what to do. I don't want any mistakes. Not now."

"Don't worry, Viktor. There won't be any mistakes. I have as much at stake as you do."

Sharkov nodded. "I'm glad you understand that."

CHAPTER TEN

Late in the evening the day after Salvato's death, Brian Mahoney knocked on Bolan's door. The kid looked as if he hadn't slept, and what he had to say sounded like something a sleepwalker might say.

"What do you mean, you don't know who they are?" Bolan couldn't believe his ears. He stared at Mahoney. "You have the bodies. The bodies have fingers. They all had papers in their pockets. What more do you need?"

"Hey, Belasko, give me a break, okay? All I'm telling you is what I know. Look, you've been around the block a few times. You know how it is. Or do you?"

"What I know is that a bunch of goons whacked out four of your men. They blew away an important witness, right after your partner gets wasted, and all you can find out is that nobody knows who these guys are."

"Look, man, I told you. We got nothing."

"I want copies of the prints. Get them for me."

"Your wish is my command," Mahoney said sarcastically. He fished into his jacket pocket and jerked out a thick envelope.

Bolan took the packet. "What's this?"

"What do you think?"

Bolan studied the DEA agent thoughtfully.

"Hey, Belasko, I know a cover-up when I smell one. The whole thing stinks. But I got my orders. I was counting on the fact that you don't have my orders. I figure you can do something with these prints. I figure you're connected."

"They can have your badge for this, Mahoney."

"Hey, what good's a badge I'm not allowed to use?"

Bolan nodded. "All right. I'll see what I can come up with."

"You have my home number, right?"

"No phones on this one, Mahoney. If I get anything, I'll be over to see you."

"I'll leave a key under the mat. I've got to get some sleep. And the funeral's tomorrow. After that..." The kid shrugged.

Bolan walked toward his car. He knew Mahoney was watching him, but he didn't want to turn around.

"Belasko?"

The Executioner stopped.

"Yeah?"

"No secrets on this, okay? If you learn anything, and I mean *anything,* I want to know about it."

"You got it."

"Tony left three kids. You know?"

Bolan knew. He'd been there before. Too many times. More times than he could count. And it never got any easier.

Bolan gunned the engine of his rental car and roared off into the afternoon sun. When he reached the outskirts of Los Angeles, he was no more comfortable with his suspicions than he had been since they'd first sneaked up on him. The old guy, the one with the hint of an accent, was the heart of the matter. He wished he had a better fix on the accent, but every time he tried to turn it up in his head, it wriggled away like a wily catfish.

Nobody chewed a capsule full of cyanide to hide a drug burn. Nobody managed that kind of hit without leaving a trail. Or almost nobody. There was somebody, but that seemed too farfetched. The kind of thing that only happened in movies—bad ones.

By the time he got to the Justice Department offices in Van Nuys, he was ready to hear the worst of his suspicions confirmed. There was simply no other explanation. The night security officer refused to let him in until a call to Hal Brognola's home got him admitted.

Brognola wanted to talk to him and insisted he call as soon as he got upstairs. He took the elevator up, and the security officer opened the door reluctantly.

"This better be important, pal," he said, letting the glass door swing closed, then turning a key in both top and bottom locks.

Bolan looked at him without answering.

"You hear me?"

The warrior nodded. "I hear you. Where's the communications room?"

"Follow me." The guy waddled down the hall, wider than he should have been, stretching the gray gabardine across a broad butt, repeatedly running one hand through thinning blond hair.

He used another key on the commo room door, grunting as he bent over for the bottom lock. When he opened the door, he reached in for the light, clicked it on and flooded the room with cool fluorescence. "You know how to use this stuff?"

Bolan grunted.

"Okay, if you say so. But do me a favor. You got any problems, keep 'em to yourself until morning. I got enough crap to deal with on this shift. You get me?"

Bolan placed one big hand on the guy's flabby shoulder, spun him around and sent him off with a shove.

Brognola picked up on the first ring. "What's going on out there?" the big Fed asked.

"Actually I was hoping you'd be able to tell me."

"Tell you what?"

Bolan sketched in the details, pausing for Brognola to ask questions, but there were none. Not until the warrior was finished.

"Look, Striker, I can't do anything from here. I'll have to go down to the office. Can this wait until morning?"

"No, I don't think so."

Brognola sighed. "Okay, look, can you fax the information to the office? I'll give you the number. I'll call you as soon as I get anything. Give me a half hour at least."

"All right." Bolan jotted down the fax number, then gave Brognola the number on the L.A. phone.

"A half hour," Brognola repeated.

"I'm not going anywhere."

Bolan cranked up the fax machine, fed the documents in one by one and transmitted the pieces of the puzzle three thousand miles. Even the fingerprints could be sent that way, enhanced automatically, digitalized on one coast and reconstructed on the other.

When it was all done, he sat back and stared at the clock. It was eleven-thirty his time, three hours later for Brognola. The second hand seemed to take forever to make a single circuit. Only twenty-five more to go. Then twenty-four. And twenty-three.

Bolan heard a tap on the doorframe and turned to see the night man holding two cups of coffee. "Figured you could use this." His tone was less hostile than it had been, and Bolan wondered whether the guy had been the recipient of one of Brognola's famous sermons on agency responsibility and cooperation.

The coffee reminded him of axle grease, but it was hot, and he welcomed it. The guard took a sip of his own, swallowed hard, then waved a hand for Bolan's attention. "Look, I'm sorry I gave you a hard time. You know how it is. There's a routine you fall into. It's hard sometimes to change. You work the graveyard like I have for six or seven years, you start to think you're alone on the planet."

"No offense taken," Bolan said.

"If I can do anything, let me know."

"I will."

The guard took another drink of his coffee, then got up to leave. "I'll be down the hall."

Bolan was grateful for the coffee, even more grateful to have some of the dead time wasted. There was too much as it was. The clock showed another five minutes.

Then the phone finally rang. "Hello," he said, after picking up the receiver.

"Where'd you get these prints, Mack?"

"Why?"

"Just answer the question."

Bolan told him. "What's the problem?"

"I can't get a positive ID on four of the sets. Nothing at all."

"And the fifth?"

"Classified. Stone wall. No access. Company stuff."

"He was CIA?"

"I don't know yet. I'm waiting for a call now. Let me call you back as soon as I hear something."

More waiting.

When the phone finally rang again, it seemed as if he'd been in a holding pattern forever. He picked up the receiver instantly. "So, was he CIA?"

"No," Brognola replied. "But they aren't happy about letting us know anything."

"But did they?"

"After the attorney general made a couple of phone calls, yeah."

"That big?"

"That big."

"So? Who was he?"

"You did use the past tense, didn't you?"

"He's dead, if that's what you mean, yeah."

"His name is...was Marko Mirtis. A Lithuanian."

"That explains the accent. What else have you got?"

"He was a defector, Striker. A heavy one. A KGB colonel until he came over three years ago, out of Afghanistan. Made his way into Turkey. Blue sky, too. Unrecruited. His bona fides checked out okay, so we bought the whole package.''

''You telling me a KGB defector is running heroin? And nobody knew about it?''

''No. I'm telling you what they told me. They didn't say anything about heroin. But then if they *did* know, they wouldn't exactly blow a horn, you know?''

''This a CIA operation, Hal?''

''They say not.''

''Then what the hell's going on?''

''That's what they want to know. You'll have a visitor tomorrow morning. From Virginia. Meantime, this is buttoned-lip time.''

''That depends on the visitor, Hal.''

''You walk on eggs, Mack. I don't know if I can cover you on this one.''

''But you'll do what you can, right?''

''Don't I always?''

CHAPTER ELEVEN

Goncharov stared in disbelief as the horsemen closed in on the transport truck. Infantrymen spilled out of the back and started firing their weapons, but the charge of the mounted men sent them scattering. Stunned by the suddenness of the attack, the troops lost their nerve. They had the edge in firepower, but didn't take advantage of it.

The one remaining APC, lying on its side, disgorged a handful of men who crawled out of the hatch one by one. A lieutenant rallied them, and half a dozen strong they charged across the rocky wasteland. At a signal from the lieutenant they opened fire, killing three or four of the mujahadeen. The riderless horses bolted away, in one instance dragging its lifeless rider behind.

But the sudden diversion quickly spent itself. The horsemen regrouped, charging the six men at a dead trot and firing every weapon they had. Goncharov recognized three old British Enfields, weapons so ancient that they might have seen service at the Khyber Pass during the Raj.

A few of the mujahadeen had more modern weapons, but they were in the minority. Goncharov fought against the urge to charge headlong into the battle; he knew he was lost if he did that. And he had no way of getting help for the others. They were on their own.

Stumbling toward a small cluster of broken boulders, Goncharov lay flat and watched the battle slowly wind down. The horsemen wheeled like cossacks, bearing down on the infantrymen, heedless of the AK-47s hammering sporadically. Another of the rebels went down when his horse was shot from under him. But the tide was slowly turning against the army men.

In a pitched battle the mujahadeen wouldn't have stood a chance. But it wasn't a pitched battle; it was a carefully executed suicide attack. Surprise, the only ally the Afghan rebels could count on, had done the trick for them. In the first wave they had cut the odds and fractured the opposition. Man for man they were outgunned, but the numbers were about even, and the mujahadeen wanted to fight.

It was obvious the Afghan army troops didn't. It was more than the reluctance to fire on countrymen. There was no heart to their fight, as if they believed in nothing, while their opponents were fighting for something bigger than any of them could imagine.

Suddenly the firing grew more continuous. Goncharov peered out from his cover and saw that the horsemen had dismounted. They were charging the scattered infantrymen on foot now. Several brandished swords. The long, curved blades caught the brilliant sunlight and flashed like beacons as the swordsmen waved the terrible weapons high over their heads.

And just as suddenly the firing stopped. A cold stillness settled like a blanket over the valley floor. Men still moved, but no one fired a shot. The army regulars lay crumpled on the ground, some sprawled where they'd fallen, too close to death even to wrap an arm around their heads, others curled in balls.

Carelessly, more like schoolboys surveying a junkyard than warriors policing a field of battle, the mujahadeen strode among the fallen men. Casually a foot would prod one of the balls, or a sword would poke at a midsection. Sometimes, even when there was no movement, the man with the sword would lean on it and pin the body to the ground for a few seconds. Then there would be a sound. The swordsman would grunt as he stepped on the victim's ribs and tugged to dislodge the blade.

One man, reacting to the booted toe in his ribs, screamed once and fired his pistol at the man standing over him. The shot seemed obscene, like a curse in an empty cathedral. It echoed off the surrounding hills, then faded away like distantly clapping hands. The scream, reduced to a thin howl, continued to bounce off the rocks and the hillsides for a few moments, then it, too, was gone.

The standing man turned then, as if to ask if anyone had seen what had happened, then he fell to the ground. Like locusts, several of the mujahadeen swarmed around the fallen regular, slashing wildly with their swords until one man, one of the lucky few with a modern gun, emptied the last of his magazine into the body. Through the tangle of legs Goncharov saw the body bounce and twitch, even after the firing stopped, and then, just as the last echo of the gunfire died away, the body lay still.

The rebels began to sift the field, stripping the bodies of weapons and ammunition. As they worked, they looked like harvesters stacking sheaves of lethal wheat. The mound of weaponry grew as one man remounted and rode off. Goncharov wondered where the horseman was headed until he saw him stop alongside the transport truck. Then the man waved a fist in the air and shouted something Goncharov couldn't understand. Dismounting, he tied his horse to the tailgate and climbed into the cab. Goncharov heard the whine of a starter. The engine resisted at first, then broke into a rumble.

The new driver was anything but expert. The truck lunged and bucked as it made a wide circle, then headed back toward the rest of the band. When he jumped down, the driver was surrounded by the others, who clapped him on the back and thrust their fists into the air in celebration.

The armament harvest continued until the rebels were satisfied every weapon on the field had been recovered. Then two men climbed into the ruined vehicles and sifted through the wreckage until they, too, had yielded everything of value, including several dozen cannon shells from one of the tanks.

Goncharov knew the rebels had no cannon that could use the shells, but he also knew, firsthand, how ingenious they were at disassembling everything from mines to artillery shells and recycling the high explosives. It was dangerous work, and many of them had been killed, while others had lost a hand or an arm or both. But the rebels were desperate, and both fear and reason had a way of diminishing under the pressure of desperation.

The matériel was loaded into the back of the truck, the weapons tied together in groups of three or four, then stacked against one wall. To keep them from sliding around the truck bed, crates of ammunition were stacked alongside.

When everything was loaded, a hurried conference took place beside the driver's door of the truck. A search of the APC turned up three eighty-liter fuel cans. They were empty, and tolled mournfully as they clanged together. Stripping a length of hose from the engine compartment of one of the APCs, the men siphoned as much diesel fuel as they could from the remaining vehicles. Two hundred and forty liters wasn't much, but the truck was useless without it, and Goncharov felt sure the mujahadeen would find some way to get more fuel as long as the truck was serviceable.

This time they were definitely leaving. The men mounted their horses, all except for the man who had driven the truck. He climbed back into the cab, slammed the door and started the engine again. Goncharov watched them go, the truck rolling obediently after the horsemen, rocking from side to side, its engine whining and snarling as the driver struggled to master the rudiments of shifting gears in concert with the clutch.

Goncharov stood to watch the strange caravan vanish across the valley. It didn't hit him until then. What the hell was he going to do now?

He started walking after the caravan, then started to run. His breath ripped through his throat like hot knives, and he could hear his heart pounding in his ears. A small fist hammered inside his chest, its rhythm getting more and more insistent as it grew in force, as if the fist were slowly getting larger.

He'd gone more than a kilometer when he realized how foolish he was. He could never catch them on foot, unless they were camped somewhere close by. But he doubted that. They were too smart to attack too close to home. The sky would be alive with helicopters in a few hours, as soon as the leader of the convoy missed his next call-in time.

That meant the caravan would keep moving, possibly all night. And every hour the distance between him and it would grow larger until he would no longer be able to see them, even through his binoculars. Once they slipped beyond his visual range, there would be little hope of ever finding them again.

The mazelike valleys and tortuous mountain passes could conceal fifty times that many men and animals from anything but infrared gear. What chance did one man, and a stranger at that, have of finding anything, then?

He walked another half kilometer when he heard something that gave him hope. He listened to make sure he wasn't hallucinating in his desperation. It came again, somewhere off to the left. He couldn't see anything, but knew he wasn't dreaming. He changed course, unlimbering his rifle, just to be on the safe side. It was a horse. He was sure of that. But only one, or a dozen? He wasn't sure. And the odds were no better than fifty-fifty that the animal was without human company.

He started up a slight incline, realized the horse was just over the far side of the ridge and broke into a run. He jerked the rifle off his shoulder and cradled it in his arms. He hadn't done that in three years, but it felt comforting. He ran more easily now despite the ascent. His heart was less insistent, his breathing less ragged.

Twenty meters below the ridge he stopped to listen for a moment. He heard it again, a nicker, almost forlorn, and he knew then the animal was alone. Taking the last few meters slowly, with a steady stride, he stopped again at the ridge line. And there it was.

Not two hundred meters away, halfway down the steeper far side, the animal struggled to free itself. Its reins appeared to have gotten tangled on something between a pair of boulders. He sprinted toward the rocks in his excitement. Then, realizing it just might be enough to spook the horse and enable it in its fear to jerk free, he slowed to a fast walk. Even that seemed too precipitous, and he stopped altogether. Holding the rifle in one hand, he held the other out as if he thought he could stroke the beast from fifty meters.

The horse stopped struggling long enough to stare at him. It seemed somehow reassured by his presence. He didn't want to speak for fear of scaring it again. Slowly, one foot placed behind the other, he moved toward the horse. He could see its saddle still in place, and realized the animal had belonged to one of the mujahadeen killed in the firefight.

At ten meters he changed direction slightly, careful to let the horse see him at all times, but cautious not to move too far. Whatever was holding the animal might be dislodged if the angle changed too much. At five meters he could see in among the rocks, and he knew what held the horse.

The dead man, his head bashed and broken from being hauled across the rocky terrain, lay wedged between two sharp-edged rocks. His foot was still hooked through the saddle's stirrup, and it had been enough to keep the frightened animal from breaking free. But the toe of the boot was on the verge of slipping free. Any sudden movement might cause the horse to make one last desperate try for freedom, and it just might do the trick.

Goncharov moved in slowly, his hand trembling as he reached to stroke the animal's muzzle. The horse calmed down, straining its head toward Goncharov's fingers.

He held his breath, and the horse watched him, canting its head to one side. When his fingers finally scratched at the horse's muzzle, the animal nickered again, then pawed the ground, its nervousness starting to reassert itself.

"Steady...steady...I won't hurt you," he said in Russian.

Then his hand closed over the reins, and he locked his fingers around the stiff leather. Holding tight, Goncharov moved around the far side, then dislodged the dead man's foot. He bent to perform a perfunctory search and found a small transmitter and a Chinese revolver. He stuck both in his coat and started back around the animal when he had an idea.

The man was almost his size. The goatskin coat, heavily embroidered in intricate green and blue lines, a flower pattern on each breast, just might fit. The coat was dirty, and a little ragged from having been dragged across the valley, but it was relatively free of blood, and much of the dirt would shake loose. Goncharov shrugged. It couldn't hurt, and it might help.

He bent again, undid the bone hooks and tugged one sleeve from the corpse. He thought he was going to be sick and turned away until the surge of nausea passed.

Goncharov forced himself to hurry. If the caravan made it into the foothills, a dozen coats like this one wouldn't help him.

CHAPTER TWELVE

As the plane touched down in Islamabad, Mahoney said, "I don't know what the hell we're doing here."

"We were looking at the wrong end of the telescope," Bolan said. "The answer is here, not in Mexico."

"I don't even know what the questions are anymore."

"You will." Bolan looked at his watch. "We have a meeting in an hour. That should fill in some of the missing pieces."

"I don't know about that. I've been here before. I've never found anything but bullshit and paranoia."

"Get used to it, Mahoney."

"You think I'm not?"

The plane taxied to the terminal, and Bolan was on his feet before it stopped moving. He reached down and grabbed Mahoney by the shoulder and pulled him up. "Come on, we don't want to miss our ride."

As the door opened and Bolan stepped out into the jet bridge, he wondered whether Mahoney was right. It was almost too impetuous to travel halfway around the world on the basis of such sketchy information. He had accepted the assignment. He'd had strings pulled, at no little effort, to get Mahoney released for this operation. It was necessary, even urgent. But his impatience was getting the best of him. He felt as if his hands were manacled, and he wanted to get out and do something about it.

At the entrance to the terminal Bolan spotted a man in a gray suit who stood to one side, scanning faces anxiously. He looked at Bolan, then at Mahoney, and took a tentative step forward. Bolan stepped aside to let the passengers behind him get past. Mahoney followed him.

The man in the suit, his pinched features squeezed even further by the effort of scrutinizing the deplaning passengers, looked at Bolan again. He took a couple of steps, stopped, then started forward again, sticking out a handful of bony fingers. "Mr. Mahoney?"

Bolan nodded. "Royce, isn't it?"

The guy tried to relax, but his face still looked tight. "Charles Royce, yes. How was your flight?"

Bolan ignored the question. He'd had his fill of small talk. "This is Mr. Mahoney," he said, indicating the DEA agent.

Royce seemed puzzled. "But I thought you...?"

"It was easier that way. Where's the car?"

"What? Oh, yes, I see. What about your bags?"

Bolan indicated the small carryall in his left hand.

"That's all?"

"That's all. Let's go, Mr. Royce."

Royce led the way through the crowded terminal. He carried himself as if he were afraid of everyone, dodging unnecessarily whenever it looked as if he would pass too close to someone. He even gave children a wide berth. The Executioner walked silently behind him. Royce turned once to make sure Bolan and Mahoney were behind him, then passed out into the noisy traffic on the concrete walk. Taxicabs and shuddering buses blared horns as they jockeyed for access to the curb.

Royce slipped into the traffic, apparently more at home with vehicles than people. He dodged between two cabs, slid along the side of a bus, then darted across the opposite lane into a parking zone. He waited for his passengers, nervously tapping his fingers on the roof of the car. Opening the back door, he waited for Bolan and Mahoney to climb in, then closed the door and got into the front.

The traffic was typical Third World chaos, but Royce handled it like a veteran. He talked while watching his passengers in the rearview mirror. "First time in this part of the world?"

"No," Bolan said.

"Yes," Mahoney answered.

Not knowing which answer to pick up on, Royce changed the subject. "There's a briefing scheduled at four."

"I know," Bolan said.

"What's going on? Everything was so hurried and so hush-hush." The question hung in the air. When it was obvious it wasn't going to be answered, Royce nodded. "I understand. The embassy isn't far."

That, too, received no response.

"You fellows don't talk much, do you?"

"Not much, no," Mahoney replied. "We like to know what we're talking about before we say anything."

"You mean you don't know why you're here?"

This, too, was greeted with silence.

"Sorry. I guess I talk too much."

"You could say that," Mahoney agreed.

When they reached the embassy compound, Royce rolled down the window and stopped to show his credentials to the Marine at the gate. Like most American embassies since the Beirut episode, this one had beefed up its security. The Marine leaned down to peer into the back seat. "Gentlemen."

Mahoney waved, and Bolan said, "Corporal..."

When the guard backed away, Royce rolled the window back up. They pulled up to the side of the building, and Royce climbed out of the car.

Bolan followed him out onto the concrete walk, Mahoney right behind him. "This way," Royce said.

The building was one of those experimental blocks of glass and stone that seemed to be all the rage with Western governments. Royce glanced up at it for a moment, then walked to a pair of glass doors, pushed one aside and stepped through. They made their way down a long, tiled corridor. Royce stopped in front of an elevator and pressed a series of numbers into the electronic lock. The door opened and he waved them in.

Bolan was thrown off balance for a moment when the elevator dropped. He had expected to be taken to an upper floor. The light bar above the door showed they were going to descend four levels. Then the door hissed open, and they found themselves facing another long corridor, this one floored in painted concrete. The fluorescent lights overhead made everything, even the air, seem cold. Under this kind of light distance seemed exaggerated.

Royce led them all the way down the hall, stopping in front of a metal door. He pressed a buzzer, and the view port mounted in the door snapped. "We're here," Royce announced.

The view port was shut smartly, then the door rolled aside with the whine of a servo motor. Royce again led the way. Bolan looked around dispassionately while Mahoney seemed almost goggle-eyed. "Holy shit, what is this place?" he wondered out loud.

Royce smiled thinly. "There's a good reason for all of this. One has to assume the worst and adopt a siege mentality in this part of the world."

A large man in shirtsleeves, his tie tugged away from an unbuttoned collar, stepped into the interior hallway. "Royce, it's about time. This them?"

Royce nodded.

"All right, I'll take it from here." He walked toward them. Bolan noticed he limped a bit, and the big man slapped his leg and grinned. "Plastic. But it holds me up." Then, sticking out a large hand, he said, "Tim Rucker. You're Belasko, right? So that makes you—" he turned to the DEA agent "—Mahoney. Process of elimination."

Rucker waved a hand vaguely as he turned to limp back down the hall. He waited in front of an open door as Royce slipped back through the security door and disappeared.

Inside, Bolan found himself in a large but claustrophobic office. "Not exactly comfortable, is it?" Rucker commented. "But the chairs are okay. Have a seat." When the men were seated, he asked, "Now, what exactly do you want to know? The cable traffic was . . . elliptical, to say the least."

"Marko Mirtis. What do you know about him?"

Rucker laughed. "Why? Is he shoplifting again? You guys came a long way for information on a kleptomaniac."

"No. Not shoplifting. He's dead. We want to know what you know about him."

"Dead? How? The son of a bitch was a fool, but—"

This time Mahoney answered. "He was responsible for five murders that we know of, possibly six. DEA agents and a witness."

"Drugs? You telling me Mirtis was a drug smuggler? Is that it?"

"Look, Rucker, we don't know much about him. We know what Mahoney just told you and not a hell of a lot more. We know he was out here, we know he was in Kabul for a while, and Turkey. That's ancient history. But maybe that history can explain what happened."

"I thought coke was a Colombian thing."

"Not coke, heroin," Mahoney said. "Lots of it. High-grade Turkish. The witness, a guy named Johnny Rivera, was nailed with a truck full of it. Mirtis took him out before we got a chance to fully interrogate him. That says to me that Rivera knew something. It also tells me that Mirtis knew at least that much, and maybe more."

"But if he's dead, what difference does it make?"

"We don't think Mirtis was the brains, just one of the higher-ups. But we lost the end of the string. It's out here somewhere, and we have to find it."

"Here? In Pakistan?"

"It's a way station. We think the stuff is coming through here. That means it probably comes through Afghanistan, as well. Now, do you have anything you want to tell us? Or don't you?"

"No need to get testy, Mahoney. I'm just trying to piece it together. I don't know what I can do to help unless I know what the problem is. Now I know, don't I?"

"Yes, you do."

"All right. Here's what I can tell you. Mirtis, before he defected, was working with a guy named Viktor Sharkov. Also, obviously, KGB. They both did time in Kabul during the war. Sharkov was still there after the withdrawal started. That was two and a half, three years after Mirtis came over to our side."

"What about Sharkov?" Mahoney asked.

"What about him?"

"Where is he now?"

Rucker shook his head. He took a sip of cold coffee and swallowed hard. "We don't know." He grinned apologetically.

"You don't know, or you'd rather not say?"

"We don't know. He dropped out of sight a little over a year ago. You have to understand that we don't have the best pipeline into Afghanistan. What information we do get often can't be verified. Even some of the intel that is verified turns out to be garbage. Anyway, Sharkov's gone, plain and simple."

"Who else was he tight with? What about them? You lose them, too?"

Rucker exploded. "Now look, damn it. Don't you high-horse me, buddy. We didn't *lose* Sharkov. He vanished. Pffft!" He snapped his fingers. "Just like that. No reassignment, as far as we know. Word is the Russkies are looking for him, too."

"You believe it?"

Rucker nodded.

"That official, or gut?"

"Gut, with confirmation, off the record, of course, from somebody I know on the red team."

"You believe it?"

"Yes."

"Can you get us in touch with your source?"

Rucker shook his head. "I don't know. I'm not sure that's a good idea."

"What about Afghanistan? Can you get me in?" Bolan asked, finally joining the conversation.

"Are you nuts?"

"Can you do it?"

"Maybe."

"Do it."

"You have authorization?"

Bolan nodded.

"Him, too?" Rucker asked, pointing at Mahoney.

"No. Just me."

"Wait a minute, Belasko," Mahoney protested. "I'm in this all the way. You can't just waltz off like that. What am I supposed to do—go to the library?"

"There's plenty to do here. You work on Rucker's KGB source. Get whatever you can."

"I don't like it," Rucker said. "As a form of suicide, it's refreshingly original. As an idea, it stinks."

"Just do it," Bolan told him. "You want to confirm the operational authorization, go ahead."

"Don't think I won't, Belasko. Wait here."

Rucker got up heavily, flexed his good leg, then left the office. When he was gone, Mahoney demanded, "Belasko, what the hell are you doing? I didn't come all the way out here to sit around a hotel lobby and watch the ferns die."

"Look, we have next to nothing. Sharkov's the only lead we have. If he's connected to this thing, he's going to find out about Mirtis. Maybe he already knows. But if we wait, he's going to burrow so deep we'll never find him."

"But—"

"Forget about it, Mahoney. It's already done."

CHAPTER THIRTEEN

Goncharov reined in to watch the caravan work its way through a narrow defile four kilometers ahead. The sun was turning a dark copper now, glowing as it grew larger and slipped toward the horizon. His shadow spilled over the rocks ahead of him, tinged with a dark bronze color at its edges.

Far ahead and below, the truck waddled like a crippled duck as it trailed behind the horsemen. Through the binoculars, Goncharov could watch the leader of the rebel contingent urging his men on, letting the single file move past him until he could lean over and talk to the driver of the truck. Behind his beard his face was lively and almost pleasant, in a rough-hewn way. It was a good face, Goncharov thought, the face of a man who might have been good to know. If only the world was a different place.

Goncharov wanted to get closer to the caravan because he was afraid of losing them in the dark. But until they passed through the narrow defile, it was too risky. He could do nothing for the moment but wait. It was apparent by now that the truck was hampering the rebels' progress. The horses could go places where the truck couldn't. Goncharov suspected the route had been changed to accommodate the unexpected bounty.

And he kept reminding himself that he didn't even know for sure that the rebels were leading him where he wanted to go. Gut reactions were fine, but they went against the textbook. Still, they sometimes worked. He hoped this was one of those times. But ultimately it didn't make any difference. The men who were supposed to ferry him to Kabul were so much raw meat lying in the dirt now. He might gain nothing by following the rebels, but it was abundantly clear he would lose nothing, either.

The truck was struggling up a steep incline, its canvas cover shuddering like a flag in a stiff breeze. Up above, at the far end of the narrow canyon, the going had to get easier. Either that or there was some sort of camp just out of sight in the defile. It had to be one or the other, because even the most determined antitechnologist would understand that the truck couldn't endure much more abuse.

And then, like a bad dream, the truck, the horses and the men vanished. He kicked his heels into his own mount, urging the horse to go faster. He was no horseman, but the tension was tearing him apart, making his nerves sing like wires stretched to the breaking point. If he didn't do something, anything, and soon, he was certain he would lose control of himself. And that would be his death warrant.

The horse hit a stride it found comfortable on the downslope and wouldn't go faster despite Goncharov's prodding. For the next hour, until the sun finally set, he would have his best, and perhaps only, chance to draw closer. While the caravan struggled uphill, he would have the luxury of going downhill, then straight ahead across the valley floor.

He had no idea what he would do when he finally got closer, but anything had to be better than this.

Purple light began to spill into the canyon, wrapping the western wall in shadows and painting the eastern wall lavender. The sun was sinking fast now, faster than he had imagined it could. A sense of urgency, almost of desperation, swept over him, and he tried again to make the horse go faster. This time it responded. The saddle was primitive and uncomfortable, but he held on as best he could, taking most of the shock against the base of his spine.

At sundown Goncharov started up the incline that funneled into the narrow canyon. He stopped to listen but heard nothing. A chilly wind blew into his face, but it was noiseless. There would be a moon, but not for a couple of hours.

Goncharov slid off his horse, grabbed the reins and looped them around his right forearm. He started slowly, letting the horse find a comfortable pace behind him. As long as the animal didn't balk, he figured he would be all right. He pressed a bit until he felt the horse pull back, then settled into a steady rhythm, climbing for nearly an hour, eventually reaching a flat, barren plateau.

The walls of the canyon still towered over him. He could sense them in the dark. They blotted out the stars on either side and were so high that he couldn't actually see the rim. It was a matter of contrast. Directly overhead, a band of stars glittered, brilliant points as hard as diamonds, cold as ice. On either side, nothing. Just emptiness. An absence of light—the very definition of darkness.

The ground sloped more sharply upward, and he could sense the walls getting closer. He was just about at the point where the truck had disappeared from view so many hours before. He wished he could risk a light, but it was too dangerous. Even with their old Enfields, the mujahadeen were superb marksmen. Now, with the newly captured modern weapons available, he would be an easy target, stumbling along behind a flashlight.

Instead, he stopped every fifty or sixty meters and ran his fingers across the ground. Faintly the ridges of the tire treads revealed themselves. The ground was too hard for anything more than that, but for the time being it was enough.

The canyon broke sharply to the left, and far ahead he could see a faint light dancing on the walls. At first he thought he was seeing things, but then he realized he wasn't. It was definitely firelight. Not much, but enough.

The light was too distant for him to do more than guess the range, but he estimated three kilometers, perhaps a bit less. He continued the climb, conscious now that the air was getting thinner. It was harder to breathe, and he felt as if something were trying to smother him.

The light grew a little brighter, then seemed almost motionless for a long time, as if he and the horse were on a treadmill, every stride leaving him just as far away as the one before and the one before that. He wanted to run, but couldn't, even if he was to let go of the reins and leave the horse behind.

And then the light started to dim. At first he thought the Afghans were leaving again. After a moment of panic, he realized the fires were being allowed to die. They must have been for cooking rather than heat. The mujahadeen were used to a more severe climate than this. Heat would have been the last thing on their minds.

As it was, the fires were risky. Not only could they be seen from the air, they could be picked up by infrared, even after they'd been out for hours. The men ahead of him were either braver than they were smart, or they knew something he didn't. It almost seemed as if they knew they wouldn't be pursued.

He pushed on for another four hundred meters. Again he stopped to listen. Again he heard nothing. But he was getting closer. He could feel it. His skin tingled, and the hair on his neck seemed to have a life of its own.

Goncharov groped in the dark for a rock big enough to hold the horse in check and small enough to wrap the reins around. After several false starts, he found an elongated rock. Its edges weren't sharp enough to saw through the leather, and it was rooted in the ground. He looped the reins around it, tying a double knot, even though he realized he might have to leave in a hurry. He still didn't want to run the risk of losing the horse through negligence.

Five hundred meters later he wondered whether he'd been too optimistic. He hadn't seen any signs of a camp. The moon was starting to come up, and pale light filtered down between the canyon walls. Everything looked gray in the moonlight, even the ground.

Goncharov cut toward the right-hand wall, actually reaching out for it several meters before he found it. He eased along the wall now, brushing it with his right shoulder, the rifle in his left hand. Every few steps he paused to listen, and every time he heard nothing.

After another hundred meters he was ready to give up. He hunkered down against the rock face, completely exhausted. For a moment he almost fell asleep. Instead, he hauled himself up after fifteen minutes, his eyes heavy and his legs aching.

The rifle slipped from his hands, and he thought about leaving it. But he couldn't give in to the temptation, no matter how tired he was. He bent to retrieve the weapon, his thighs screaming at the sudden strain.

His fingers closed over the barrel, and as he started to straighten up, something caught his eye. He felt a cold, dry breeze whip past him. Ahead, about two hundred meters, something turned red for a second, then disappeared, then came back, this time orange. At first he was confused. It seemed to vanish and reappear in time to the wind. Then he understood—coals. It was the remains of one of the fires.

The realization sent a surge of adrenaline through him. His legs still ached, but he was able to focus on something outside his skull or his skin for a moment. He started moving again, carefully, one step at a time. He felt for small rocks with the soles of his boots, pressing straight down to avoid kicking one. Then, when he'd halved the distance, he heard something behind him.

A voice. Speaking Pushtu.

Then a small circle of cold metal pressed against his neck. This time he didn't worry about noise. He let the rifle fall.

CHAPTER FOURTEEN

The bazaar was a nightmare of blind alleys. Teeming with people, it seemed to pulse like a living thing. Mahoney stood out like a red flag. A foot taller than most of those around him, his head and shoulders seemed to float on the surging crowd. He twisted and turned to get through. His progress was slow and his temper short.

He still cursed Belasko for treating him like an errand boy, sending him off for what he considered housework. He hadn't flown ten thousand miles to talk to some damn pencil pusher, no matter who owned the pencil being pushed.

It was hot and oppressively muggy. He felt as if he were melting inside his clothes, as if he might dissolve in his own sweat and wind up a puddle on the grimy street.

The scents of warring spices assaulted him from every side. Clouds of acrid smoke swirled around him, making his skin feel greasy. There had to be more to life than this, he thought. Then, remembering Tony Salvato sprawled in the dirt, bleeding from half a dozen holes in his chest, he remembered, too, why he was here. He knew he'd endure a lot worse than this to even the score. And something told him he couldn't do it without Belasko's help.

He could see far ahead, over the heads of the crowd, and the sign he was looking for floated like a mirage nearly three blocks away. Mahoney was nervous. He'd dealt with lots of unusual people. But this was a first. He'd never had a meeting with a Soviet agent before. He didn't know what to expect, and felt as if he'd been cut loose without an oar.

The sun grew a little larger, and the crowd was beginning to thin a bit. He'd gone through most of the bazaar, and wondered whether there was an easier way than through its heart. Not that it would help now.

Finally he reached the steps. He looked around out of habit, but there were too many people for him even to begin to notice something out of the ordinary. He shrugged, pushed open the glass door and stepped through. It was dark in the hall, and he patted his rib cage to make sure the Browning was where it was supposed to be.

The wooden stairs creaked under his weight, and he took them slowly, trying to keep the noise to a minimum. Up on the second flight he had a little light from a small bulb over the third-floor landing. The place smelled old and musty, as if the wood were slowly decaying around him as he climbed.

The last flight he took even more cautiously. Appointment or not, Mahoney wasn't about to trust anybody more than he had to. That meant not at all whenever possible. That was more than habit; it was instinct.

Down the hall he spotted three doors, all on the rear wall. The building was silent, more silent than it should have been with the teeming bazaar just outside. He wondered whether this was a KGB building, maybe soundproofed or something.

Mahoney found the door he wanted, which bore a tiny plastic sign that read Romanov Imports. The DEA agent pressed the buzzer, but didn't hear anything inside. He stood to one side of the door and knocked.

The sound of his knuckles on the wood landed with a dull thud in the hall. The door felt more solid than he'd expected under his knock. He pressed the buzzer again, this time impatiently tapping it several times with his thumb. He still heard nothing and sighed in exasperation.

That was how they always treated messenger boys, he thought. It didn't matter what side he was on—a lackey was a lackey. Mahoney started counting in his head, giving the man thirty, and not one second more. For good measure he tapped the buzzer two more times. Then a bolt slid back and the door swung open.

He found himself staring at a man his own size, which surprised him. He expected some little toad in wire-rim glasses. The man smiled and reached for his hand. He took it firmly and pulled Mahoney into the office. "It's better to close the door before formalities," he said.

Mahoney grunted, then shook the man's hand. "I'm Brian Mahoney. I believe you were expecting me?"

"A pleasure, Mr. Mahoney. My name is Yuri Kostikian. Please, come in and sit down."

He led Mahoney to a comfortable office. When he saw the Naugahyde, Mahoney grinned. Things really were the same all over. Maybe this wouldn't be so bad, after all, he thought.

Kostikian sat on a sofa and waved Mahoney to a chair. "Now, what can I do for you?"

"I understand you can give me some information on a man named Marko Mirtis. Is that right?"

Kostikian leaned back as if to dodge the question. "What exactly do you want to know?"

"Everything you can tell me."

"What do you already know?"

Mahoney lost his patience. "Look, I didn't fly halfway around the goddamn world to play twenty-questions with you, Kostikian. I came for information: You either have it or you don't. If you have it, give it to me. If you don't, let's save everybody's time. All right?"

Kostikian smiled. "You're in a hurry, aren't you?"

Mahoney stood. "Look, thanks but no thanks. I have better things to do."

"Of course you do. And so do I. But I just want to make sure we're talking about the same Marko Mirtis. In Lithuania it isn't that unusual a name. Not exactly like your John Smith, but I can tell you I have used it myself more than once, checking into a hotel. For a little recreation." He winked. "You understand?"

"I don't give a damn. Sign any name you want. Hell, use mine. Just give me what I came for."

"Please, Mr. Mahoney. This is a very sensitive matter. Try to be patient."

Mahoney let the air balloon his lips. He tapped a finger on the arm of his chair. "Look, my Mirtis is dead, to begin with. He was apparently rather adept at certain forms of witness relocation."

"Witness relocation? I don't understand."

"Let me put it another way. He wasted somebody in our custody. Iced him. You understand?"

Kostikian nodded. "Marko was an assassin, yes. A very good assassin. One of the best."

"You sound like you respect that."

"I do, Mr. Mahoney. In my line of work, you understand, I . . .

Let's just say he was a professional, and I admire his professionalism. Or did.''

"Look, Kostikian...Yuri. Mirtis attacked a safehouse. We were interrogating a witness in a smuggling operation. The guy was a mule, a nobody. But you're telling me the man who wasted him was a KGB assassin. Doesn't that seem strange to you?''

Kostikian stared up at the ceiling. His lips moved, but he said nothing for a long time. When he finally spoke, he seemed weighted down by the words. "Mr. Mahoney, a year ago the answer to your question would have been yes. It would have surprised me very much.''

"And now?''

"And now I have nothing but surprises. Mirtis vanished three years ago. No trace. We didn't find out until two years later that he'd defected. At around the same time two of our agents also disappeared. One of them was a man named Viktor Sharkov, who was a high-ranking officer of the KGB. A colonel, in fact. Do you understand what that means? A man of that rank simply vanishing into thin air, as if he'd been sucked up by a vacuum cleaner? It isn't done. It's unheard-of. The other was Sharkov's second-in-command in Turkey, Vasily Chebrikov.''

"I don't see the connection.''

"You will. If I understand correctly, you work for your government's Drug Enforcement Administration."

"So?"

"So, we've been hearing all sorts of rumors. Rumors about Sharkov. And drugs. We think he's smuggling drugs out of south-central Asia. We have no proof, but I personally believe it. I've spoken to Tim Rucker about it, more than once, in fact. We're trying to be helpful. This is a new day for all of us. It will take some getting used to."

"I still don't see—"

"Sharkov was Mirtis's superior. Not at the time he disappeared, but before that. Sharkov spent a considerable amount of time in Turkey and later in Afghanistan. He was back in Turkey at the time he vanished. I think there's a connection, but I can't prove it."

"And you don't know where Sharkov is now?"

"Not for certain. Again there are rumors, but only that. He seems to be moving around, almost constantly."

"And you think he and Mirtis were working together?"

"Yes, I do. They used to work very well together before Marko defected. I don't think this was planned that far back, but I think it is happening, yes."

"And what are you doing about it?"

"Officially, nothing."

Mahoney waited a beat before asking, "And unofficially?"

"I can't answer that. I'm sorry."

"Why not?"

Kostikian shook his head.

"But you are doing something?"

"Mr. Mahoney, America isn't the only place on the planet with a drug problem. We have our disaffected, we have our unemployed and we have our criminals. People in Georgia, in Armenia, in Lithuania have drug habits, too. Not as many as you have, maybe. At least not yet. But it will continue to worsen. One of the assets of a police state is the ability to control such things as smuggling more effectively than you could ever hope to do. Not completely. But now all that's changing. That's why I expect the problem to grow. That's why I'm talking to you now. Two years ago, even a year ago, this conversation would never have taken place."

"Look, Yuri, I'm concerned about one thing. Do you know where Sharkov is, or don't you?"

Kostikian covered his eyes with one hand. He looked as if he might be falling asleep. Then he dropped the hand, and was about to answer, when a phone rang in an adjacent office. The Russian sighed and stood. He walked toward the second office, and Mahoney sighed impatiently.

Kostikian put the phone down with a frown. He turned to Mahoney, and all hell broke loose. A loud bang, like a large firecracker, went off. Both men looked toward the front door as it came crashing into the room, propelled by a booted foot. Mahoney dived for the floor as Kostikian backed up a step, a look of surprise on his face. Everything seemed to slow down.

The man in the doorway aimed an ugly-looking automatic pistol deliberately. Mahoney reached for his Browning as Kostikian groped under his jacket. The pistol hissed, and the Russian staggered backward, slamming into the doorframe and falling to one knee. The gunman fired again, and the splat of the bullet told Mahoney that Kostikian was dead. He heard the Russian hit the floor as his Browning cleared its holster.

Mahoney rolled as the gunman turned toward him. He squeezed off a shot, and the killer fired back. Mahoney's shot went wide, but it threw the gunman off balance. The DEA agent fired again, this time taking the gunman high on the shoulder. Before the guy could recover, Mahoney fired again. The pistol seemed so heavy in his hand that he was sure he was going to drop it.

The assassin staggered back toward the door, missed it and slammed into the wall just beside the doorway. Mahoney fired once more, and the gunman lay still. The rattled DEA agent got out of there fast.

"WHAT THE HELL HAPPENED?" Bolan asked when Mahoney opened the door for him.

The DEA agent shook his head. "I'm still not sure. I went to meet the Russkie and somebody blew him away. That's all I know. They were after me, too. But I lucked out. Royce said he didn't know how to reach you or Rucker, so I told him I'd wait here in the hotel."

Bolan frowned. "Rucker and I met with Randy Macmillan, the Aussie merc who's going to take me to the border."

"I think Rucker has some explaining to do," Mahoney said.

"You may be right, but I don't want to jump to conclusions. We need him right now. Still, it does seem odd. I just don't know whether it was a setup or a coincidence."

"There's no such thing as coincidence, Belasko. You know better than that."

"Maybe. I'm not sure. When we heard about the attack from Royce, Rucker seemed genuinely upset."

Mahoney snorted. "I bet."

Bolan sat down, letting the musty-smelling sofa take his full weight. He let his breath out in a long, silent stream. "Rucker says the only way I'm going to get to the border is with Macmillan's help. But I don't trust mercs. Still, this is Rucker's turf. It's his ball game."

"As far as I'm concerned, the less Rucker knows about our plans, the more likely we are to live long enough to carry them out."

"You really don't trust him, do you?"

"Look, I don't know how much experience you've had dealing with spooks, but I've had a bellyful. I'm not saying Rucker's dirty, necessarily, but I'm pretty sure a few of his buddies might be. These guys are all the same. They've raised looking the other way to a high art. What I'd like to do, in case you're asking, is hoist Rucker by his ankles and shake the change out of his pockets. You just might be surprised at what we find."

"If he's dirty."

"Right. And if he isn't, then somebody else is feeding our schedule to the bad guys. Either way we're living on borrowed time, and I don't like it."

"I don't, either," Bolan agreed. "But if we want to get to this guy Sharkov, we have to play by the rules."

"That's what I'm trying to tell you, Belasko. There are no rules. Not here, and not in this business."

"Then we'll make a few of our own."

"Such as?"

"Such as no solo missions from now on."

"Meaning?"

"Meaning we're both going over the wire."

Mahoney grinned. "Now you're talking. I hear Afghanistan's lovely in the fall."

CHAPTER FIFTEEN

Viktor Sharkov watched quietly as the canvas bags were ferried up the hillside and stacked in one of the roofed buildings. Vasily, as was his habit, played the overseer. He seemed to relish giving orders to the others. It was a trait Sharkov used, but didn't like in his lieutenant.

Having someone to play the heavy was often valuable. But when that same man betrayed—no matter how carefully he tried to hide it—the desire to take orders from no one else, he posed a problem. For now it was a problem Sharkov could live with. But how much longer was unclear.

The bags weren't that heavy, but the men handled them so carefully they looked as if they were handling lead bars. That was Chebrikov. He had browbeaten the others to the point where they walked on eggs constantly.

Sharkov stood with his hands on his hips as the last half-dozen bags made their way up the hill. When the last man deposited the last sack, he came out of the mud-and-stone hut, clapped his hands together and looked at Chebrikov, who sent him off with a nod of his head. Chebrikov then turned and started back down the hill toward Sharkov. "All done, Viktor," he said, smiling broadly.

Sharkov watched quietly, his head tilted to one side, as Chebrikov took long, sliding steps down the dry, barren hill.

"Where's Hikmal, your Afghan?" Chebrikov asked, the smile stretching his mouth even more.

"He'll be here tomorrow."

"I thought you said today."

"I did. But it doesn't pay to be too precise, does it? There are too many people interested in our little shipment. I thought it best to play it safe."

"You should have told me, Viktor." Chebrikov's smile was replaced by a pout.

"Don't be a child, Vasily."

"You keep too many secrets, Viktor. You shouldn't exclude me so much."

"You always learn what you need to know."

"Eventually, yes, but—"

"Don't worry about it. Just make sure you have two men on watch at all times. I'm not sure I trust these buffoons."

"I'll stay up all night if you like."

"That won't be necessary. Just make sure there are no slipups. We've already lost one shipment. I don't want to think about losing another. And I especially don't want to have to worry about it. Understood?"

Chebrikov nodded. "Of course. What do we do about Mirtis?"

"What's there to be done? He did what he was paid to do. It's unfortunate that we have to find a replacement for him, but it can be managed. There's no shortage of men like Marko. You ought to know that better than anyone."

"I do. Of course I do! But the Americans aren't stupid. They might be able to trace him."

"They might be able to identify him, yes. Trace him? Never. Besides, we're paying good money to make sure we're protected on that end. I hope we're getting our money's worth."

"You talk too much about money, Viktor. You should be careful. It isn't something you know that much about. Besides, if we can buy someone, there's always the possibility that someone else will pay more."

"And I'm paying you to make sure that doesn't happen. I'm getting my money's worth from you, Vasily, am I not?"

Chebrikov didn't answer right away. He didn't like Sharkov's tone. But then, he realized, he didn't much like Sharkov. The man had changed, slowly but certainly, in the past year. The wonderful idea that had brought them together was looking less wonderful every day.

For the time being he would put up with Viktor's moods, but there were limits. If Viktor didn't know that, someone would have to teach him. Soon.

The afternoon wore on, and Sharkov was beginning to get antsy. Twice he walked to the bottom of the hill, and Chebrikov wondered whether he was waiting for someone other than the Afghan. He didn't think Viktor was fool enough to try to pull a fast one. Not here, anyway, and certainly not yet. Chebrikov was his link to the others. None of them spoke Russian, and Viktor didn't speak Pushtu. That, for the time being, was as good an insurance policy as any. But if Sharkov had made other plans and was expecting someone else, someone who, perhaps, did speak Pushtu, then Chebrikov would have to watch his back.

As the sun began to set, the wind picked up. Snow came suddenly at this altitude, almost without warning. If it did snow, Hikmal would be delayed. Even the best horsemen would have trouble pushing their mounts through a heavy snowfall. Chebrikov thought about warning Viktor, but he decided against it. Better, he thought, to keep a few secrets of his own. Viktor wasn't the only one who knew how to use surprise to good advantage.

But Sharkov, too, was looking at the sky. Then he glanced at Chebrikov, as if to blame him for the sudden change in weather. "It's colder," he muttered. "And it looks like snow."

"It will snow, and soon," Chebrikov said.

"How much?"

Chebrikov shrugged. "Who knows. This time of year anything's possible. Maybe a couple of centimeters, maybe a meter."

Sharkov swore under his breath, turned away and started off into the darkness. Chebrikov heard the man's footfalls below. He was about to say something about the mines when a light clicked on halfway down the hill. Then he realized just how dangerous the weather could be. The mines were pressure-detonated. Under a covering of snow, no one, not even the men who had planted them, would know precisely where they were. A little flaw in Sharkov's planning.

Chebrikov watched Sharkov's flashlight bobbing down the hill, then stopping where the ground leveled off. He was through the mine field now, and he turned off the light. Immediately he was lost from sight.

What now? Chebrikov wondered. He didn't like it one bit, but there was no way he could follow Sharkov without being seen. He would have to use a light to get past the mines, and if the man didn't want to be followed, he'd be watching for just that.

It was a stalemate, and Chebrikov knew it. He shook his head in disgust, realizing he'd been outsmarted yet again. Sharkov was infuriating, but Chebrikov had to hand it to him. He stared out into the darkness, listening to the wind. It moaned like a lost soul in torment. The flames in front of him danced faster, like mad dervishes. Then he heard another sound, distant and irregular. He stepped past the fire, as if its light was interfering with the sound. The noise rose and fell. He couldn't place it, not yet, but it seemed as if it were getting closer.

Then, far out over the valley floor, he saw a single red light, its glow washed out by the thickly swirling clouds starting to fill the valley. It was a helicopter, and Sharkov had known it would be coming. He had gone out to meet it.

Chebrikov cursed and started down the hill. He was almost to the mines before he remembered they were there. He reached into his pocket for a flashlight, clicked it on and played the beam across the ground. In its light he could see swirls of dust coiling in tiny funnels as the wind rushed up the hill and around the rocks littering the dry earth.

He picked his way carefully, looking for the slight mounds under which the mines lay buried. Slowly he stepped around one, then rushed several meters downhill until he spotted another. They were arranged in concentric rings a few meters apart. Staggered and only roughly patterned, they littered the hill just under the surface. Chebrikov shuddered as he thought about what would happen to him if he made a mistake.

Then he was through. By this time the chopper was hovering just above the ground, not far away.

He could hear the sound of the rotor clearly now and saw the cloud of dust it kicked up, reddened by the single light.

He started to run, his legs pumping, and every step jarring his spine and rattling his teeth. A finger of bright light speared out, and he could see a figure moving toward the chopper. He didn't have to see clearly to recognize Sharkov's stiff walk, his head thrown back over impossibly squared shoulders.

Then someone jumped out of the chopper and walked toward Sharkov. Before Chebrikov could get much closer the man turned and started back toward the helicopter. Sharkov stood and watched him climb in, and instantly the chopper began to lift off. It rotated on its rotor once, slowly drifted to one side, then rose straight up. The finger of light disappeared, and Chebrikov realized with a start that the aircraft wasn't a Soviet helicopter. It was a Cobra.

The chopper was unmarked, as far as he could tell, but there was no doubt in his mind. It was American-made. He closed in on Sharkov almost without realizing it, then stared skyward. The chopper had already vanished.

Sharkov smiled at him. "So, Vasily, you're worried, eh?"

"Should I be?"

"Yes, you should."

"Why?"

"Hikmal has been delayed."

"That was his helicopter?"

"Do you have to know everything, Vasily?"

CHAPTER SIXTEEN

"There's the border, mate," Randy Macmillan said as he killed the jeep engine and pointed a grimy finger westward. Bolan and Mahoney looked at the saw-toothed mountains, their peaks twinkling in the late-afternoon sunlight. "Never thought you'd get this close to hell without an asbestos suit, did you?"

The Australian laughed, then pulled field glasses out of the back seat. Bolan sat patiently while Macmillan scanned the road ahead. When he was finished, he looked at the Executioner. "Rucker says you're to meet an Afghan named Hikmal in twenty-four hours or he won't be there. That right?"

"That's what he says."

"Rucker's an idiot. You know that, don't you?"

"He likes you, too," Mahoney said.

"It's not about liking, mate. It's about living. Rucker's the kind of bloke who can get you killed without even thinkin' about it. It's not that he's a bad man, not even that he's a lousy agent. He just doesn't know how to run people. And that's the plain and simple truth of it."

"Then why are you here?" Bolan asked.

The Australian winked. "Money. I have my needs, mate. Don't you know? And that's the only reason that really counts."

"Remind me of that every hour or so, will you?" Mahoney cracked.

"Oh, now, ain't you the funny one? And I suppose you're not here for the same bloody reason, eh, Mahoney? Money don't count for you, eh?"

"That's right."

"Have it your way." Macmillan sighed loud enough to show how tolerant he could be.

Bolan listened to the exchange without speaking. Rucker had said Macmillan was annoying. But he'd also said he was good. Now, sitting next to the Australian in the jeep, he wasn't so sure. But they needed someone who knew the border country and who could get them to the rendezvous in a hurry.

"We have to wait an hour or so," Macmillan told them. "We made better time than I thought. And we don't want to cross the border during daylight."

"How bad is it?" Mahoney asked.

"Pretty bad. The border patrols are one thing. We can work around that, but there's every sort of scum you can imagine out there. Pirates, bandits, I don't know what the hell to call them. They swoop down on the refugees and take everything they've got. With the Russkies gone it's hell on earth."

Bolan climbed out of the jeep and walked off the road a few steps. He could see downhill nearly three miles into the relative tranquillity of Pakistan. The countryside was wild, but nothing compared to the Afghan side of the border.

Macmillan started the engine and tossed away a cigarette, which arced through the gathering dusk and disappeared. Bolan climbed back into the jeep. "Second thoughts?" the Aussie asked.

"Always."

"Good way to be."

"Have you met Hikmal?" Bolan asked as the jeep started to roll.

"Three or four times. Don't know him all that well, but he seems like a straight shooter. As much as any, and more than a few I've met. Watch your back, though. Fact is, Belasko, you're probably worth your weight in gold to the man. Most everybody is. There's a buyer for just about anything. Slave labor, white slaves, ransom. You'd be surprised how much folks are willing to pay." The jeep seemed to rise slowly into the air, then hung suspended for a moment, slamming back to earth almost as suddenly. "That's it. We're in Afghanistan now," the Aussie announced.

"How far to the rendezvous?" Bolan asked.

"Not far, maybe sixty miles or so. But it's about the roughest sixty you'll ever want to see. Man has to be crazy or unlucky to want to live here." Macmillan sniffed. "Smells like snow. Keep your fingers crossed. It can get bad in a hurry."

The rising moon washed everything out, diminishing color to shades of gray, but Bolan noticed a haze beginning to drift across the sky. It was tough to see, and the warrior was impressed by Macmillan's handling of the jeep.

Bolan kept sweeping his eyes across the terrain on either side of the road. The Aussie had his hands full with the jeep, and security was the warrior's job. They were about ten miles over the border when Bolan reached out and tapped Macmillan on the arm. "Hold it a minute, Randy."

"What's the problem?" The jeep whined to a standstill. "You see something?"

"I'm not sure. I thought I did."

"Where?"

Bolan pointed off the road at a forty-five-degree angle. "Over there. Just movement. I couldn't make out any details."

They sat quietly, Bolan squinting through the moonlight. The road itself was little more than a rock-free track through a jumble of broken stone. There was little vegetation, most of it gnarled and stunted. Enough for a man to hide behind, but not much else. In the dim light the leaves looked like little pieces of ancient tinfoil.

"I guess it was a false alarm, mate." Macmillan laughed. He was nervous, and the laughter sounded forced. Letting out the clutch, he gunned the engine enough to keep it from stalling and started to roll in jerking spurts. Two hundred yards more and he stopped again. "Maybe you were right. Look there."

Something lay in the road ahead. It was dark and oblong but too far away for either of them to see any more details. Bolan turned the glasses on it. "Looks like a body. I'm not sure. I better take a look."

"I'll come with you," Mahoney offered.

Bolan waved him off. "You stay here and watch our backs."

He started to get out of the jeep, but Macmillan grabbed him. "Hold on. Not a good idea."

"You can't use the lights," Bolan said.

"We can roll up to it and over it if we have to."

The Aussie gunned the engine and the jeep lurched ahead. It picked up a little speed as it approached the object in the road. They were only fifty yards away now. The body, if that was what it was, remained motionless.

"Fucker's either dead or a sound sleeper," Macmillan muttered.

"I don't like it," Bolan said. "Wait here." He climbed out of the jeep before Macmillan could object, making sure his CAR-15 was ready. He stepped off the road and started moving parallel to it, about twenty yards to the right.

He was only ten yards from the object now, but well to one side. He swiveled his head, listening to the night. All he could hear was the rumble of the jeep's engine, its muffler coughing every few seconds. He crouched and started ahead. Something moved off to the left on the far side of the road. "Look out, Macmillan!" he yelled.

Bolan hit the deck as a single shot cracked. He could see the bright muzzle-flash and knew it was an old weapon. He could hear footsteps, and suddenly the road was bathed in light. Macmillan had flicked on the headlights and jammed the jeep into gear. The engine roared, and the lights wobbled as the vehicle rolled forward.

Bolan could see them now—seven, eight, maybe nine men charging toward the road. Several veered in the direction of the jeep. Bolan swept his muzzle across a wide arc in front of him, the CAR-15 hammering in the night.

There were more gunshots from the charging men. One of them had an automatic pistol, but they seemed to be lightly armed. Two men darted straight across the road at him. He could see the old rifles in their hands, held like clubs as if they were out of ammunition.

The Executioner fired a short burst and took out one of the advancing men, but the second either tripped or dived out of harm's way. He heard glass shatter and looked toward the jeep. Three holes, only dimly lit by the backwash of the headlights, pocked the windshield. The engine still raced, but the jeep was slowing down. Neither Mahoney nor Macmillan returned fire.

Bolan got to his feet as someone tackled him. He saw the flash of a knife blade, caught the wrist and twisted. A sharp crack sent the knife clattering away into the darkness. The man on top of him moaned, and Bolan swung his fist, slamming it into the man's jaw and sending him sprawling.

Out of the corner of one eye he saw Macmillan spring up and onto the jeep's hood, his automatic rifle spitting fire. Two pistol shots rang out, and the Aussie tumbled over the windshield and back into the jeep. Three men swarmed toward the vehicle, and Bolan jammed another clip home, then opened up on the assault team.

He nailed one man, but the other two scampered off into the darkness. It was over as suddenly as it had begun.

Bolan raced toward the jeep and reached in to kill the headlights. He turned the key, and the rolling jeep ground to a halt. Mahoney lay across the back seat, a dark stain on his left shoulder. Bolan felt for a pulse, found a faint one, then turned to the Australian.

Macmillan lay on his side, moaning. Blood covered the left shoulder of his shirt. Then he fell silent.

CHAPTER SEVENTEEN

Mahoney was losing a lot of blood. Bolan kept glancing at him, but he couldn't really take his eyes off the road for long. It was too treacherous, and the curves too frequent. The kid kept moaning, but there wasn't anything the warrior could do about it except get him to medical attention as soon as possible.

He drove with his headlights on high. If anybody wanted to ambush him, he thought, just let them try. He was in no mood to be cautious, or forgiving. What he wanted more than anything was to get Tim Rucker in a room for an hour. The guy would make a good speed bag. Rucker was either incompetent or reckless, maybe both. He couldn't blame Macmillan for any of this. The poor dead bastard had tried his best. He'd even warned Bolan about Rucker.

The Executioner had run out of faith in coincidence. It had been nothing more than an ambush, plain and simple. And the attackers had been well informed.

Macmillan had a big mouth, true enough. But the guy was no fool. He wouldn't have gabbed about his own mission, not one like this, with his own life on the line. They had either been compromised somehow, or it had been a setup. Either way the finger kept pointing to Tim Rucker. No one else was so directly involved. Sure, the guy had pulled some strings, had probably gone through channels, but still, something stank, and the odor was getting stronger by the minute.

Rucker had led them to Kostikian. Whatever else he was, the man wasn't a complete idiot. He wouldn't have been stupid enough to point him and Mahoney toward the KGB contact and then leak the information, especially since Mahoney had gone alone. If you were going to exterminate pests, you did it in one fell swoop, not piecemeal.

So that left one big question mark. So far the only name in front of it was Rucker's, but there could be other candidates, people he didn't know about yet. But he'd sure as hell find out. And damn quick.

His first problem was finding a doctor. They were two hundred miles from the nearest large city. The chances of a total stranger, and a foreigner at that, getting help in the middle of the night were slim at best.

Mahoney had stopped moaning, and that was a bad sign. The kid had lapsed into unconsciousness, which meant he was no longer able to keep the pressure on his wound. Bolan pulled the jeep over reluctantly. Stopping in the middle of nowhere seemed tantamount to suicide, but he had no choice.

He left the engine running and jumped down to lean into the back. Mahoney had slipped halfway to the floor. His head was in Macmillan's lap, but the Australian wouldn't mind. He'd never care about anything anymore.

Mahoney was still breathing, but it was rapid and shallow. He was probably going into shock from the loss of blood. Bolan had more than his share of combat medical experience, but he'd always had a few necessities to work with. This was next to impossible.

He stripped Macmillan's belt, then took Mahoney's, as well. Hooking them together, he made a cincture long enough to encircle Mahoney's chest. He had to pull the kid forward, loop the leather around his shoulders, then try to tighten it enough to keep the makeshift compression bandage in place. Together the belts were too long, so he unbuckled them again and made a hole in the leather, just big enough to admit the tongue of Macmillan's buckle. He had to put his weight into it this time, but too tight was better than not tight enough.

Mahoney winced slightly as Bolan tugged the leather tight enough to buckle the belts again. The bandage was already blood-soaked, but the warrior was more concerned with getting back on the road than tidiness. He tugged the belt once more to make sure it would hold, then let Mahoney lean against Macmillan's knees.

Climbing back into the driver's seat, Bolan looked once more over his shoulder to make sure the kid wouldn't fall over, then kicked the clutch, jammed the jeep into first and let the thick tires bite into the dry, loose dirt just off the road. The road was too steep for him to shift into second, so he had to content himself with the angry snarl of first.

He drove for what seemed like hours. Trying to rack his brain to reconstruct their route out, he had to slow at an intersection near the top of the low range of mountains. He knew they had made a turn, and he remembered it being from right to left. That meant he should turn left, but it looked wrong somehow. He let the jeep coast a few yards, stopping with its nose just edging into the intersection.

The splintered end of a signpost jutted into the darkness, but the post and the sign itself, along with whatever information it might have yielded, were long gone. Trusting his instincts, he made the left and pushed the jeep into the rutted road. It was less than a mile to the top of the mountain. From there maybe he'd be able to spot some hint of civilization, or whatever passed for it this far from the real world.

On the ridge line he saw a light and breathed a silent prayer of thanks. He checked Mahoney once more, then let the jeep pick up speed as he started downhill and toward the light. It was nearly five miles away in a straight line, but the way the road snaked down the face of the mountain, it was more like ten or twelve. At least a half-hour drive yet, even if he pushed it.

Bolan felt the first flakes of snow on his cheeks without realizing what they were. He brushed absently at the moisture. When it dawned on him, he cursed. Now he could barely see ahead of him.

The Executioner hoped that the light wouldn't go out before he got close enough to see whatever building housed it. If it did go out, or if the weather got worse, he might never find the building, and Mahoney might not make it. The warrior needed to know where the nearest medical help could be found, and a half hour was the most he could spare. Any longer than that and Mahoney's chances would start to evaporate.

But he caught a break. The snow stopped and the light stayed on. Still, he found himself driving faster and faster, as if the jeep and gravity were doing what he was unwilling to do himself. He steered through turn after turn, switchback after switchback, barely using the brake.

The light was close enough now that he could see the dim outline of a building, dark gray against the much darker horizon. The road started to flatten out, and he shifted into second, giving the old jeep as much gas as he dared. Its muffler rumbled in protest, but Bolan ignored it.

As he drew closer, he realized it was a farm of some kind. Several buildings, most much larger than the one with the light, loomed out of the darkness. Bolan rolled into a broad, unfenced lane, shifted down and let the jeep drift all the way to the front porch of the ramshackle farmhouse. Another light went on, this one in an upper story, and a block of light spilled out onto the dusty ground as he stepped down.

The front door flew open, and someone appeared on the porch. Bolan heard the telltale click of a shotgun being pumped. A second later a bright glare hit him in the face. He held up a bloody hand to ward off the probing blade of light and he heard someone gasp, "My God, man, what happened to you?"

The last thing Bolan expected was to hear an English accent. Footsteps thumped on the wooden porch, and the light swept away from him and over the jeep as the figure approached.

"We need a doctor," Bolan said.

The figure was almost up to him now. He could see the shotgun cradled in one arm, the flashlight in the same hand. "Sarah," the man called. "Sarah, come quick. We have to get them inside."

The man stood back as Bolan reached for Mahoney, pulled the unconscious DEA agent out of the jeep and arranged him for a fireman's carry. The warrior struggled with the deadweight and got onto the porch with some difficulty because of the high step. He saw a woman outlined against the light spilling through the front door.

"Sarah," the man said again, "get Dr. Singh on the radio. Quickly."

The woman vanished as the man slipped past Bolan to open the screen door. "Inside," he directed, stepping back to let the warrior pass. Then, once Bolan was inside, the Englishman brushed past and said, "Follow me."

He led the way into a back room. A double bed, neatly made up as if for guests, filled one corner of the small room. "Set him down," the man said.

"We need a doctor," Bolan repeated.

"Sarah will take care of that. He's not far. We should bring the man in now."

"No need," Bolan said, shaking his head.

"What in heaven's name happened to you?"

"I'm not sure. Bandits, I think."

"You should never have been out there at night. Even armed it's too dangerous after dark. That's why I sleep with the shotgun close at hand."

"Do you have a phone?"

"Sorry, no."

"I have to get in touch with someone in Islamabad."

"We can use the radio. Someone can patch us through. That's how I do it when I have to call someone. You better sit down, son. You look dreadful. Are you sure you're not hurt?"

"I'm sure."

The woman reappeared. "Dr. Singh will be here in twenty minutes."

"I better tend to my friend," Bolan said. "He's bleeding pretty badly."

"Best leave it to Dr. Singh. Sarah will keep an eye on him until then." The man stuck out a hand. "Reese Childress," he said.

Bolan shook the hand without giving his own name. "Can we make that call, then?"

"Of course. Come with me."

He led the way into another room. An elaborate radio setup sat on a handmade wooden table. Bolan gave him the information and sat on the edge of his chair, waiting for Childress to make the connections. The process seemed to take forever, but finally he heard Rucker's voice crackle through the speaker.

"Belasko?" he said. "Belasko, you there? What happened?"

Childress waved him over, and Bolan sat in front of the mike. He covered it with one hand. "Where are we?"

His host told him and explained as best he could the location. Bolan relayed it to Rucker.

"What do you want me to do, Belasko?"

"Get here as quickly as you can. We have a lot to talk about."

"Can't it wait until you get back here?"

"No, it can't. Macmillan's down for the count. Mahoney's badly hurt. I don't know how long before he can be moved, or where he'll be moved to. If he makes it."

"That bad?"

"Yeah, that bad."

Rucker sighed. "All right, give me six hours. That's as soon as I can make it."

"Six hours. At the outside, Rucker."

"Don't threaten me, Belasko."

"Too late for that."

Too late for Macmillan, too, he thought.

CHAPTER EIGHTEEN

Tim Rucker stood on the asphalt pad near Peshawar, leaning on a polished wooden cane. Its silver head picked up the glow of the chopper's lights. His hair swirled in the prop wash, and he watched Bolan climb into the Huey. He cupped his hands around his mouth, letting the cane lean against one hip.

"This is it, Belasko. I'm overextended as it is. If anything happens, I never heard of you."

Bolan stopped halfway in and looked over his shoulder. "Anything happens, Rucker, and you better believe I'll be seeing you."

"Don't push your luck. There's too much going on out here for some asshole who doesn't know diddly-squat to come in and start throwing his weight around."

"Tell me about it. Keep an eye on Mahoney. Make sure he stays in the hospital for a couple of days. And don't let him do anything stupid."

Rucker nodded. "Look, we'll talk. I don't mean to bust your hump, but—"

Bolan waved him off, and the chopper started to lift off. He sat on one of the benches bolted to the wall. Two surly-looking door gunners leaned against their M-60s.

The chopper was painted black. Like the aircraft, the gunners were deliberately anonymous. Even their faces seemed part of the deniability. They looked like a million other men, decked out in jeans and denim shirts. They might have been going to the mall to pick up some do-it-yourself supplies on a Saturday morning.

Only what they were going to do, nobody knew, not even the men themselves. Rucker was right. This was bending the rules so far out of shape that it was a wonder they didn't snap altogether. Or maybe they already had.

Rucker had gotten Bolan and Mahoney out of Afghanistan without a hitch, and now the warrior was heading back. Solo, with all kinds of unanswered questions buzzing in his brain. He still didn't believe Rucker was dirty, but his faith was shot full of holes. He only hoped his body wasn't next.

Bolan closed his eyes for a moment. When he opened them again, one of the gunners was lighting a cigarette. Casually the man shook his match, checked to see the small puff of smoke, snapped it in half and flicked the broken ends out into the night. The Executioner watched the gunner because he had nothing else to do, and because it was easier to focus on something meaningless.

The man betrayed no emotion whatsoever. One arm was draped over his machine gun. He stared off into the blackness below the chopper, dragging on the cigarette deeply.

The other gunner sat on the floor beside the door. Bolan shifted on his bench, waiting for one of the men to say something, if not to him, then at least to each other. But they were as silent as death.

The man with the cigarette finished his smoke, squeezed the butt and flipped it out into the night. He was a big man, six-two or so, and a good 220 pounds at least. He had a slight paunch, but it looked hard, as if he had a rock under his shirt. His sleeves were rolled up past his elbows. A tattoo, its details blurry in the dim light, spiraled up one forearm. The other was unadorned. His hair was longish and a bit thin on top. Bolan put his age at somewhere in the late thirties.

The other man had more hair and no tattoo, but otherwise they could have been taken from the same mold. The man on the floor looked as if he were falling asleep. He seemed relaxed to the point of unconsciousness, his head lolling on its thick neck with every shift in direction the chopper made.

Bolan stood and walked to the door, slipped into a harness and locked it onto the bar. The tattooed man spoke for the first time.

"Don't get too close, buddy." His Texas drawl was unmistakable. "You don't want to fall out of this thing. Old Roy is known to give people some wild rides, especially when he don't like where he's going.''

The warrior flicked the harness with a finger.

Tattoo smiled. "You think that thing'll hold you? I seen guys a lot smaller than you take a header. Them harnesses ain't worth spit.''

Bolan backed away from the door and sat on the bench again. "You go into Afghanistan much?''

Tattoo shook his head. "Too much. It's crazy in there, man. People shoot at anything that moves.''

"You know this Hikmal?''

"I know him, yeah. Why?''

"What can you tell me about him?''

"Not much. Bugger keeps to himself pretty much. Seems like he knows what he wants, but ain't too anxious for other folks to know what that might be. We cut him off a couple of times because he wasn't toeing the mark, you know?''

"Rucker said he was a good man.''

"Rucker says a lot of things. If I was you, I'd watch out for ol' Hikky. What do you want to see him for, anyway?''

"I have to get to Kabul. According to Rucker, he can get me there.''

"He can, yeah. Whether he will is something else.''

"I think he's already agreed. No point in going all this way if he hasn't.''

"He's agreed to lots of stuff he never done. That's how it is with him. Unpredictable as a rattler. And twice as dangerous. He gets a burr under his saddle, you might as well cut your own throat. Saves him the trouble, and it don't hurt as much."

"What about Rucker?"

"No comment."

"You don't like him?"

"What's to like or not, partner? Whether I like it or not don't enter the picture. Man signs the paycheck, you cut him some slack. Know what I mean?" The chopper lurched wildly before Bolan could answer. Tattoo laughed. "Downdraft, that's all. Hit them all the time over this goddamn place."

The squawk box squealed for a split second, then crackled. "We got company." The voice on the speaker was tinny and sounded tight, as if it had been squeezed through clenched teeth. "Ten o'clock," the pilot said. "One bogie."

Tattoo unhooked his belt and crossed the cabin. The chopper lurched again, and Tattoo had to drop to one knee to keep from falling over. The other gunner woke in a hurry. "What's happening? What the hell's going on?"

"Roy says we got company," Tattoo told him. "I was just going to check it out." The Texan hooked on next to Bolan and leaned toward the door. He jerked a headset off the wall and slipped it on, swinging the mike around to get it into position. "Roy," he shouted, "what you got?"

"Don't know. A chopper. That's all I can see."

"Hind?"

"Too far to tell."

Bolan leaned behind Tattoo, but he couldn't see anything in the darkness. Apparently Tattoo couldn't, either.

"You sure?" the Texan asked.

"Saw something, man. I'm tellin' you. It's out there."

Tattoo shook his head. "Don't see a thing." Turning to the other gunner, he said, "Andy, you'd best get your headset on. We better be ready. And put your damn harness on. If that's a Hind, things'll get hot in a hurry."

Andy grumbled as he slipped the headset on. "I'll take your door. Roy's probably seeing things again."

"Roy always does. You know that. But most of the time it's out there. You got to give him that."

"I'd like to give him a swift kick in the butt," Andy muttered.

"There it is," Bolan said. The chopper was running without lights, like their own, but he'd seen a small flash of light from an exhaust tube, a finger of flame that winked on and off before Tattoo could pick it up.

"You sure? Don't go gettin' silly now. We can't afford that."

"I saw it, all right. Exhaust. He's running too rich a mixture. Some of the fuel's burning off in the tube. Watch." He pointed just short of ten o'clock. Against the black sky, the flame flickered again, a small orange comet, its tail wagging, then disappearing.

"Got it," Tattoo said. "Can't see the machine, though. Must be one of them goat-eater patrols."

"Not this close to the Pakistan border," Andy said.

Tattoo didn't answer. He raised Roy on the mike. "Got him, Roy. What do you figure?"

"Afghan patrol, most likely."

"That's what Andy said."

"You don't buy it?"

"What's to buy? Can't see nothin' out there to buy."

"Hang on. We're going up to five grand and see if we can get a look at him."

The chopper strained to climb as Roy pulled it up as fast as he could. At five thousand feet he leveled off, but they still couldn't see the outline of the chopper. It was too far away for its bulk to show against the sky.

"I'm going toward the mountains," Roy barked. "You watch for that bastard. You see anything,

anything at all, let me know. Fucker's probably carrying air-to-air. We can't outrun that shit.''

The chopper swooped toward the distant teeth of the mountains. It felt strange running from something they couldn't see. Bolan peered into the night, hoping to get another glimpse of the flame. He wanted to know how fast they were closing.

"We got one bit of luck," Tattoo said.

"What's that?" Bolan asked.

"Them goat-eaters ain't too good with the high-tech shit. Fight like tigers when they want to, but this stuff's too complicated. They never got enough training. The Russkies just put the shit in their hands and told them to point.''

"Sounds familiar," Bolan said.

Tattoo nodded. Neither one of them had to say Vietnam. It was always there.

"Oh-oh!" Roy shouted into the squawk box. "Hang on."

The chopper screamed to the right, the floor tilting wildly under the three men in the cabin. Bolan slammed into the wall, and Tattoo pitched toward the open door. The warrior grabbed for him, catching the big man by the belt as his body hit the harness. The strap snapped, and Bolan took the full weight on his arm.

Andy saw what was happening and scrambled toward the opposite door. His safety harness wouldn't let him get close enough, and he couldn't afford to take it off.

Tattoo's feet scratched at the floor of the chopper, and one arm grabbed for the doorframe. He swung out over thin air, balancing on one foot as Bolan struggled to hang on. The chopper rolled the other way, and the shift threw Tattoo's weight back in toward the door.

He caught the doorframe again, and Bolan jerked the big man toward him. His elbow screamed in its socket. It felt as if someone had injected molten lead into the joint, but he refused to let go. Tattoo got a hand on the safety rail, then swung his other hand around as Bolan pulled him again.

The chopper leveled off, and the warrior could see the ground rushing by them a hundred feet below. Roy was racing along the lip of a canyon. Something glowed yellowish-green as the chopper dipped again, this time sailing down into the canyon. The impact of the missile rumbled around them, and the brilliant glow was almost blinding in its intensity.

"That was close," Roy said over the speaker.

Tattoo shook his head. "You can say that again!" He looked at Bolan. "Thanks, man. I owe you one."

Bolan shrugged.

Tattoo was suddenly thrown into bold relief. The bogie was overhead, flying the lip just as Roy had done. The searchlight speared through the cabin, picking Tattoo out as a machine gun opened up.

"Christ!" Andy shouted. He spun his gun and aimed high as Roy banked to the left. Andy started hammering away as bullets sailed through one door and out the other. With the steep bank it was next to impossible to keep on his feet, but Bolan struggled to get to Andy's door. He was almost there when the chopper shifted under him and he lost his footing. As he fell, a slice of machine-gun fire, laced with green tracers, ripped into the wall behind him.

Andy groaned and fell to the cabin floor. He had been holding himself up with the machine gun, and as he lost his grip, he slid across the floor toward the open door. Tattoo reached for him, lost his own footing and had to grab the safety rail. He scrabbled desperately to grab Andy, but couldn't hold him.

The unconscious man slid out the door and disappeared. Tattoo screamed into his mike, pleading with Roy to right the ship long enough to regain their footing. The pilot swung in a tight one-eighty and dropped the Huey like a hot rock.

Bolan scrambled across to Andy's gun and hauled himself to his feet as Roy banked again. Another rocket sailed past and slammed into the canyon wall, mushrooming orange all over the face of the cliff.

The Executioner opened up but kept losing his balance. The M-60 hammered away, but the pilot of the attacking chopper had the advantage. Bolan slipped on Andy's headset and shouted to get Roy's attention. He barked a series of commands, and Roy rogered. "On three," Bolan said. "One . . . two . . . three."

Roy banked sharply left, throwing the Huey over on its side. Bolan, hanging on for dear life, raked the bottom of the chopper above them. He saw the enemy pilot open his mouth in surprise, then the chopper veered away. But they were too close. The rotor snagged the wall, snapped off and sailed away like a blade of grass in a high wind.

The rest of the rotor, unbalanced by the missing blade, tore loose, and the chopper tipped over, nosed down and bounced off the rim of the canyon. It burst into flame as it fell, spewing burning fuel over the rocky walls.

Roy pulled the Huey over, and Bolan heard him sigh into the open mike. "That was too damn close."

Tattoo looked at Bolan, then smiled. "I guess I owe you two."

"Before this is all over," Bolan said, "I just might collect."

CHAPTER NINETEEN

Tattoo sat by the door, the wind whipping through as the chopper began to climb. He kept shaking his head, as if he couldn't believe what he'd just seen.

"You guys were close?" Bolan asked.

Tattoo nodded. "We were in Nam together. Been out here for years. Mostly working for Rucker, and Royce, the guy who had his job before."

"Tell me about Royce," Bolan said.

"Nothing to tell, really. Knew his stuff, did his job. Better than some. Better than Rucker, actually."

"What happened?"

"Nobody knows. Except Royce, I guess."

"And Rucker."

"Yeah, and Rucker."

Bolan filed the information away. One more little scrap of history, maybe meaningless, maybe not.

Tattoo slumped against the cabin wall, his face heavy with grief. The chopper dipped suddenly, and Bolan glanced out the open door. He couldn't see anything, but Roy was dropping closer, leveling off not more than a hundred feet above the ground. Walking closer to the door and looking down, Bolan could make out the dark, rough terrain, barely illuminated by moonlight. It looked as if it stretched from one end of the world to the other, so forbidding and so monotonous that he wondered why anyone would want to live there, let alone attempt to scratch sustenance out of the barren waste.

"We're getting close," Tattoo said, shifting his weight.

Somewhere off to the west, Bolan knew, lay the city of Kabul, his ultimate destination. Ahead, steep cliffs climbed straight up, their walls a dull gray, looking almost smooth in the pale light. The pilot began to slow the Huey, then angled toward one of the cliffs. The engine roared and the chopper climbed suddenly. The ground fell away as the face of solid rock rushed straight toward them. The thundering engine and the steady, straining rhythm of the rotors slammed into the wall and bounced back at them.

Then they were above the canyon wall. The ground hundreds of feet below looked like a smooth gray sheet. Roy skirted the rim, following its zigzag pattern, staying as close to the rocky plateau as he dared. Veering left, he dropped the Huey precipitously, then stabilized the ship just a few feet off the ground, where it hovered for a moment. Slowly settling the last few feet, it touched down just as three men rushed out of the shadows at the base of the cliff.

"This is it, Belasko," Roy barked over the squawk box. "Grand Central Station, Afghanstyle."

Bolan jumped to the ground, then stuck his head back in. Tattoo still leaned against the wall. He watched the Executioner, his eyes bright and alert, despite his slack posture. "You said you owed me one."

"Actually I said I owed you two."

Quickly Bolan sketched in the details on Mahoney, and Tattoo promised to keep an eye on him. "Whatever you do, though, don't tell Rucker anything."

Tattoo nodded. "Hey, man, I already told you I don't like the guy much. Don't worry about it. I'll watch your buddy. You watch your ass."

The chopper started to lift off as Bolan backed away. He watched it climb straight up, drift over the canyon rim and disappear. The three men who had rushed to meet the chopper chatted among themselves, and the warrior turned to them curiously.

One of the men nudged the other two, and the chatter stopped abruptly. The same man said, "This way quickly, please." He tugged on Bolan's sleeve, pulling him in toward the base of the cliff. Without another word he turned and started to follow the snaking edge of stone, keeping close enough to the wall to brush it with the fingers of his right hand. Bolan stayed on his tail, and the other two came right behind him. The warrior was wary. Too many coincidences had cropped up on this mission. More than were healthy.

He marveled that Roy had been able to pick out the landing zone. The face of the cliff was all but anonymous. In the pale moonlight, what features it had were washed out. But the men with him seemed almost as remarkable. True, they were just following the wall. But the broken rock underfoot and the high altitude did nothing to slow them down. They moved as easily and as monotonously as if they were out for a Sunday stroll. None of them paid any attention to Bolan.

When they'd traveled for a half hour, the warrior realized Hikmal had been more than careful. Rather than give away his location, he'd chosen to send his men a considerable distance. If it had been a trap, the three guides would have been lost, but Hikmal himself would have been uncompromised.

Bolan noticed that the ground was sloping gently uphill now, and they were climbing higher into the mountains. The air was getting colder, but the exertion of the climb more than compensated for the drop in temperature.

He was starting to wonder if they would ever stop walking when the man ahead of him held up a hand. Bolan nearly bumped into him. The two men in the rear brushed past, talked briefly to the leader, then moved on, leaving Bolan alone with the point man.

The guide dropped to the ground and leaned against the rock wall. He looked at Bolan with an emotionless gaze. The big man wondered whether the guide was studying him or looking past him at the emptiness behind him. He wanted to ask questions, but something in the guide's manner told him he'd be wasting his breath.

He heard voices in the darkness, and a moment later the two men returned. With them was a fourth man. Even in the dim light, Bolan could see this was no ordinary man. The others seemed to hang back a little. The guide jumped to his feet and stepped away from the new arrival, who advanced toward Bolan with his arms behind his back. He nodded, said something in a language the warrior recognized as Pushtu, then waited for them to leave.

"Arbak Hikmal?" Bolan asked, extending a hand.

The man looked at the offered hand curiously, his arms still behind his back. "Yet another visitor. Why am I suddenly so much in demand?"

Bolan was confused for a moment. He hadn't expected such good English, and the reference to another visitor had caught him off balance. He stared at the heavily bearded mujahadeen. The man's black eyes had the fierceness of a hawk.

Hikmal jerked his head as a sign for Bolan to follow him, turned abruptly, then started back along the base of the cliff. "What do you want from me?" he asked over his shoulder.

"I need your help."

"So strange—a man who has nothing, besieged on all sides by men who have everything. What makes you think I can help you? More to the point, why should I?"

Bolan reached out and grabbed Hikmal by the arm.

Hikmal whirled so suddenly that Bolan didn't even see it coming. The knife was under his chin in a split second, the point prodding at the soft tissue between the jawbone and the larynx. "Don't ever put your hands on me!" Hikmal's voice was soft, almost tender. "There won't be another warning. Understood?"

"Understood," Bolan said, refusing to flinch from the cold steel.

Hikmal must have seen something he liked, because he smiled, his white teeth splitting his bushy beard. "All right. You have questions. We'll talk." He sank to the ground, leaned against the wall and patted the earth beside him. "Sit. Ask."

"You know why I'm here."

"Yes. You want to get to Kabul. I'm a travel agent and I make the arrangements. Very simple."

"It's not that simple and you know it."

"Yes, of course, I know it. But I don't know what the real truth is, either."

"You don't need to know that."

"No, I don't."

"Who's your other visitor?"

"You don't need to know that."

"Touché."

"I'd be glad to tell you if I knew the answer. Unfortunately, I don't. Still, it seems odd, no? First he shows up and then you. Even though I knew you were coming, it seems to me there must be a connection."

"Maybe. I've seen more than a few coincidences lately myself."

"So...well, you'll meet the Russian. Maybe then you'll know something you don't know now."

"Russian?" Bolan sat forward. He watched Hikmal intently in the dim light.

"No, not Viktor Sharkov."

"So you do know Sharkov."

"I know him, yes. And I know that you're going to Kabul to find him." Hikmal paused. "I know what you're thinking, but it wasn't Rucker who told me about your mission."

"Then how did you know?"

"Think about it," Hikmal said, getting to his feet, "while we walk."

After fifteen minutes of rough going, Bolan spotted a makeshift corral with several dozen horses. On the far side several small fires, already beginning to die out, stirred in the wind, giving off columns of brilliant sparks.

Hikmal paused at the edge of the corral. "I'll take you to the Russian. Maybe he'll tell you what he won't tell me."

The Afghan walked past the first of the fires and headed toward the face of the cliff. Bolan followed him cautiously, not quite sure what was happening.

Hikmal entered a small opening in the rock. Shrugging, Bolan followed him into the cave. On the far side of a small fire a figure sat on his haunches, leaning back against the wall. The crouching man watched Hikmal intently, looked at Bolan, then back at the Afghan.

The warrior looked at the man curiously. The man stared back, his face emotionless. Hikmal turned to Bolan. "I have important business to attend to. We'll talk in the morning." He brushed past Bolan and was gone.

CHAPTER TWENTY

Chebrikov kept tapping his foot, and the sound was driving Viktor Sharkov mad. He wanted to shout at the man, even physically assault him, but he just kept on grinding his teeth. Both men were on edge. The opium sitting under the tarpaulin was worth a fortune, and he was in the middle of nowhere, hoping like hell he could hang on to it long enough to make that fortune his own.

"Vasily, can't you find some other way to deal with your anxiety?"

"What?"

"Your foot, man, your foot. It's driving me crazy."

Chebrikov looked at the offending appendage as if he'd never seen it before. He sighed. "I don't know. Maybe I'm not cut out for this, Viktor. Maybe you're not, either."

"Nonsense. We've done more dangerous things. We've been in tighter corners. What can go wrong?"

"You trust that Turk, Kemal?"

"Of course. Why shouldn't I?"

Chebrikov shrugged. "No reason, I guess. It's just—"

"It's just that we're new at this, Vasily. That's all it is. We're so used to working for someone else. We're just a little confused by the freedom we have."

"Is that what you call it? Freedom?"

"What else should I call it? We're making our own decisions. We're doing things because we want to, not because someone else told us we ought to. That's the very essence of freedom, isn't it?"

"I can't imagine why everyone wants it so much if this is what it feels like."

"You'll get used to it."

"Where's the Afghan? He's two days late already."

"That isn't a very long time. Not here. Have a drink and forget about it, Vasily. It won't be much longer."

"That's what you said yesterday."

Sharkov stood and walked to the doorway. He looked out and down into the dark valley, then stepped through the doorway and walked away from the building. He wished Chebrikov was more stable, or at least more subdued. He had the vague sense that things were slipping out of control, just a little bit, but enough to make him wonder what else would go wrong, and when.

"If only Vasily holds together," he whispered to himself. And Sharkov knew he was talking about himself, as well.

The Uzi draped over his shoulder made him feel uncomfortable. He walked away from the buildings and started down the hillside, then found a rock he could sit on. Crouching under the stars, he wondered what would happen if he was wrong. It wasn't a new feeling, but this time he was working without the comfortable net of the KGB stretched beneath him. If he fell off this wire, he'd break his neck . . . if someone didn't break it for him.

Sharkov heard the footsteps at the last second. He turned, thinking Chebrikov had followed him down the side of the hill. A hand clamped his mouth and an arm slithered over his collarbone, then squeezed his windpipe.

He groped for the Uzi, but he was too late. He felt it slide over his arm and away from him. Steeling himself, he waited for the slice of cold metal against his throat.

But it didn't come.

Someone grabbed his legs, and he felt his feet leave the ground. He tried to shout, but the hand over his mouth made it impossible. Wriggling like an angry snake, he tried to kick away the hands around his ankles, but they closed even tighter, and his feet went numb with the pressure.

It felt as if he'd been in the air for an eternity when he was dumped unceremoniously onto the ground. A sharp rock jabbed into his back, another cracked against his ankle.

"Let him up." The voice wasn't unpleasant, and the language was Russian.

He sat up slowly, rubbing his bruised back. "What the hell's going on?"

"No questions, please," the voice said.

A pale light bathed him, and he looked up into the center of the dim beam. But even the faint light was enough to obscure the face of the man behind the torch.

"Who are you?" Sharkov demanded. "What do you want?"

"Viktor Sharkov, I presume?" The voice sounded faintly amused.

Sharkov nodded and tried to rise, but a pair of hands pressed him back down. "Don't get up on my account," the voice said. "We don't stand on ceremony here."

"Damn it, tell me what you want!"

"This isn't your country, Sharkov. It's mine. I don't take Russian orders here. Not anymore."

The hands released him, and Sharkov heard the shuffle of several pairs of feet on the rocky ground.

"Did you bring the shipment?" the voice asked.

"What shipment?"

"If you don't know, then perhaps I have the wrong man, after all."

"Hikmal?"

"Did you bring it?"

"What's going on?"

"I told you when we first discussed this matter. I trust no one. That includes you. I can't afford to make mistakes. Trusting the wrong man is the worst mistake one can make."

"Then why did you agree to the deal?"

"Because I have needs that you can satisfy, Sharkov. We both know that. I was quite explicit, in fact."

"Then why the damn theatrics?"

"I'm a careful man."

"Hikmal, if you double-cross me, I'll have you hanged. If you're lucky."

"I don't believe in luck, Sharkov. Where's the opium?"

"It's here. Don't worry."

"And the weapons?"

"All in good time. If I tell you now, you don't need me."

"I don't need you in any case. You make things easier, not possible."

"That's what you think."

"You talk a great deal for a man who has no guarantees. And who gives none."

"I gave you a guarantee. You deliver the shipment, and you'll get what you want."

"And if I don't get it?"

"Then you have the shipment. What more insurance do you want?"

"I've been thinking about that very thing."

"And...?"

"I'll get back to you on that. Where's the opium?"

"You can't take it in the middle of the night."

"What better time?"

"But—"

"Do you want the delivery made or don't you?"

The Afghan had him over a barrel. He stalled for time, but there was nothing he could do to change the equation. Right now Hikmal held all the cards. "I'll show you," he said, again trying to rise. This time no one held him down.

He tried to get a look at Hikmal, but the Afghan stayed out of sight. Each time Sharkov tried to turn around, he felt something poke him in the back. He didn't need to see it to recognize it as a rifle.

"I should warn the others we're coming," Sharkov said.

"No need."

At the top of the hill he saw why. In the dim light of the main quarters he saw several men lined against the wall. A half-dozen of the wildest-looking men he'd ever seen held them at bay with automatic rifles. He tried again to look at Hikmal, and again the rifle nudged his spine.

"This wasn't necessary." Sharkov exaggerated the resentment in his voice, but it just sounded silly, even to him. Hikmal didn't bother to comment. "This way," he told the Afghan, veering to the right and heading for another of the ruined buildings. At the doorway he stopped. "It's in there."

Hikmal shouted something in Pushtu, and suddenly two dozen men swarmed up the hillside. One carried a torch and stood just inside the shattered hovel. Like ants, the others darted through the doorway, only to reappear moments later with three or four of the burlap sacks on their shoulders.

It all happened so quickly that Sharkov wondered whether it was happening at all. The situation, plainly, was out of his control. Before the staggering possibilities had fully sunk in, the mujahadeen were gone. He was alone now on the hillside with Hikmal.

"Four days," the Afghan said.

"What?"

"Four days. I make the delivery. If the payment isn't there . . ."

"It will be."

"For your sake I hope so."

Sharkov turned just in time to see the Afghan vanish into the night. He wanted to run after him, but somehow knew that was unwise. He stood there, staring into the darkness. When the numbness wore off, he turned to the other building. His men were spewing out now, illuminated only from their shoulders down by the dim light inside the building.

This wasn't at all what he'd planned.

CHAPTER TWENTY-ONE

Tim Rucker stared at the wall, his hands tapping on the polished wood of his desk. The clock, its hands jerking spasmodically in perfect time to the dictates of the quartz crystal at its heart, had irritated him for some time. He remembered the old days when clock hands moved smoothly, perfect circles scored one by one as the second hand swept again and again around the face. Maybe the quartz was better, but he didn't think so. At least in the old days it was possible to see time as one continuously unwinding string. Now all you could see was one spastic second after another, each unit of time cleanly and completely segregated from those on either side. It didn't seem like progress.

He had an appointment, but not for an hour yet. Killing time was something he no longer did well. Maybe it was the clock, or maybe he was getting too long in the tooth for the job. He ate antacid tablets in assorted flavors as if they were going out of style. The stress was eating him up inside.

He hated his work sometimes, and this was one of them. He'd been too carefully schooled to accept change so easily. But change was all there was these days, the sands shifting under him as he stared at his feet, wondering where to take the next step, and how long he could risk staying put. Like the clock on the wall, his life was recreated. It looked the same, but it didn't work the way it used to. It was supposed to be better, but all it was was different.

The old rules didn't work anymore, and he didn't know what the new rules were. Sometimes he wondered if there were any rules at all. Besides, what difference would it make if he screwed up? There was nothing at stake, nothing that really mattered, anyway. The boobs in D.C. were always getting their balls in a knot. If nothing was happening, they had to make something up. He was getting damn tired of the games. It had been different in the old days. He kept coming back to that, the old days, like some old coot rocking away on a front porch. Maybe that was what he'd become. Old.

He pulled his Browning automatic out of his desk drawer. Hefting the cold, heavy metal, he felt as if he were in control again. It was an illusion. He knew that. But illusions were all that mattered now. He remembered the old days in San Francisco when people honestly believed a goddamn flower could stop a bullet. Talk about pipe dreams. The guy who thought that one up must have had some really good hash.

Guns were what made the world go round. Rucker lifted the pistol and sighted along the gleaming barrel. The clock was an easy target. He could probably drill it dead center. But if he did that, he'd be hip-deep in assholes in nothing flat. They'd come swarming in, wondering what the hell was going on.

And he'd never be able to explain it, not to their satisfaction. The next thing he'd know, he'd be on the way home, maybe to some decompression tank in the Blue Ridge Mountains, maybe just to jockey a desk until the big twenty rolled around. That was what it was all coming to. He knew that, too. That was what everything was for. Retirement. Serenity. The easy peace that came when you knew you'd done your job and nothing happened on your watch. Or nothing that anybody wanted to talk about.

Rucker snorted and stood. He took his jacket off and bent over the open bottom drawer of his desk. The holster was right where it always was. He undid the buckle and slipped it on. It was getting a little snug, and he had to adjust the cinch before the gun would sit comfortably under his arm. With his jacket back on, it was barely noticeable.

Letting the jacket hang open, he stepped into the small washroom and ran a fistful of damp fingers through his hair. He slapped himself with water-cooled palms, then shook himself as if he had something in his eye. Leaning in close, he looked at the bags under his eyes, the slight bluish color, and remembered he hadn't been sleeping very well lately.

One more hazard.

Stepping out of the washroom, he turned the light off and walked back to the desk. He didn't think he'd even need the gun, but what the hell? He took a second magazine from the middle drawer, tucked it into his jacket pocket and turned off the desk lamp. Then, taking his cane off the wall hook, he left his office.

Out in the hall he nodded to Frank Flannigan, who rode herd on the nighttime crew, mostly ripping and reading cables. It was a dull job, but somebody had to do it. Maybe that was what they'd have him do when he got too old for his current job. Hell, Flannigan didn't seem to mind. He was overseas, getting the extra bucks, and had a damn good standard of living, what with the exchange rate being what it was.

It might not be so bad.

He waited for the elevator after punching in his code on the electronic security panel. The elevator hummed quietly as it descended, whispering to a halt right behind the door. It opened and he stepped in, not bothering to turn around until it had started up.

On the main floor he stopped to sign out, then walked to his car in the embassy parking lot. He hated meetings. This one was no different. It was a bit more intriguing, but then, in the business of intrigue, that was to be expected. Even the unusual quickly became commonplace.

He waved to the Marine corporal at the gate and nosed out into the broad, tree-lined avenue. Islamabad was trying so damn hard to be modern. The rumor was that it even hoped to become some sort of tourist mecca. Fat chance.

And like most Asian capitals, Islamabad admired the wrong things about the West. For some reason he'd never understand, architecture was always the first casualty when a Third World country entered the modern age. Islamabad was no exception. It was full of glass-and-aluminum cubes. The glass was tinted, in deference to the summer sun, but it still looked like Erno Rubik had brainwashed everyone in town who owned a drafting table and a set of triangles.

He drove without paying much attention, as he always did. His leg hurt most when he had to sit behind the wheel, and he was never able to concentrate much on where he was going, let alone on the various local ordinances.

Moving into the bazaar area, he rolled his window down and turned off the air-conditioning. It was late, and the crowds were gone, but the spices still hung in the air. It was what he liked most about this part of the world. The food was no bullshit. The spices meant business. He had enjoyed Thailand when he was stationed there, and two tours in India had given him a lifelong addiction to curry. If he did retire, he'd have to make sure he was near New York or Washington, maybe Boston. He'd need a hit of Asian cooking at least once a week, just to keep his sinuses clear, if for no other reason.

The streets were getting narrower. The cleanliness of the main business district was a distant memory. Papers littered the pavement, and stray dogs nosed around the battered doorways. On the far side of the bazaar was the import-export district, where huge old warehouses lined block after block. Shops sometimes occupied the front, but long- and short-term storage, cubic miles of it, was the main business.

He almost missed the place he was looking for. He had to go out of his way, squeezing through a narrow alley and circling the block once. He rapped the horn twice, then once, then twice, and the huge freight door rolled to one side. He drove in and listened to the big door close behind him. Another car was already inside. He stayed behind the steering wheel. This was an away game, and he didn't know the ground rules. Somebody would tell him soon enough, so he stayed put, rapping the wheel with the heels of both hands and whistling through his teeth.

A rear door on the other car opened, throwing light on the driver, whom he didn't recognize, and the man climbing out of the back, whom he did, but only just.

The door closed, and the gloom returned. The man passed behind his own car, then behind Rucker's, and stood at the passenger door until Rucker leaned over and unlocked it. The man opened the door and took a seat, closing the door again almost as an afterthought. Rucker thought wryly that this was a man no longer used to opening and closing doors on his own. He had climbed too far up the ladder for such things.

"It's been a long time, Timothy."

"Eight years. I guess that's long in this business."

"Especially these days."

"You seem to have held up rather well."

"And you."

"Yeah, well, I'm not so sure."

"Battle fatigue, Timothy?"

"Not for attribution, but, yeah, I guess so."

The man nodded. "I know how it is."

"I don't think so."

"I know more than you think. This is a strange and wearing profession we've chosen. I sometimes think it has chosen us."

"Well, every sacrifice needs a lamb."

"You always did have a rather pithy way of expressing the harsh realities."

"That's what losing a leg will do for you. Gives you perspective, you know?"

"I've never been able to forgive myself for that."

"It wasn't your fault. Hell, if it hadn't been for you, I'd have cashed it in then and there. I suppose you've come to collect a due bill?"

"Not exactly."

"Don't beat around the bush."

"All right, then, we have a problem. A joint one, I might add."

"Come on, Peter, we're both too old for this. Stop being coy."

Grebnov sighed.

CHAPTER TWENTY-TWO

The Russian was stubborn. Bolan kept prodding him, trying to get him to reveal anything to hang another question on, but it was no use. A smile, even a laugh, from time to time was the best he could get. So far not even the man's name had been volunteered. Bolan wished he had a name to stick on the guy, anything to make him more human, more a person and less of a cipher.

Frustrated, he sat down across the fire from the taciturn man. He watched the Russian quietly, hoping the pressure would force the man to break his silence, but that didn't work, either. He ran back through the past few days while he waited, trying to find something he could use. He remembered Rucker saying Kostikian had hinted the Russians were after Sharkov themselves. Mahoney had said the same thing. Could the silent man across from him be his Soviet counterpart?

It was worth a chance.

"All right," Bolan said, "since you don't want to talk about yourself, let me tell you about me."

The Russian didn't say anything, but his eyes seemed to brighten. He was interested.

"I'm looking for another Russian, a former KGB agent gone off the deep end. He was a colonel. He worked in Turkey and Afghanistan, as well as London and Paris. Ring a bell?"

The quiet man looked as if he wanted to say something. His lips twitched, and he had to compress them to try to conceal the impulse. Bolan waited, but the composure returned, and he pushed on.

"The man in question is running heroin into the United States. He's new at it, and not very good. Not yet. But he seems to be a quick study. I'm here to put an end to it. That means if I find him I'll probably have to kill him."

The Russian tilted his head back, looking down along his nose, but still he said nothing.

"The man's name is Viktor Sharkov. He also used another former Soviet agent named Marko Mirtis. Sound familiar?"

The man's eyes flickered. He was listening intently now, almost expectantly. Bolan had guessed right, but so far he couldn't prove it.

"Mirtis was a defector. He came over to our side three years ago. We figure Sharkov got in touch with him, promised him the moon, and the guy bought in. It got him killed."

"Marko is dead?"

"So, you do know what I'm talking about."

"Is he really dead?"

Bolan nodded. "Why do you care?"

The man lapsed back into silence.

"I figure," Bolan continued, "that you're here for the same reason I am. Yuri Kostikian said you guys were doing something about Sharkov, but he didn't say what."

"Why don't you ask him again? You're so fond of asking pointless questions, go badger him for a while and leave me alone."

"Can't do that."

"Why not? You got here. You can get out, too."

"Kostikian's dead."

This time Bolan scored a direct hit. "What did you say?" the Russian gasped.

"I said Kostikian's dead. You didn't know that?"

The Russian shook his head. "No, I didn't." For some reason that seemed to change everything. The Russian looked less sure of himself now, confused, almost frightened. "Did you kill him?"

"No. I don't know who did, but whoever it was almost got a friend of mine. In fact, I think he was supposed to."

"Viktor..."

"Yeah, what about Viktor?"

"Never mind." The Russian stood and pawed at his face, scraping at the stubble on his chin, then rubbing his eyes with his fingertips. "I'm tired. Please be quiet so I can sleep."

Bolan sensed that this might be his only opportunity to break through. "Look, I told you why I'm here. It's no secret why you're here, either. But maybe you know something I don't. Maybe I know something you don't."

The Russian smiled. "You think so, do you?"

"Yes, I do."

"Maybe you're right. But I have to sleep."

"We don't have time to sleep, guy."

"Why should I tell you anything?"

"Because you have a job to do. Because you're just like me. You take your work seriously. In this case that means taking down Viktor Sharkov. I can do it with or without you. Maybe you can do it without me. I don't know. But I do know that we have a better chance working together. You know that as well as I do. This is no time for pride, or for suspicion."

"If you know so much, why are you here?"

"I already told you. I have to get to Kabul. Hikmal can get me there."

"If Sharkov is such a menace, why do you trust those who work with him?"

"I don't trust them. I don't even know who they are."

The Russian laughed.

"What's so funny?"

"The very man you expect to take you to Kabul carries the heroin to Pakistan for Sharkov. That's what's funny."

Bolan frowned. "Hikmal's a courier for Sharkov? I don't believe it."

"Not a courier, my friend. *The* courier. Where do you think he is at this very moment?"

"Suppose you tell me."

"He's gone to meet with Viktor to pick up the next shipment."

"How do you know that?"

"I have my ways."

"You're sure?"

"Positive."

"Then why didn't you go along? Why are you here?"

"Because Hikmal kidnapped me. And, after all, I'm a Russian. He doesn't trust Viktor, either, but he needs him. He needs the money Viktor can pay him for weapons. You freedom-loving Americans haven't seen fit to supply Hikmal and dozens like him because he's too independent. He won't toe the line, so he has to go begging for assistance. People aren't in the habit of giving beggars weapons and missiles, so he has to find a way to pay for them. Viktor knew that, and since he no longer cares what Soviet policy might be, he uses Hikmal, just like you Americans use other Afghans."

Bolan shook his head. He turned and walked toward the mouth of the tiny cavern and looked out at the camp. He didn't want to believe what the man was telling him, but he knew it was true. The evidence was everywhere. The weapons of Hikmal's men were anything but modern. Obviously they weren't getting help from Rucker. Maybe that was the carrot that had gotten Hikmal involved in the first place. But there had to be more. Maybe Hikmal was playing both sides.

He turned back to the Russian, staying in the mouth of the cave. "You're certain?"

The Russian nodded. He got to his feet and walked toward Bolan. Tilting his head to one side, he watched the big man quizzically. "You seem surprised."

"I am," Bolan admitted.

"And you don't like it."

"No, I don't like it."

"But you're a pragmatist and will go along until you see things more clearly."

Bolan nodded.

The Russian smiled again. "My name is Maxim Goncharov," he said, extending a hand. "KGB."

Bolan took the proffered hand. "Mike Belasko."

"CIA?"

Bolan shook his head.

"I see. Military Intelligence, then?"

"Look, Goncharov, we have a lot to talk about. So let's skip my life story. Let's just say I'm a civil servant and leave it at that."

Bolan told the Russian everything, from Rivera's interrogation to the chopper ambush the previous night. When he was finished, Goncharov looked at him quietly for a long moment before saying, "It appears you have more trouble on your end than I have on mine. All I have to worry about is Sharkov himself."

Bolan nodded. "You may be right. Tell me everything you know about Sharkov as far back as you can. There has to be a connection here, something we don't know about. If Sharkov has a pipeline to our side, it's somewhere in the past, some chance encounter, some operation that brought him into contact with somebody on our side."

Goncharov took his time. At first Bolan thought he was being careful, but as the Russian talked, it was apparent he was just being thoughtful, sifting every little detail, looking for something that might fit, some little piece to fill in one of the holes in the puzzle.

The sun was up by the time the two men finished talking. Now all they could do was wait for Arbak Hikmal to return. Bolan lay back against the rock, cradling his head in folded arms. He was exhausted, and there was so much to do. And so much he still didn't know. He closed his eyes. But he didn't sleep.

CHAPTER TWENTY-THREE

From the hillside the building looked innocuous enough. A ramshackle, barnlike structure, it sat off to one side of the valley. Half of the floor of the valley was taken up with rows of fruit trees. The orchard stopped abruptly at the edge of a dirt road. Beyond it several small buildings lay to the right, their target to the left.

Bolan watched through binoculars. The place looked deserted. Two battered jeeps nosed against the side of the barn, but they had been that way for hours. He was taking a calculated risk, and he was uneasy.

Hikmal had driven a hard bargain. He'd agreed to hold off on the opium delivery and to lead Bolan to the processing plant. In exchange Bolan guaranteed him the same money Sharkov was willing to pay—five hundred thousand dollars. And a little grease for the arms purchase. Rucker had balked, then reluctantly caved in. But it was a crapshoot and Bolan had a cold hand. It would only take one screw-up and he would lose Hikmal and, in all probability, any shot at Viktor Sharkov.

He'd be lucky if that was all he lost. But he was here to make it work, and he'd give it his best shot.

Bolan turned to Hikmal. "You're sure that's the place?"

The man nodded. "Yes, I'm sure."

Goncharov was getting impatient. "What are we waiting for? Why don't we just do it?"

Bolan tried to brake the Russian's emotions. "We want to be absolutely certain."

Goncharov jerked a thumb at the Afghan. "He's certain. We don't know anything to the contrary. What's the problem?"

"This is Pakistan, Goncharov. We don't have the authority to do anything here. If we move and we make a mistake, it's worse than doing nothing."

"I know. But I'm tired of all this nonsense about jurisdiction. Where I come from, you do what you're sent to do. Someone else has to worry about jurisdiction. We're not diplomats. We're not even policemen. I think we should go now."

"After dark we'll handle it. Don't you worry about that. But we can't get close now without being seen, and we can't afford that."

Goncharov listened to the argument impatiently. This sort of quibbling was new to him. He was used to a more direct approach. The American commando looked at him as if waiting for him to say something. He looked back, his face blank. The big American made sense, but he understood only one way to proceed. "Suppose I went down by myself and took a look around?" Goncharov suggested.

"What good would that do?" Bolan asked. "If they get suspicious of you, it could blow the whole thing. Right now they don't know we're here. That's the best time to move. Why give them a chance to get ready for us?"

"Goncharov's right," Hikmal said. "Why not let him try it?"

Bolan said nothing. He was trying to maintain control of a very precarious situation. Goncharov had his own agenda, and Hikmal was still unsure he'd made the right decision. Bolan himself was here for one reason and one reason only. Everything else was secondary. "All right," the warrior said reluctantly. "Go ahead."

The Russian started down the hill, half expecting one of them to object. When he had gone fifty meters and no one did, he settled into a steady lope. It felt good to be moving through a place with a little greenery. The air was warm, the sun hot on his back. It was altogether more pleasant than the past few days had been.

Bolan watched him through the glasses, occasionally shifting his gaze to the buildings, then picked the Russian up again as he worked his way toward the leading edge of the orchard.

Goncharov was in the trees now, and Bolan lost him for a few seconds. The rows of trees were at a slight angle, and the man appeared and disappeared as he passed through. The closer he got to the buildings, the less often he was visible.

Bolan trained the glasses on the road now, waiting impatiently for the Russian to break into the open. A door on the barn swung back, and two men could be seen in the doorway. They stood there talking. The warrior watched closely, but there was nothing unusual about the men. They looked like farm workers taking a break from heavy work.

Then one of them stepped out into the sunlight. He turned to watch his companion close the door, waved just as the door was about to shut, then started toward one of the smaller buildings across the narrow valley. Bolan watched him closely, but there was no sense of urgency in the man's movements. No need to worry. Yet.

Then Goncharov was in the open. The Russian walked slowly toward the big barn. He approached the door that had just been opened, and Bolan saw him reach for a cord of some kind and jerk it twice. Probably a bell, he thought.

The Russian turned his back to the door, a nice touch, and surveyed the orchard as if he were considering making an offer for it. After a minute he turned again to jerk the cord twice more. A loft door swung open above him, and Goncharov stepped back. Bolan watched him shield his eyes with one hand as he spoke to the man leaning out above him.

The man kept shaking his head, but Goncharov refused to take no for an answer. Finally the loft door slammed shut. Goncharov walked to one corner of the building and disappeared behind it. The front door swung open, and the man from the loft stepped through a narrow opening. He pulled the door closed behind him and started toward the corner of the building. It looked as if he were shouting something.

While Bolan watched, a plume of pale smoke appeared over the roof of the barn. There was no chimney, and he couldn't tell where the smoke was coming from. It looked as if it issued from somewhere on the other side of the barn.

The man turned the same corner as Goncharov.

"What's going on?" Hikmal asked, getting to his feet.

"Not sure," Bolan replied. "Goncharov has gotten somebody out of the building, but that's all I know for sure. I don't like it. Now they know we're here."

"Not necessarily."

"I wish I had your confidence."

Goncharov reappeared. The man was behind him, waving his arms. It was strange to see his mouth opening and closing and not be able to hear anything. He was irritated, yelling something at the Russian, who seemed to be explaining himself and trying to calm the man down.

Then, with a final wave of one hand, like an angry parent pushing a kid onto a school bus, the man stood still and watched Goncharov walk away. Finally, seemingly satisfied, he turned and reentered the barn.

The smoke continued on the far side, but there was no apparent concern. Whatever it was, it was supposed to be there. Bolan kept the glasses on the barn. The loft door reopened, and the same man reappeared. He seemed to be watching to make sure Goncharov left. After ten minutes the door closed again, and once more the barn looked deserted, except for the pale smoke swirling up into the sunlight.

Bolan could see the Russian through gaps in the orchard now. He was running. When he broke into the open and started up the hill, he never broke stride. The warrior started down toward him, letting the glasses dangle from a strap. He expected Hikmal to follow him down, but the Afghan stayed where he was, sitting on the grass.

Goncharov was out of breath. He sucked air for a few moments, licking his dry lips and coughing from his exertion.

"So," Bolan asked, "what good did that do?"

Goncharov smiled. "Hikmal's right. It's a processing lab. I could smell the chemicals. Around the back I found empty drums. I told them I was looking for a job, and I think they bought it. Anyway, it shouldn't be too difficult getting inside tonight. The barn's just that, a plain wooden building. There's some security. I could see locks on the loft door and the main door, and the windows around the back are barred. But there's no reinforcement. We should be able to smash through the door easily."

"How many men?" Bolan asked.

"I don't know. Besides, that could change, depending on whether they work around the clock. I would guess they do. I'm sure they want to get the opium in and the heroin out as quickly as they can."

"So we wait until dark," Bolan said.

"Then what?" Goncharov was even more impatient now.

"Then we take it down. Hard."

"The harder the better," Goncharov said. "This should get Viktor's attention, maybe even smoke him out."

"Let's get busy." Bolan walked back to the jeep, the Russian following. He grabbed a pencil and paper from a pouch and drew a quick sketch of the barn and the surrounding area. They discussed the plan for the next hour, trying to consider every possible contingency. Hikmal stayed aloof, nodding when he agreed, but saying nothing.

By sundown they'd finalized the plan. Then they checked their weapons and made sure they had enough ammunition. The jeep was out, since it would make too much noise. And if they were to pull this off with as little bloodshed as possible, they'd have to surprise the men in the barn.

The sky turned violet, then indigo. The first handful of stars appeared, and it was time to go.

Bolan led the way down the hill. The others followed in single file, Goncharov right on the Executioner's heels. They entered the orchard, and Bolan picked a route that would take them to the left corner of the barn, keeping as far away from the other buildings as possible.

When they reached the last few rows of trees, the Executioner held up a hand. Squatting behind a thick trunk, he watched the barn for a moment. The smoke was still spewing from the far side, thicker now in the cooler night air. The front of the barn had only two windows. Heavy cloth hung over them, but light leaked around the edges.

"Okay, Goncharov, this is it." He patted the Russian on the shoulder and gave him a gentle shove.

The KGB man sprinted for the left-hand corner of the big building, then flattened himself against the wall. He listened for a moment, then waved a hand. Hikmal went next, taking the opposite corner. He vanished behind it and made a quick circuit, reappearing at Goncharov's shoulder. The Russian waved and Bolan went next, taking the right-hand corner.

There was a small door at the rear, and Hikmal worked his way around the back. Bolan signaled to Goncharov, then moved to the front door. He pressed an ear to the rough wood, then placed two grenades at the unhinged end of the big sliding door, using some sticky clay. Finally he pulled both pins and sprinted for the corner.

The grenades went off almost simultaneously. Bolan was back around the corner before the smoke cleared. Goncharov raced toward him as he shoved the door back on its ancient rollers.

A chorus of shouts erupted inside the barn. The place was dimly lit, and as Bolan stepped through the door, he could see men scurrying like frightened mice. Several of them ran toward the rear exit and slammed into one another as the first of them struggled to get the door open.

So far not a shot had been fired.

CHAPTER TWENTY-FOUR

Bolan thought they were home free.

Then he heard the choppers. He sprinted out into the open in time to see a pair of Soviet Hinds moving in fast. He ducked back into the barn.

"What's going on?" Goncharov shouted.

"Choppers. Two of them. Soviet-made."

"Here? Impossible! We're in Pakistan. You must be mistaken."

"We're just barely over the border," Bolan reminded him. He turned to Hikmal. "Has this happened before?"

"Many times. Borders don't mean much in this part of the world."

"Are they Russians?" Bolan asked.

Hikmal smiled at Goncharov. "Probably Afghan regulars. The Russians are supposed to be gone, no?"

"We better get the hell out of here," Bolan said. "If they take this barn out, we'll be fried."

"There's no cover," Goncharov reminded him.

"The pilots aren't very good," Hikmal said, "and they don't really understand the weapons systems. They might hit the barn by accident. Out in the open we have a chance. If we get to the orchard, we'll be safe.''

Bolan moved to the door. He watched as the choppers made a crude circle, then swept over the outbuildings. They were about a thousand feet up, and one machine wobbled a bit as the pilot tried to hold it steady. "How the hell did they even know we were here?" Bolan asked.

Hikmal laughed. "There are Russians everywhere. There are KGB spies in the mujahadeen. There are mujahadeen sympathizers in the Afghan army. No one knows where anyone else really stands. And there are no secrets. More than likely Sharkov has connections in the regular army."

"We can figure that out later," Bolan said. "Let's get out of here. Now!"

He grabbed Hikmal and tugged him toward the door. "Go. Goncharov, you're next." The Russian stepped to the door, waited for Bolan to rap him on the back, then sprinted across the open field to the tree line.

Bolan didn't wait for a signal. He broke for the trees, loping easily in a zigzag pattern. He didn't even glance at the circling choppers. When he reached the first row of trees, he slowed. "Don't anybody fire!" he shouted. "Don't call attention to us."

The three men huddled in the trees. One of the two helicopters veered off to the left, then pivoted.

A white streak swept down from the sky, and a moment later the barn mushroomed up and out. At first it was just light, as if a new sun had been born behind the weathered wood. Then pieces of the building spiraled away and the first thunderclap reached them. Thick black smoke swirled like dark water around the bright flames.

"That was closer than I care to think about," Bolan said.

"What now?" Goncharov asked.

"I want the money Sharkov promised me," Hikmal said. His matter-of-fact tone was controlled, but there was a steel backbone buried in the calm words.

"Sharkov wouldn't be stupid enough to leave the money before you delivered the goods," Bolan told him.

"No. That was the deal. It's in the house. I'm sure of it."

"You want to ransack that place with two helicopters flying around? You must be out of your mind."

"Far from it," Hikmal said. "I need it to buy weapons. American aid is slow, when it comes at all. I can do better on the black market, and have. Your Mr. Rucker might not come through as he promised. I need that money."

"Is the house defended?" Bolan asked.

"Maybe a half-dozen men," Hikmal replied. "Automatic weapons, but nothing else to worry about. It's just a farmhouse. Nothing more."

"I still think it's risky. Besides, we want Sharkov. I, for one, don't give a damn about the politics."

"I can get you to Sharkov," Hikmal said. "You know that."

"And if we help you, how do we know you'll keep your end of the bargain?"

"Why wouldn't I?"

"Maybe we ought to think this through," Bolan suggested.

"I have time," Hikmal said. "But not too much." He walked off into the trees.

Bolan shook his head, then turned to Goncharov. "If we help him, he'll have what he wants. He has no reason to give us Sharkov then."

"Of course he does," Goncharov said. "Viktor will never trust him again. He'll lose his connection. Where does he get the money for more weapons, then?"

"You tell me."

The Russian poked a finger into Bolan's chest. "From your government, my friend. It's the only place he can get it."

"But you heard what he said—it's slow when it comes at all."

"Slow is better than never. When you have nothing, slow is something you can live with. Besides, if he helps you, you'll owe him a favor. He means to collect it."

"Maybe you're right," Bolan said. "I don't like it, but I guess we should give him what he wants. We're his best bet. But he's our only one. Without him we can't get to Sharkov. We don't know where he is, and we couldn't get to him even if we did."

"You don't trust him, do you?"

"Maybe I don't," Bolan said. "But I guess we should do it. I don't think we can pull this off without him. If you have any other ideas, I'll listen."

Bolan was exasperated. He knew the Russian's argument made sense, but he was trying to talk himself into accepting it, and he felt uncomfortable. He felt as if the Afghan were holding a gun to his head.

"All right," the warrior said, "let's do it." Bolan stepped into the trees. He found Hikmal sitting on his heels, leaning against a tree.

The Afghan looked up at him. "Did you decide?"

"It's a deal. But I'm warning you right now. You already screwed around with the arrangements once. It better not happen again."

"Things aren't always under control out here, Belasko. I do what I can and what I have to. My people come first."

"I don't think that's it, Hikmal. I think you have some personal agenda. I'm not even sure you know what it is yourself. But it better not get in the way."

Hikmal seemed to consider the threat. He didn't seem flustered, just thoughtful. Then he straightened. "All right. What you say is fair."

The choppers still whirled around, circling the ruined and blazing barn, but they were spiraling higher on every pass. There had been no return fire, and there was nothing left for them to shoot at as far as they could tell.

In the meantime the house remained silent. Lights burned, but no one had come out. "You sure the house is defended, Hikmal?" Bolan asked.

"It's supposed to be. You don't leave that much money unattended."

"If it's there."

"It's there."

The choppers made a final pass, then climbed rapidly and sped for the border. Bolan watched them leave, more than a little uneasy at the recent chain of events. "I guess we might as well get rolling," he told the Afghan.

The two men walked back to join Goncharov, who watched them expectantly. "Well?" he demanded.

"Mount up," Bolan said.

Hikmal led the way this time. They fanned out, moving one at a time, the other two providing cover just in case. When they were within fifty yards, Bolan held up a hand. He scrutinized the place from end to end. The lights burned, but there was no movement. No shadows moved behind the curtains. It looked almost as if the place had been deserted in a hurry.

Hikmal took Goncharov around the back way while Bolan moved in on the side door. Flat against the wall, the Executioner heard nothing. He didn't like the setup. It was too quiet.

Bolan moved along the wall, skirting a low hedge, and took up a position on the far side of the door, ducking under the half-glass panel darkened by a cheap shade. Easing up against the door frame on his side, he reached out to try the door.

It opened easily. He pushed, yanking his arm back quickly, but nothing happened as the door swung inward and hung, swinging back and forth on its hinges.

He shook his head. Something was definitely odd. Taking a deep breath, he ducked into a crouch and darted through, hitting the first cover he could see, behind an old china cabinet. Then he raced through the hallway and into a kitchen. There was no sign of life.

Hikmal and Goncharov entered from their end, and the three men stood there, looking at one another and wondering what the hell was going on.

Bolan led them from room to room, alternating with Hikmal and leaving Goncharov to bring up the rear. Every room on the first floor was deserted. Hikmal, his anger growing, charged upstairs. The warrior dashed after him, but the Afghan had half a flight's lead.

The big man gestured to Goncharov to wait below, then followed Hikmal down an upstairs hall. As with the first floor, they found each room deserted. Some were lit, some were dark, but all were quiet.

"What's going on?" Bolan growled.

"I don't know," Hikmal said. "Something's wrong."

"I don't think you're going to find the money."

Hikmal looked at him sadly. "I don't, either."

"I think we better go down."

"There's still the cellar," the Afghan said. "I want to check it out."

"You won't find anything."

"I want to be sure."

"Okay, go ahead."

Hikmal started down to the first floor. He ignored the quizzical look Goncharov gave him, brushed past him and reentered the kitchen. Bolan ran after him. A doorknob rattled, and Hikmal flung the door open, clicked on a light and started down the steps before Bolan could cross the kitchen.

The Executioner shouted down the steps. "Damn it, Hikmal! That could have been booby-trapped."

"It wasn't," Hikmal muttered. He started to say something else, then stopped in midword.

"What is it?" Bolan asked.

"I think you better see for yourself."

Bolan entered the stairwell and moved down the rickety wooden steps. The smell of damp stone assaulted him, and something else he couldn't put his finger on.

On the bottom step he turned. Hikmal was pointing. Bolan followed the finger, then shook his head. Against the base of the wall a half-dozen bodies lay like toy soldiers, their heads against the stone foundation. Their feet pointed at the ceiling. A half-dozen pools of blood, swollen to one small pond, seeped into the damp earth along the edge of the stone.

Next to the last body a briefcase yawned open.

Hikmal had his money, after all.

CHAPTER TWENTY-FIVE

Tim Rucker left his office after midnight and went down to the basement garage. As soon as he was ensconced in the backseat of his car, his driver left the compound and nosed out onto the tree-lined Islamabad avenue.

Rucker settled back in the car, letting his driver decide on the route. The only hard-and-fast rule was that no two days should be the same. He decided only when he would go home. His driver decided how they would go.

The ride went smoothly, and it was over almost before he realized it. The gates closed behind him and the driver let the big Oldsmobile roll almost to the garage door before pressing the button to open the automatic door. Then, gunning the engine, he pressed the button again. When the door swung shut, he killed the engine.

The overhead light would go off automatically in three minutes, plenty of time for both of them to enter the house. The driver opened the door to the basement, stepped through and then waved Rucker to follow.

Shifting his cane to his left hand, the CIA man closed the door and locked it. He dismissed the driver for the night and climbed up the stairs to the foyer, then went to his study. After turning on the light, he crossed wearily to his desk and sat in the big leather chair. He placed his briefcase on the desk, twirled the combination dials and popped the latches.

The CIA agent pulled out a stack of files, closed the briefcase and put it on the floor. He opened the first file, started to read, then blinked away a watery haze. The letters swam like small fish through the haze, darting and wiggling. He was too damn tired to bother with anything. So he sighed and closed the file. It would wait until morning, or until the inevitable bout of insomnia later that night.

He wished Tania, his wife, and the kids were home, but they wouldn't be back for another two weeks. They had to get out once in a while and go someplace normal. He understood that and he encouraged them.

Rucker looked around the study once before walking to the door. Clicking off the light, he padded down the hall to the stairs. Out of habit he kicked off his shoes and pushed them against the newel. Too many late nights had taught him not to wake Tania if he could avoid it. The habit stuck even when she was away.

As he passed by, he pressed the light switch for the upstairs hall. The indirect lighting filled the stairwell, and he enjoyed, as he always did, looking back at his shadow on the stairs behind him. He enjoyed, too, the feel of the thick carpet under his stockinged foot.

At the top of the stairs he pushed another switch, turning off the overhead light. The small night-light was on in the master bedroom, enough to see by for the rest of his trip. He half stumbled into the room, again pressing tired fingers against his eyes.

"It's about time," the voice said.

Rucker froze in his tracks. He let his hand fall slowly, like a piece of tissue paper drifting on a slight breeze. "What the hell are you doing here, Mahoney?" he demanded. "How did you get in?"

"You thought your little security system was enough, did you?"

"Damn it! I can have you arrested for this."

"So call a cop."

"Aren't you supposed to be in the hospital?"

"I had a miraculous recovery."

"Always the wise guy, Mahoney. What do you want?"

"What do you think I want?"

"How the hell should I know? What does a crazy man usually want?"

"Crazy? Is that what you think I am?"

"What else could you be, breaking in here like a common criminal?"

"Oh, I'm anything but common, Rucker. You ought to realize that."

The CIA man sighed, then walked to the bed. "Do you mind if I sit down? I'm exhausted."

"Just keep your hands where I can see them."

"I'm not a fool."

"I didn't think so. That's why I warned you. See, I figure, having been warned, you'll know better than to do anything dangerous to your health. Or have you already done that?"

"What are you talking about? Make sense, damn it."

"Can I run a little number past you, Rucker?"

"Number? What number?"

"Five followed by five zeros."

"So? Five hundred thousand. What about it?"

"There's a dollar sign in front of the five, Rucker. Mean anything now?"

"Should it?"

"All right, let me try another number on you. What about six? That do anything for you?"

"Six dollars? Why should it?"

"Not dollars, Rucker. Corpses. Six corpses."

"Look, Mahoney, if you can't make sense, I'm going to sleep. Wake me up when you figure out what you're talking about." Rucker leaned back on the bed, draping a hand over his eyes.

"Pretty cool customer. I'll give you that. But six is a lot of dead bodies, Rucker. Takes a lot of holes. And a lot of dirt to fill them up. You really expect to be able to get away with it?"

Rucker said nothing.

"Look, I know about the money. And I know about the dead bodies. What I don't know is the connection between them. But it won't take me long to figure it out."

Rucker sat up abruptly. "Listen to me, you dumb fuck. Didn't you get enough lead in Afghanistan? You don't have any idea what you're getting yourself into here. It can get you killed. Snuffed." He snapped his fingers. "Like that. For all I know maybe it already has. I might not hear about it until later."

"Come on, Rucker. That won't cut it."

"I don't give a damn what you think. You're in over your fat head."

"Watch your mouth."

"Fuck you. Get out of here before it's too late."

"I want you to tell me about it."

"I'm not telling you anything."

"Why not? Is it classified?"

"You bet your ass it's classified."

"I want a piece, Rucker."

"Piece of what?"

"The action. What else? You think I don't know what you're doing? You think you can dip into the petty-cash fund and turn half a mill around without anybody noticing? Hey, and for drugs yet. What a naughty boy. Suppose the vice president heard about it? He's leading the war against drugs, you know. He'd be pretty miffed.''

''Is that what you think I'm doing? You're a bigger jerk than I thought.''

''Nice try, Rucker, but I don't bluff.''

''I don't, either, Mahoney. And you couldn't be farther off base.''

''Then tell me about it.''

''I can't.''

''You have to, or I'll blow the whistle. Even if what you're doing is cleared, you don't want it out in the open.''

''Hey, you think I give a damn what you say? You think you'll even get a chance to say anything? Forget about it, Mahoney. Your ass has just gone south. This is bigger than you can imagine.''

''I suppose you're going to tell me that the money was for the mujahadeen?''

''Would you believe it if I did?''

''Depends on what kind of support you can give me.''

''Support? You want support? I'll give it to you. Arbak Hikmal was bringing in a couple hundred pounds of opium. He was supposed to get half a million dollars for his troubles from Viktor Sharkov. Only somebody convinced him to trash the dope. No dope, no money. Stop me if this gets too boring for you.''

"Keep going. So far I like it. It has a nice ring to it.''

"No money, no guns. That means about a half-dozen operations come to a screeching halt. Operations we didn't set up, but that we wouldn't mind seeing pan out. It was a good idea, using Sharkov's money to fight his former employer. Only you fucked it up.''

"So you dig into Uncle Sam's pocket to make up the shortfall.''

"You're not as dumb as you look, Mahoney. Anyway, to keep Hikmal going, we cough up. Nothing sinister in that, just the usual black ops. In other words, I'm doing my job, and you come in here acting like I'm some big-time mafioso. I should be pissed, but actually it's kind of flattering. Maybe it's even a good idea. Unfortunately for me, and my bank account, I don't work that way. Now I'm asking you, as one of Uncle Sam's nephews to another, get out of my face. I have enough problems. As far as I'm concerned, this conversation never took place. Against my better judgment I'll let you walk out of here. Don't make me regret it. Things could get real nasty then.''

"You still didn't tell me about the bodies.''

"What bodies?''

"In the basement with the money.''

"Shit happens."

"And the choppers?"

"What choppers?"

"At the lab."

"I don't know what you mean."

"The two choppers that nearly nailed Belasko when he took down the lab. You mean to say you don't know anything about them?"

"No."

Mahoney coughed. "Excuse me if I have trouble swallowing that one."

Rucker seemed distracted for a moment. The DEA agent was starting to think Rucker was telling the truth. He just wasn't sure. Rucker seemed suddenly uneasy, as if something were going on he didn't know about.

"Okay, guys, you can come out now," Mahoney said.

Rucker's eyes popped. "What guys?"

"Me," Bolan said. He opened the closet door. "And Hikmal and Goncharov."

The other two came in off the patio.

Rucker looked at them for a long moment. His gaze shifted to Goncharov. It was the presence of the Russian that really spooked him. When he spoke, his voice was funereal. "I'm a goddamn dead man. Do you know that? I'm dead."

"Don't worry about it," Bolan said. "Your secret's safe. We need your help."

"You think I'd help you bastards now? You've got to be kidding."

"No joke, Rucker," Bolan said. "Believe me."

Rucker sighed. "Tell me what you want."

CHAPTER TWENTY-SIX

"Look, Belasko," Rucker said. "You have to understand that there isn't much more I can do. We have limited resources. And I'm not sure the jerks on the Hill would be too sympathetic if this got out. We're not supposed to be in the business of busting drug smugglers, you know."

"Don't worry about it. Your little secret will be safe. And as far as I'm concerned, this makes a lot more sense than most of the things you guys try."

"Where's the national security angle? What's my hook if I get nailed on this?"

"You'll think of something."

"You bastard." But Rucker grinned. "You'd get along just fine with my boss."

"No, thanks," Bolan said.

"The contact will meet you at the warehouse. You tell him what you want, then you're on your own. I'll cover the difference, if any. He already knows that."

"Fair enough."

Bolan started the engine, letting the jeep roll down the driveway. Rucker hobbled alongside for a few feet. "I'm going back to Islamabad in the morning," he said. "If you have to reach me there, try not to compromise yourself. Or me."

Bolan nodded.

Rucker opened the electronic gate and watched the jeep pass through. Bolan glanced back once as the gate rolled closed. He saw Rucker wave, then disappear inside.

Hikmal seemed subdued. "What's wrong?" Bolan asked.

"Too much politics," the Afghan answered. "I hate politics. I don't understand why freedom is always hostage to politics."

"Anything worth having is hostage to politics, Hikmal. Welcome to the real world."

"For you, maybe."

"For you, too, whether you want to believe it or not."

The warehouse was north of Peshawar. It was an hour's drive, and for the rest of the trip no one said a thing. When the warehouse came into view, a huge, ugly building advertising itself as the home of modern plumbing, Mahoney laughed. "That's where we're going, all right. Right down the toilet."

They pulled into a rutted road alongside the warehouse, and Bolan swung the jeep around to the back door. The place looked deserted. A single red bulb burned over the steel door. There was no other sign the building was even in use.

Bolan climbed out of the jeep. "Mahoney, get behind the wheel. Anything happens, get out of here. Don't stop for me. I'll find you in Islamabad."

"No gung-ho shit, Belasko. We're all in this together. Get used to it. I didn't come this far to turn tail when trouble rears its ugly head."

"This isn't your world. It's mine. And you do what I say. When we're done here, you go back to Islamabad. Somebody has to keep an eye on Rucker. And besides, you're still too weak. There's no way you could handle it out there."

"But—"

"He will," Goncharov put in. "I'll make certain of that."

Bolan left the jeep about fifty yards from the door and approached the warehouse cautiously. There was little cover for an ambush behind the building, just knee-high grass stretching up a gentle hill for a quarter of a mile. If trouble was coming, it would strike from inside the warehouse.

As Bolan drew near the door, it swung open. A small man wearing mandarin robes and wire-rimmed glasses stood in the doorway. He was outlined by a dim light issuing from somewhere deep inside the building. The Chinese nodded as Bolan approached. "You're punctual, Mr. Belasko."

Bolan said nothing.

"Are your friends coming in?"

"Just one." He turned and waved to Hikmal.

The Afghan walked toward them, and the Chinese bowed. "Arbak Hikmal?"

"Yes."

"I have heard of you."

"Do you have what we need?"

"I'm a businessman, Mr. Hikmal. I have what everybody needs."

Hikmal grunted. That wasn't what he wanted to hear—one more tick getting fat on Afghanistan's bleeding flanks.

Carrying an electric lantern, the Chinese led them into the depths of the warehouse. He escorted them into an office, took a seat at an old metal desk and aimed the lantern at the ceiling. "Now, gentlemen, what can I do for you?"

"You know why I'm here," Hikmal said.

"Of course, you wish to buy plumbing supplies. That's why all my customers come here."

"I'm not accustomed to joking about such matters," Hikmal said.

"We Chinese are longtime veterans of commerce, my friend. You must learn to relax. This is a business transaction like any other."

"Not to me."

"Then indulge me. What do you want?"

Hikmal reached into his pocket, removed an envelope and opened it. He withdrew three sheets of ruled paper, soiled from frequent handling, and pushed them across the desk.

The arms merchant looked at the sheets without picking them up. Then, with one delicate hand, he separated the sheets and leaned forward, peering over the top of his glasses. He hummed to himself, made a comment occasionally in Chinese, then sat back in his chair. "I'm surprised."

"Why?" Hikmal asked.

"I had expected heavier arms to be your priority."

Hikmal smiled. "You're not used to dealing with men who have to transport their purchases on horseback."

"You should modernize, my friend."

"Have you ever been to Afghanistan?"

"Many times. To Kabul and to Kandahar."

"Then you haven't been to Afghanistan. Those cities are as much like the rest of the country as Beijing is to the Mongolian desert."

"I have trucks."

"Helicopters are used to horses and camels. They look more closely at trucks. We can only use them partway."

"Of course."

"Do you have what I need?"

"Do you have what it will cost?"

Hikmal nodded.

"Then let's talk about it."

Bolan leaned back. It was obvious the Afghan knew what he was doing. It was equally obvious the Chinese would do business. The logistics weren't his problem. He stood, and the other two men looked at him, annoyed at having their discussion interrupted. "I'll wait outside," he told them.

The arms merchant nodded absently. Hikmal didn't acknowledge the remark at all. His mind was elsewhere. Bolan left the office and walked back toward the door. He had to go slowly because the Chinese had the only light.

Mahoney was leaning against the jeep. Goncharov still sat in the back.

"How'd it go?" Mahoney asked.

Bolan shrugged. "They're talking."

"I'm tired of talking."

"You should be more patient," Goncharov said. "Nobody wants Sharkov more than I do."

"Wanna bet?"

"Betting is for fools," the Russian said, snorting.

"You calling me a fool?"

"If you bet, yes."

Mahoney glared at the Russian. Bolan looked at the sky. He was sitting on nitroglycerin. In an earthquake. This ad hoc coalition was precarious at best. There were too many axes and only one wheel to grind them on. He wished he could figure out a way to hold it together, but that was next to impossible, and he knew it. The best he could hope for was a temporary unity under pressure. When this was over, he didn't give a damn if he ever saw any of these guys again.

"Tell me some more about Sharkov," Bolan said to Goncharov.

The Russian climbed out of the jeep. "I've already told you everything I know." Goncharov seemed relieved to have the subject changed. Even Mahoney seemed interested.

"Not the file data," Bolan said. "The personal. I need to get a sense of the man himself. Tell me anything you can think of."

"He was a good intelligence officer. One of the best."

"You know him personally?"

"I thought so. Now I'm not so sure."

"What happened to him?"

Goncharov shrugged. "Who knows? If I had to guess, I'd say he saw himself getting old, and since the old ways are changing, he thought perhaps he'd become expendable. Nobody likes to have that happen."

"He's not alone in that. You're in the same boat."

"I'm not as old. I'm more flexible, and my life's work isn't under attack."

"You think that's all there is to it?"

"What do you mean?"

"You think he's a rogue, acting on his own?"

"Insofar as I know, yes."

"Do you believe it?"

"I don't know what to believe. I've seen a lot of strange things in my career, things that made me shake my head because no other response was possible, things that turned my stomach. But that's always the way it is. I can't change that. Neither can Viktor. But I think he feels betrayed. I think he just wants to get even in some small way by becoming the ultimate capitalist. What better way to thumb your nose at the old ways than by going overboard to embrace the new?"

"You like him, don't you?" Bolan watched while the Russian thought about the question.

"Why do you ask?"

"Because if you're in a bind, if you don't know where your sympathies lie, I want to know about it."

"Fair enough. I don't like him. I never did, really. But I respected him once, even admired him. He was what I wanted to be—the ultimate professional, serving the state without question because he believed in it. Now... I just don't know."

"What about the man who sent you after Sharkov?"

"Peter Grebnov is a good man, what you Americans would call a liberal, I suppose. He was never comfortable with some of the more brutal excesses.''

"So he could be using you?''

"How do you mean?''

"In an attempt to undercut a sanctioned operation. Maybe Grebnov's the rogue.''

"Maybe he is.''

"That doesn't bother you?''

"No, because Peter is right. I have children, Belasko, two of them. Whatever happens, it's the children who suffer with drugs. If they don't use them, their parents do, and still they suffer.''

"Pretty sentiments,'' Mahoney said. "But Sharkov's one of yours.''

"So he is. But I'll bet you he had one of yours in his pocket.''

"Betting's for fools,'' Mahoney reminded him.

"Touché,'' Goncharov said, reaching into his pocket.

He pulled out a crisp ruble note and extended it to Mahoney. The DEA kid jerked a dollar from his pants and covered the Russian bill. "You're on,'' he said.

CHAPTER TWENTY-SEVEN

Bolan felt the truck wobble beneath him. He was in the last vehicle to leave, and he was getting uneasy. Three truckloads in all, the purchase represented just a small part of what Hikmal needed, and since the five hundred thousand dollars didn't go very far on the arms market, just a fraction of what he could use to meet those needs.

Even knowing what to do with the remainder of the money, after he'd paid Li Po, the Chinese arms merchant, for the first shipment, was a problem. Hikmal refused to use a commercial bank, claiming the money wouldn't be safe. Bolan had offered to help, but the Afghan was suspicious of the offer. He seemed to be turning inward, as if the sheer prosperity of the moment were a burden he didn't know how to cope with.

Where the rest of the money was now, only Hikmal himself knew. That it was still a considerable sum for the Afghan was certain, but even the exact amount was something Hikmal wouldn't divulge.

Now, sitting in the front of the truck, conscious of the explosive freight behind him, Bolan wondered where it was all leading. It seemed such a strange and circuitous route to take down a drug dealer. But the modern world was anything but simple. There were no direct routes anymore, not when there was a fortune to be made and no lack of willing fortune hunters.

In the back of the rusty truck, disguised as a bakery wagon, were thousands of rounds of ammunition for an assortment of black-market assault rifles, everything from AK-47s to CAR-15s. The Pakistani army was moderately sympathetic to its Islamic brethren in Afghanistan, so the patrols, if they were to encounter contraband, tended to look the other way. But sometimes it took cash, and sometimes there was nothing you could do to convince a pissed-off army officer to go momentarily blind. Worse than that was the possibility that one of the infinite number of spies and near spies swarming like locusts along the border would get curious.

The guns and ammunition were useless without men to use them. Hikmal had men, but they were hours away. If anyone was to stop them before the rendezvous, neither of them might live to see another sunrise. And Bolan was savvy enough to know that Li Po wouldn't be averse to selling the same matériel a second time for a second juicy profit. He was, after all, as he had taken great pains to point out, just a businessman.

Hikmal, though, seemed almost blithely unconcerned. He hummed scraps of melody in a craggy baritone, sometimes whistled or patted his hands on the steering wheel. The songs and the rhythms were alien to Bolan's ears, but he said nothing. Let the man enjoy himself, he thought. It might not last very long.

They were still an hour from the border. That meant that Mahoney should just about be crossing the city line into Peshawar. Bolan had had to argue with the Afghan to get him to stagger the shipment. Three trucks, three different routes, three different arrival times. It was safer but less fun. Hikmal had pouted for a while, even when he conceded that Bolan was right. Better to lose a third of the load than to lose it all.

Glancing in his side mirror, Bolan noticed a pair of headlights well behind them on the barren road. They were climbing slowly, and the road snaked back and forth across the rugged mountainside.

He watched the lights without calling Hikmal's attention to them. They seemed to be gaining, but slowly. If the vehicle behind was in pursuit, the driver was in no hurry. He watched closely, looking for any change in speed.

Then the headlights got closer. On high beams the lights bounced and slashed across the rocky ground. Hikmal couldn't fail to notice them now, but if he was concerned, he didn't show it. Bolan watched the Afghan's eyes darting now and then from the surface of the road ahead of him to the careening lights.

"You think that's an army patrol behind us?" Bolan asked.

Hikmal shrugged. "Perhaps."

The Afghan said nothing more, and Bolan chose to let the subject drop. But he kept watching. They were still several terraces below the crest of the mountain, but the higher they climbed, the more isolated they became. Bolan fiddled with the AK-47 in his lap.

For a moment the sky grew almost white, then they heard a chopper. Bolan craned his neck to look up at the sky. A bright finger of light swept along the road, passed over them and kept going. The chopper followed right behind the beam, as if pulled along by it. He couldn't see the contours of the helicopter, but the engine sounded familiar. It was American-made; he was almost certain.

That made it almost equally certain that it was the Pakistani army. No one else out here could afford that kind of hardware. Bolan steeled himself for the chopper's return, but the beat of the rotors gradually diminished. The pilot continued to follow the road, and the chopper suddenly appeared in Bolan's mirror. The bird pivoted and swept back toward them, this time following the next lowest loop of the serpentine highway.

The lights on the following vehicle suddenly went out, and Bolan caught a glimpse of red as the brake lights flashed once, then again. The chopper bore down on the darkened vehicle, then the finger of light swept over it, and Bolan could clearly see a jeep. Two men jumped from the vehicle and started to scramble down the mountainside.

"Stop the truck, Hikmal," Bolan ordered.

"It's no concern of ours."

"How do you know that?"

"I don't. It's what I believe that counts. And I believe it's no concern of ours."

The chopper spun on a dime and came back toward the jeep. In the cold air Bolan could see a thin wisp of smoke coiling up from the jeep's exhaust. The chopper hovered now, the beam pointing straight down. Then the aircraft started to descend.

The searchlight spun away, a brilliant parabola spilling down the mountain like quicksilver avoiding a thumb. One of the fleeing men was caught in the egg-shaped disk of illumination. He looked up at the chopper, then ran until he stumbled, the searchlight's beam following him every step of the way. He tried to claw his way back to his feet, but the slope and his terror kept pulling him off balance. He fell again and lay still, his arms curled over his head.

Bolan steeled himself for a sudden burst of machine-gun fire, but it never came. The chopper descended the rest of the way, and three men spilled out of the open door. The truck still groaned upward, and Bolan was on the verge of losing sight of them when Hikmal slammed on the brakes. The warrior jerked his head around in time to see a shadowy figure disappearing on his side of the road, sprinting straight up the side of the mountain. It was the second man from the jeep. Hikmal ground the gears, jammed the truck into first and gunned the engine. The truck lurched jerkily ahead as the engine roared.

"Stop!" Bolan shouted, grabbing Hikmal's arm. He shoved the door open and jumped out.

Running after the fugitive, he was barely able to pick him out in the dim gray light. The man was tired, and his legs seemed to flail uselessly as he tried to reach the next loop of the highway. Far fresher, Bolan closed on him rapidly and he caught him after another fifty yards.

The man clawed at his belt for a gun, but the Executioner covered the last ten yards in a sprint, reaching the man just as the gun barrel cleared the canvas holster on his hip. Putting his head down, Bolan slammed into him with a shoulder and knocked him down. The gun went flying, and the warrior grabbed the man's shirt as he tried to scramble away. Tugging him to his feet, Bolan jerked him roughly and started to drag him back down toward the truck.

As he descended, the Executioner watched the action on the mountainside far below. The three men from the chopper had caught the other man and were bundling him back up the hill. As Bolan and his prisoner reached the truck, the chopper lifted off and Hikmal gunned the engine.

"They're coming!" the Afghan shouted.

The chopper spun on its rotor shaft, climbed three hundred feet, then banked toward them, seeming to fall uphill as the distance between it and the side of the mountain shrank. Bolan swung around the AK-47, but the chopper banked again, climbed straight up and roared down the mountain. The searchlight went out. In the renewed darkness the engines sounded thunderous, then the chopper was gone, and the truck rumbled on alone.

Bolan shoved his prisoner up into the cab and climbed in after him. He leaned over and clicked on the cab's interior light, then shook his head. He had seen the man earlier at the warehouse. The guy worked for Li Po.

CHAPTER TWENTY-EIGHT

Fifteen horsemen moved down out of the rocky defile. A broad canyon stretched ahead of them, slowly widening out like a funnel. Dead center ahead, framed by the steep walls on either side, snowcapped mountains in rank after rank stretched off to the horizon. Bolan and Hikmal had made their rendezvous with the horses and had shifted the arms onto the pack animals.

"This is the worst part," Hikmal said, letting his horse hang back a little.

"Are you expecting anything particular?" Bolan asked.

The Afghan shook his head. "No, but this is one of the key approaches to the city for shipments from Pakistan. The army, of course, knows this. They patrol from the air. No schedule. Some say they're too smart for that. The truth, though, is that their hearts aren't in it. Maintenance is bad, and the skill to perform repairs is even worse. There's bad morale. All of this is good for us. But we have a long way to go."

As they reached the mouth of the funnel, Hikmal drove his horse a little harder, widening the gap

between himself and the others. The second man
followed while the third sat on his restless mount,
tugging on the reins to hold him back. When the
third man started down the slope, Bolan realized
what was going on.

These men were so well drilled that defensive
measures were second nature to them. They were
stretching the column deliberately. A single mine
would then kill only one man and two horses, and
a sudden helicopter assault wouldn't eliminate the
whole band in the wink of an eye. Death from the
sky was part of their world. Outgunned, techno-
logically outstripped, they had to adapt the little
they had to the reality they faced.

Bolan was the last man down the hill. By this
time he could barely see Hikmal, who was nearly a
mile ahead. A hundred yards, at least, separated
each man from his neighbor.

Much later, they were nearly at the final rendezvous point when the first distant thump of rotor
blades echoed off the mountains. By this time
Hikmal and Bolan were riding together again.

"We have to hurry," the Afghan said. He dismounted and took the pack horses from Bolan. He
cut his own loose and quickly hobbled all three.
"We'll have to come back for them."

Back on his horse, he didn't wait for Bolan. They
plunged through the near darkness at breakneck
speed.

"There's two of them!" Bolan shouted.

Hikmal didn't answer. It took them fifteen minutes, and the sound of the choppers grew louder and louder. By the time they reached the campsite, the drone was echoing off the high walls of the cliff towering above it.

The rebel leader ordered his men to pull the horses in close to the wall. Some of the animals had already been unloaded, and the crates lay scattered.

Barking commands, Hikmal ran among the men, trying to keep them from panicking. Slowly they fell into line, working in pairs to ferry the crates up against the rock wall. Where possible they crammed them in among the broken boulders littering the shallow bowl in which they'd camped.

Bolan snatched a blanket from his horse. It was GI brown, and he draped the cloth over a stack of crates, tucking it in to cover the lighter color of the raw wood. Hikmal noticed, and ordered three men to strip the other horses. Then he tugged one crate aside and started to rip it open with a rusty crowbar.

The nails screamed as he jimmied the lid off the crate. Bolan joined him to find two Redeye shoulder-launched missiles. These were the prime acquisitions of the recent purchase, and no one, least of all Hikmal himself, had expected them to be necessary so soon.

"Do you know how to use these?" the Afghan asked.

Bolan nodded. He took one of the thirty-pound Redeyes and peeled away the plastic wrapping. After the missile and launch package were clear, he peeled a second one. "Better do a third," he told the Afghan.

"No. Two helicopters, two missiles. They're too precious to us."

"Hikmal, you have to—"

"I said no! If you're afraid to use them, then tell me how. I'll do it."

Bolan brushed him aside. "Listen to me! If you don't take those choppers out, a million of these things won't do you any good. Do you want to waste everything you have here?"

"Two helicopters, two missiles."

Bolan sighed, but said nothing. He hoisted one of the Redeyes onto his shoulder and started to run. Hikmal grabbed the second and followed him. The choppers were very close now. So far there hadn't been a hint of light. Either they weren't interested in finding the rebels, or they already knew where they were.

The first spear of light slashed out of the sky as one of the choppers hung over the towering rock face, which was about three hundred yards west of the campsite. The beam swiped across the stone wall, then speared down to its base. Bolan turned for a moment, but couldn't watch because the ground was too treacherous. He nearly fell as it was, and held on to the Redeye with difficulty.

He was already a hundred yards from the campsite, but wanted to put a little more ground between him and it. He heard Hikmal shout something, but the roar of the chopper's engine drowned it out. The second chopper was farther west. So far it hadn't put its searchlight on. Bolan found a cluster of rocks and crawled in among them. Hikmal scrambled in after him, but the warrior pointed to the west. "That way, at least fifty yards!" he shouted, cupping his hands and leaning toward the Afghan.

Hikmal looked confused. "Look," Bolan said, "as soon as I fire the first missile, they'll come looking for us. If we stay together, we may not get the second one off. We have to split up. As soon as the bird's away, I'll find you."

The Afghan nodded without enthusiasm, but he did as he was told.

The first chopper was drifting along the rim rock. It was only a hundred yards west of the camp now, its searchlight probing along the base of the wall. Bolan couldn't nail it for fear of sending the wreckage down on top of the rebels hugging the wall.

The second chopper was a better bet. He could barely make it out against the black sky and was more than grateful that the Redeye was a heat seeker. Any other targeting mechanism would have been iffy at best. As it was, the Redeye was notoriously unpredictable.

He homed in on the nearly invisible chopper. Holding his breath, he counted backward from three. Squeezing the trigger, he felt the dull throb of the missile leaving its tube. His shoulder vibrated for a moment, then the bird was off, leaving a thin stream of silver smoke behind it.

He couldn't stay to watch.

Bolan ran for all he was worth. He sensed rather than saw the second searchlight go on. A heartbeat later, a deafening crack bounced off the sheer stone wall, and a huge fireball mushroomed out. Hundreds of gallons of burning fuel spewed from the ball, pouring liquid fire over the sheer face of the cliff.

And right on the money the second chopper swung its light away from the cliff. It picked up the narrow band of smoke. At almost the same instant a pair of rockets thumped from pods slung under the chopper's fuselage.

Bolan nearly missed Hikmal as he dashed through the darkness. The rockets slammed into the stone pocket behind him, their simultaneous concussions slapping him like a giant hand and sending him sprawling into the dirt.

He scrambled to his feet, aware that the huge fireball and the streams of flame gushing down along the face of the cliff threw off enough light to make him and Hikmal visible. He grappled with the second Redeye, hoisting it to his shoulder as a machine gun started to hammer. He could see his target clearly. It was a Hind, loaded for bear.

Squaring up the launch tube, he squeezed off, then hit the deck. He covered his head with his hands, dimly aware of a hurricane of hellfire slashing toward him. He could see the puffs of dust as each bullet slammed into the ground, a line of marching geysers. Then the Redeye hit.

A second fireball ignited, and the hammering machine gun stopped. The Hind had started toward him, hovering about fifty yards from the wall. The missile had taken its rotor off, and the machine dropped straight down. The tumbling rotor arced through the smoke and orange flame, slammed into the wall and shattered.

It seemed as if the clang of raining wreckage would never stop.

CHAPTER TWENTY-NINE

Two of Hikmal's men were killed by falling debris. One of them, caught by the cascading gasoline, was charred beyond recognition by the holocaust.

The rebel leader was in a foul mood. He'd spent most of the night sitting by himself on a rock. No matter who tried to approach him, he sent him away with a scorching stream of curses. Twice during the night he fired a burst from his AK-47, sending the bullets ricocheting high off the cliff and showering the men below with razor-edged shards of stone.

"The man's become a lunatic," Goncharov muttered, dropping into a crouch beside Bolan.

"He's angry, not mad," Bolan said.

"Did you ever lose a partner or a subordinate? Do you still want to avenge him?"

"Yes, of course I have, and I do. But that's different. He was my partner, not a soldier. A commander has to accept casualties. He can't afford to grieve, not when he has a responsibility to his other men."

Bolan hesitated before answering. He wondered whether Goncharov would understand what he was about to tell him. "Look, a partner is one thing. That's special, but you have to understand that a good leader worries more about his men than he does about himself. If he loses one, he takes it hard. He thinks it's his fault . . . and it is. There's no pain quite like it, Goncharov."

"You sound like you're talking from personal experience, Belasko."

"Just take my word for it, okay?"

Goncharov sighed. The Russian didn't understand Americans, and he never would. He moved back into the shadows.

Bolan heard shuffling feet behind him and turned to see Goncharov pacing. Since they'd been reunited in the camp, the Russian had said very little. He seemed to be tormented by something. Perhaps he had demons of his own, Bolan thought.

Goncharov realized he was being watched, and the awareness made him uncomfortable. He glanced at the big American, then started to move farther into the shadows, changed his mind and stopped. A moment later he was heading back in Bolan's direction. He groaned a little as he sat down on the cold ground. "I wish there was something we could do for him," he said, pointing toward Hikmal with his chin.

Bolan really wasn't in the mood to talk, but he wanted to know more about the secretive Russian.

This might be an ideal opportunity. "There isn't," he answered quietly.

"I guess I know that." Goncharov sucked in his breath, letting the air whistle between his teeth. "But I still wish it."

"Do you think Sharkov still has connections in the Afghan army?"

"I'd imagine so. Why do you ask?"

"Because I'd love to know how those two helicopters, coming out of nowhere, managed to find us. Hikmal says they almost never fly at night anymore. But these guys knew we were here. They had to. There's no luck that blind."

"He might have been able to get the Hinds sent out here. But it still doesn't explain how he knew *where* to send them."

"I know that," Bolan said. That's a separate piece of the puzzle. You have any ideas on that?"

"A hundred, but none of them very likely."

"I have one, too, and it seems feasible. Maybe even likely."

"I know what you're thinking, but, no, I didn't have anything to do with it. I'm out here for one reason and one reason only—to terminate Viktor Sharkov. I've already told you that."

"Yeah, you told me."

"But you didn't believe it."

"I don't know what to believe. I don't understand why we haven't been followed. There was that peculiar episode with the helicopter back around the border, but that didn't make any sense to me then, and it still doesn't. But I would have thought someone would have been dogging our tracks. Instead, they seem to be anticipating them. As if we're predictable."

"Not us, Belasko, but maybe him." He jerked a thumb toward Hikmal. "He is, after all, not a military man by training, but by necessity. I don't mean to demean him. He's rather a remarkable man in so many ways. But we have whole faculties full of experts who do nothing but study guerrilla tactics, both their application and ways to combat them. I don't think Hikmal could surprise them."

Two men charged up the slope on horseback, and Hikmal jumped to his feet. He ran down to meet them, hauling one of the men from his mount. Bolan and Goncharov watched as the Afghans talked among themselves.

Obviously something was up.

Hikmal ran back up the slope to the camp. He started shouting commands, and his men were galvanized by whatever it was he said. They began to gather weapons, and two men broke open a pair of crates. Bolan ran after the Afghan and caught him by the arm. "What's happening?" he asked.

"An armored column is headed this way."

"How long?"

"An hour, maybe less. They have to come through a narrow pass. If we can get there ahead of them..."

"I want to help."

"No. This is our fight, not yours."

"It doesn't matter."

Hikmal shook him off. "I have much to do."

Bolan ran to his bedroll and grabbed his own weapons. Half of the mujahadeen guerrillas were already on their horses. Bolan was amazed at their efficiency. Hikmal noticed him as he prepared to mount. "Hurry, if you're coming!" he shouted.

The warrior finished saddling his horse and swung onto the animal's back. The rebels had already started to move by the time he grabbed the reins. He pushed his horse to catch up with Hikmal, who was still barking commands as the rebels fell into a ragged line.

The rebel leader finished issuing his instructions and eased back, letting his horse walk until Bolan caught up with him. "Four tanks," he said, "and some motorized artillery. I don't think they're looking for us, but they might be. Those helicopters might have sent our location before they were destroyed."

"Wouldn't it be better to elude them?"

"It would if we had time, but we don't. I have to assume they know where we are. That means I can't afford to let them chase us. We have to hit them while we have surprise on our side."

The column angled up through a series of narrow defiles, each one a little higher than the last. The air was thinning, and Bolan grew conscious of his labored breathing. They were high above the broad valley now, but Bolan was able to see only a little V-shaped slice of it over his shoulder. Surrounded by rocky walls at every turn, he wondered if rats in a maze felt the way he did at the moment. Hikmal was quiet now, a man with a clear sense of what he had to do, and not a trace of theatrics about him.

The others were quiet, too, whether from habit or in imitation of their commander, Bolan didn't know. They'd been moving for nearly an hour when Hikmal halted the column to converse with two of his closest lieutenants. He waited to one side, where Bolan joined him. The lieutenants moved among the column, dividing the men into two large groups and one small squad.

Bolan watched quietly, impressed by the disciplined behavior of the men. At a signal from their leader one of the two large groups moved out. The men angled toward the left, then seemed to disappear. Hikmal waited until they were gone, then moved his horse closer to Bolan.

"We have to hit them from both sides at once," he explained. "We'll be nearly three hundred feet above them, the others even higher on the other side of the pass. There's no way into the valley by land without using the pass. Once they're inside, we'll strike."

"You've done this before, I gather."

"Many times. The Soviets learned to expect it, but there was little they could do about it on the ground. That's why the helicopters were so important to them. But since they've pulled out, it's a little easier for us."

"I would think your own countrymen would know even better what to expect."

"They do. But their hearts aren't really in the fight, so they get careless."

"But their lives are at stake."

"Yes, they are. That can't be helped. And we try not to be more brutal than necessary." Hikmal raised a hand, and the second column moved off. "I have work to do," he said, and prodded his own horse.

Bolan followed right behind him. There was no way he was going to sit on the sidelines. Not now when so much was at stake. He needed Hikmal, and he needed him alive. The Afghan might think it was his war, but Bolan had his own to fight, and the man was a crucial part of it.

The smallest of the three units fell in behind their leader. In the distance Bolan could hear the telltale clank of metal tracks and the monotonous drone of powerful diesels. The six men with Hikmal each carried a light antiarmor weapon. The powerful LAW rockets were a match for anything on land, but the odds were so lopsided that Bolan didn't give the rebels much of a chance.

The clanking grew louder, echoing off the walls of the pass. The thunder of the big tank engines made the ground tremble. Rocks started to shower down from high above as they entered the confines of the canyon.

Hikmal dismounted, and the men behind him jumped from their own horses, scattering among the rocks and looking for cover. Bolan jumped to the ground and unlimbered his AK-47. The thunder was continuous now.

The rebel leader crouched behind a boulder, scanning the rocky rim and keeping one eye on the advancing column. He seemed to tense up, then shot an arm straight into the air. The last of the armored vehicles was in the pass, and sudden thunder broke out behind it. Bolan looked up in time to see several huge boulders teetering on the edge of the cliffs, one already tipped over and bouncing as lightly as a pebble off the sheer cliff face as it fell.

It landed with a horrible crash, and one by one more explosions cracked and more boulders began to fall into the narrow defile. They crashed into one another on the way down, some shattering on impact, and a last, powerful blast peeled away a great slab of granite. It tumbled end over end before landing on the rubble below.

The column was trapped, it couldn't go back, and it couldn't advance without going through the semicircle of LAWs.

"Aim for the lead tank!" Hikmal shouted. His voice died away, and its echo was swallowed by the dull whoosh of a LAW. The rocket sped straight for the lead tank and detonated on impact. It tore the turret halfway off, but the tank continued to roll straight on. The driver knew he had to get out of the defile, or he wouldn't stand a chance.

The second LAW took out the left tread, and the tank spun in a half circle before the driver realized he had no traction on that side. He tried to compensate, using the right track to drag the ruined tank, clanking and smoking, another twenty-five yards. A third LAW slammed home, glancing off the underside of the turret and down into the tank itself. It went off with a roar that sounded feeble compared to the others. A geyser of flame shot up through the turret hatch, and the turret tumbled to one side. Almost immediately the ordnance in the tank started detonating. In a chain reaction, shell after shell blew, tearing the tank to pieces and showering Hikmal and his men with shrapnel. They crouched low until the last shell exploded.

The diesels of the following tanks grew to a hurricane fury. The second in line tried to ease past the wreckage. It couldn't, and the driver backed up, then gunned the engine and rode up and over the burning hulk.

While it was canted at a forty-five-degree angle, a fourth rocket was launched at its underside. A turret gunner on the third tank opened fire, cutting the rocket launcher in two with his machine gun. But the rocket found a chink and gutted the second tank.

Men began to pour out of the remaining vehicles as the tanks tried to maneuver in the tight confines of the narrow pass. More rocks began to cascade down from above, bouncing off the steel plate with horrible bell-like clangs that echoed and reechoed.

Automatic weapons' fire broke out in several places as soldiers poured from a trio of APCs. Two turret gunners began to fire at the rim of the defile, but they were far too late. The men up there had already done their work and changed positions. The distant crack of rifles rose and fell as the rebels above fired a few bursts, sprinted to another position, then fired again.

Hikmal started down toward the canyon floor, and Bolan was right behind him.

CHAPTER THIRTY

Hikmal led his men toward the bottom of the wall. The remaining LAWs were fired as the last of the mujahadeen scrambled down the slope. The crew of the third tank panicked. When Bolan hit the bottom, he heard the whine of a servo as the tank's turret swiveled. The heavy cannon opened up, blasting at the top of the canyon wall in a desperate attempt to take out men who were no longer there.

The artillery shells thundered high overhead, dislodging huge slabs of stone and sending them tumbling back into the canyon with an earthshaking roar. The debris piled down onto the tank itself, and slabs of granite landed all through the trapped armor, some flattening fleeing soldiers, others shattering on impact with the vehicles.

The APCs were empty now, and the frightened soldiers ran into one another in their haste to get out of the trap. Hikmal and his men opened fire, picking off targets at will. After three furious volleys, the rebel leader called a halt. In the sudden silence, broken only by an occasional rock falling from the shattered canyon walls, he shouted to the surviving Afghan regulars, demanding they surrender.

One man, either terrified or enraged, charged straight at Hikmal, an AK-74 in his hands. He raised the state-of-the art assault rifle and swept a vicious arc in the rebel's direction. Bolan shoved Hikmal to one side and opened up with his own weapon. The soldier stumbled, and the warrior hit him high on the shoulder. The man staggered back, and Bolan fired again. The shots went high and smashed into the canyon wall, showering sparks and razor-sharp fragments of chipped granite in a fan-shaped cascade.

The other soldiers, realizing they were trapped, and having lost all stomach for the battle, raised their hands over their heads. Hikmal, with a glance at Bolan, climbed to his feet and dusted himself off. He started to speak, shouting through cupped hands. The soldiers seemed confused. Some, not knowing whether to believe what they were hearing, backed away, clutching their rifles frantically.

Bolan looked at one of Hikmal's men, who stepped closer and translated the ultimatum. "He says if they surrender, they will not be harmed. If not..." He drew a thick finger under his chin and clicked his tongue against the back of his teeth.

One by one the soldiers took tentative steps forward. They dropped their weapons, first in ones and twos, then en masse. Several of the rebels moved down onto the canyon floor and began to gather the weapons into pyramids. The others kept their rifles ready. Everything was so carefully planned, probably from long practice, that it didn't register on Bolan at first. But then he realized the men with the best weapons kept them trained on the surrendering soldiers, while those with ancient Enfields and battered American M-1s moved into the column for the harvest, each taking a newly captured weapon and adding his own discard to the pyramids.

Hikmal asked for the commander of the column to come forward. At first no one responded. After a second and then a third demand, a frightened lieutenant stepped forward. Hikmal had the officer escorted to him and stepped aside, pulling the trembling young man by the sleeve. Bolan followed them, even when the rebel leader frowned at him.

Quickly Hikmal explained that no one would be harmed if he promised to return home instead of to his base. They were all Afghans, he said, and shouldn't be shooting one another for the benefit of outsiders.

The lieutenant nodded as if he understood, but his frightened eyes kept darting from the trapped column to the wild man in front of him. Once, he looked at Bolan in desperation, but the warrior just stared back at him. He could offer no help, and wouldn't have even if he could. This was Hikmal's turf, and Bolan was an outsider.

When the harvest was completed, several of Hikmal's men gathered around their leader. They wanted to know what to do with the prisoners. He glanced at them, then turned to the lieutenant. "You see, my men are getting impatient. You have to decide whether to accept the offer or not."

The lieutenant couldn't speak. His lips moved spasmodically, but no sound came out of his mouth. "Come on, man, decide," Hikmal urged. He was almost pleading with the soldier, but the lieutenant was paralyzed by fear. The mujahadeen were getting restless. They crowded in more tightly around Hikmal, Bolan and the lieutenant.

One by one the officer searched their faces, looking for some clue. He obviously didn't believe the offer was genuine, but he was afraid not to accept it. He licked his lips, then looked at Bolan again. Bolan nodded. The lieutenant started to speak as one of Hikmal's men brushed past the rebel leader and stood in front of the trembling man.

His arm darted forward, and the lieutenant grunted, his mouth rounding in surprise. His eyes widened, their lids flickered and he started to collapse. Only when the small trickle of blood oozed from one corner of his mouth did he seem to realize he'd been hurt. Bolan reached for the man, trying to prop him up. Hikmal's man grunted and brought his arm up, looked at the bloody blade, then started the knife forward. Bolan caught the arm in midarc.

The rebel glared at him, then turned. Bolan heard a hammer click, and Hikmal stepped forward, an old revolver in one hand. He jerked his head, signaling that Bolan should let go of the rebel's arm. The warrior shook his head.

Hikmal brought the gun closer and held it under Bolan's nose for a moment. "As you wish," he said, flicking his wrist and firing.

The crack of the gunshot stunned every man in the canyon. For a moment there was perfect silence. Then the rebel staggered back, a stunned look on his face. Hikmal gave him a shove, and the man sprawled backward on the ground, the circle widening around him as the others stepped back and let him fall.

The rebel leader shook his head. "You never listen, do you?" Kneeling by the man he had just shot, he shook his head sadly again. "You don't understand, and now you never will." He got up, turned to the lieutenant as calmly as if nothing had happened and said, "Well?" But the lieutenant was already dead.

"We have to go," Hikmal said. "Tarak, you know what to do." He looked at his second-in-command, then pulled Bolan by the arm. "We should get back to camp. I'm worried about the Russian. I don't think I trust him.''

He led the way to the horses, and Bolan followed, more confused than ever. Just when he thought he had Hikmal figured out, the man threw him a curve. The Afghan mounted without a word and didn't wait for Bolan.

The ride took nearly an hour, and Hikmal hadn't said a word by the time the camp came into view. Most of the time he was well ahead of Bolan, as if he didn't trust himself to be too close.

As Hikmal reined in, Goncharov stepped toward him, holding something in his hand. By the time Bolan got there, the Afghan was already holding whatever it was and talking anxiously to the Russian.

Bolan dismounted and sprinted the last few yards. ''What's going on?''

Hikmal turned and tossed the object to him. Bolan snatched it out of the air and looked it over carefully. ''Where did this come from?''

The Afghan turned to Goncharov for the answer.

''It was in one of the crates,'' the Russian said. ''It was found just after you left.''

''So that's how they knew where we were,'' Bolan said.

''I think so,'' Goncharov agreed.

Bolan looked over the device more carefully. It was a small radio beacon, the kind used by police and intelligence agencies to track someone without having to get too close. "It's not American-made."

"No, it's Bulgarian. I've seen them many times. Even used them on occasion."

"So how did it get into the shipment?"

"I don't know."

"Oh, don't you?"

"Look, just because this is an Eastern Bloc toy doesn't mean I planted it. When could I have done it? I wasn't even in the warehouse when the shipment was loaded."

Bolan thought about that for a moment. Goncharov was right about that part of it. But couldn't the Russian have carried it with him, then planted it sometime after the rendezvous? That made sense except for one wrinkle—the jeep and the chopper that had been following Hikmal's truck. If the jeep and the helicopter had been picking up signals from the beacon, then it hadn't been on Goncharov at all, but in the crates. That meant it had been planted at the warehouse.

Or that Hikmal had done it himself. Bolan was in a bind. One explanation complicated his problem, and the other made no sense at all.

"I think it's time we asked our Chinese friend a few questions," Bolan said, referring to the prisoner he and Hikmal had taken at the border.

"Maybe he can explain a few things for us." Bolan tapped the beacon against his palm. "But I guess we should destroy this right now before it gets us all killed."

"No," Goncharov said, stepping forward. "Not yet. I have an idea."

"What do you want to do?" Bolan asked.

"Let's talk to Li Po's man first," Hikmal said. He didn't wait for an argument and started across the camp toward the small tent where the prisoner was being held. Hikmal ducked inside. Bolan was about to follow when he heard the Afghan curse.

"What's wrong?" Bolan asked, pushing aside the door flap. Hikmal stood with his hands clenched into white-knuckled fists. He looked at Bolan, then toward the tent opening. The warrior brushed past him and stopped in his tracks. Goncharov came into the tent just as Bolan turned away.

"What happened?" the Russian asked.

"He's dead," Bolan replied.

The prisoner lay on his back, a pool of blood under his head. His throat had been cut. Recently.

Bolan looked at Goncharov. "I suppose you don't know anything about this?"

Hikmal held up a hand. "Enough. This is my camp. That means it's my problem." He turned to the Russian. "You said you had an idea. What is it?"

The Russian stared at Bolan for a long moment. "You want to get to Kabul. I think you should go now."

"What about you?" Bolan asked. "What are you going to do?"

"I'll take the beacon with me, active."

"Where to?"

Goncharov looked at Hikmal. "Wherever you meet with him. Can you do that? Can you get me there?"

"What's the point?" Hikmal asked. "If he's in Kabul, what good will it do?"

"Belasko doesn't trust me. You don't, either. So I'll be out of your way. I can't do you any harm if I'm not with you. And if the beacon is Sharkov's, he'll come. Unless Belasko gets him first."

"And if I do?" Bolan asked.

"I'll wait three days. If you don't show by then, I'll come to Kabul to look for both of you."

Hikmal watched the Russian for a long time. Just when it began to seem as if he would never speak again, he nodded. "Done."

CHAPTER THIRTY-ONE

Bolan was getting cramped in the back of the truck. The ride had lasted for hours, and the tight space left him virtually no room to move around to relieve the tightness in his muscles. The truck was old and smelled of unfamiliar spices and something stale and foul, like dead fish, only not quite as strong.

Only once on the road had he heard another vehicle. The truck had lumbered to a halt, then bounced off the road, and Bolan had tensed, expecting the worst. He'd heard the unsteady rumble of a big diesel and had snicked the safety off his rifle. But the diesel had rumbled past, and the truck had bounced back onto the potholed pavement to continue on its way.

Now that it was past, the incident had become a welcome relief from the monotony of the voyage. The trip proved that newspapers weren't always wrong. The Western press had been full of stories about how the countryside belonged to the mujahadeen and the cities to the Kabul government. The roads themselves bore that out. Traffic was almost nonexistent except for heavily armed convoys and the sporadic forays of armored patrols, but they were increasingly rare as the rebels pressed harder and harder on the cities, taking their resistance into the streets with assassinations and bombings of army and government buildings.

Bolan looked at the illuminated dial of his watch. According to Hikmal's estimate, they were less than an hour away from Kabul. That would put them little more than fifteen or twenty miles away, he figured.

He wanted to push the canvas aside and draw a breath or two of untainted air, but he knew it was too risky. He had come so far, too far, really, to put it all at risk by so simple a mistake.

The truck slowed and lurched as the driver shifted down a gear. The incessant groaning of the transmission snarled and thumped against the frame of the truck. Bolan could feel the staccato rapping through the floorboards. The driver dropped another gear, and the snarl grew louder.

Now he could hear something else. It was a bigger, more modern engine. The truck slowed to a crawl, taking the potholes in creaking slow motion, then stopping altogether. The engine hummed uncertainly, the muffler chugged and rattled, but the big diesel in the other vehicle nearly drowned it all out.

He heard voices arguing, and surmised that a patrol wanted to examine the interior of the truck.

The driver appeared to be arguing against it strenuously.

Then an engine gunned, and a second vehicle pulled up behind the truck. Its headlights filled the truck bed and seeped through the cracks between the heavy wooden crates. Bolan shifted the rifle awkwardly, trying to position it with its muzzle toward the rear of the vehicle, but he had to settle for a steep angle toward the back end of the roof.

He ground his teeth and took a deep breath as the headlights bored in a little closer. He could hear the tailgate squeak as it was lowered, and the truck shifted on its ancient springs. He heard the door slam as the driver got out, then feet shuffling along the side of the truck, but he couldn't see anything. He felt helpless, a blind fish in a small barrel.

Again the vehicle shifted as someone, probably one of the soldiers, climbed up into the bed. Bolan could see a stubby shadow as someone leaned over to peer into one of the open-topped crates near the tailgate. Backlit by the bright headlights, the man's face was a blur. He held a pistol in one hand—Bolan could see that well enough—and a flashlight in the other.

Then the driver appeared, just head and shoulders beyond the tailgate, shouting something at the soldier, who seemed to be paying no attention whatsoever. Bolan had no idea what might be in the crates, but he hoped it was innocent enough.

Farther back, he knew, were the weapons. If the soldiers found them, it was all over. If they found him, too, it was all over. There was no innocent explanation for a man hiding behind crates in a truck—none, at least, that would get him out of this bind.

The flashlight danced around the interior of the truck, and the man tugged one of the crates aside, shining the light down in behind it. He reached over and grabbed something from the floor, but Bolan couldn't see what it was. The soldier turned toward the driver, holding out the thing he had found as if it were evidence of some crime.

The driver said something, more conciliatory this time, which seemed to satisfy the soldier. He tossed his discovery back where he'd found it and squeezed between two crates to check along the next row. He was just going through the motions now, and Bolan started to relax a little. After poking about a little more, he backed toward the tailgate. The driver was still babbling, probably complaining about the intrusion.

Jumping down, the soldier said something to the driver, then stepped out of Bolan's view. The driver climbed up into the truck and made a show of rearranging the crates. Under his breath he told Bolan to stay put no matter what happened. Then, shoving one more crate, he jumped down. The warrior saw the flap of the tailgate swing up. It clanged home as the headlights behind the truck started to swing away.

The big APC rolled past, and Bolan caught a brief glimpse of its ominous profile. Another big diesel rumbled, and the other vehicle snarled past as it made a wide turn. It, too, was an APC. The driver rapped on the side of the truck as he moved toward the cab. Bolan felt the vehicle shift, then heard the door slam. The gears ground just as another pair of headlights appeared behind them, some distance up the road.

Bolan rapped on the back wall of the cab to get the driver's attention, but the headlights were closing fast. This was a smaller vehicle, probably a jeep, and it screeched to a halt with a blaring horn just as the truck started to move. The warrior heard the driver curse, and the truck stopped rolling, its brakes whining.

The jeep pulled up alongside the truck, and Bolan cursed his inability to see what was happening. Angry voices, muffled by the rumble of both engines, rose and fell. Again the tailgate was jerked down, and this time two men climbed up into the truck, each armed with a submachine gun. A bright light speared through the shadows, and Bolan was momentarily blinded by the glare.

As his vision returned, he saw the two men tugging at the crates, and beyond them the driver. He wondered where Hikmal was, but he couldn't afford to dwell on it. These soldiers were more hostile than the earlier patrol. They seemed determined to find something to warrant arresting the driver.

The driver started to climb up into the vehicle, but one of the soldiers stepped to the edge of the truck bed and kicked him in the face. The driver fell like a stone, and Bolan heard him groaning as he lay on the pavement.

Once more the soldiers attacked the crates, this time shoving the first row all the way off the truck, where they crashed to the ground. The men started on the second row as the driver got to his feet again. He had a pistol in his hand and was raising it as the shorter of the two soldiers turned toward him. The gun cracked, its echo making Bolan's ears ring. The second soldier raised his SMG, and Bolan shoved the canvas aside and raised his own weapon.

The soldier heard the rustle of the cloth and turned, but it was too late. The warrior stood and shoved the muzzle of his AK-47 into the soldier's midsection. The man raised his hands, and his SMG dropped to the floor of the truck with a rattle. He backed toward the edge of the truck as Bolan climbed over the crates, pinning him in place.

Backing to the very edge, he jumped down, still facing the Executioner as the driver backed up to give the soldier room. With his hands on the truck bed, he looked up at Bolan with a sneer. Then, as if it had just occurred to him, he looked at his comrade's gun and reached for the weapon in the same instant. The driver saw the sudden lurch and fired.

The soldier groaned, then slowly sagged to the ground, his hands clawing at the splintered wooden floor of the truck before they disappeared. The passenger door slammed and Hikmal rushed around the corner of the truck. He spoke quietly to the driver, then the two Afghans dragged the wounded soldier to the jeep.

Hikmal reappeared and grabbed the dead man by the ankles, then tugged him off the truck. The soldier's head slammed onto the pavement with a sickening thud. The driver grabbed him under the shoulders and he, too, was hustled away.

As Bolan jumped down, he saw the jeep lurch off the road and out into the barren countryside.

"We have to hurry now," Hikmal said. "They may have called in. There's no point in hiding in the back now. You might as well ride up front with me."

CHAPTER THIRTY-TWO

The streets of the city were almost pitch-black. Bolan had never seen a major city so dark.

As they rolled along, Bolan realized he was holding his breath. The tension was thick enough to feel with his fingers, filling the cab like an invisible gel. Hikmal, too, seemed to be growing more tense as they plunged deeper into the city. The buildings were mostly dark, as if even having a light on behind your own draperies might elicit unwanted attention.

Here and there half-finished blocks of high-rise apartment buildings, some still little more than I-beam skeletons, stretched down side streets, towering over the plywood barricades and heaps of excavated soil. Kabul looked more prosperous than Bolan had expected, and more desolate. In some ways it reminded him of a ghost town. They passed building after building, dark from basement to roof, showing no sign of life whatsoever, as if they were the only living things in town. So far not even a dog or a cat had moved in the shadows on either side.

Hikmal checked his watch again, then made a sharp turn to the left. The truck traveled through a narrow side street, then into a broad, desolate plaza. Signs were posted everywhere, but there was no one abroad to read them.

They crossed the plaza, and Hikmal tossed a casual salute to a pair of policemen on motorcycles, sitting on the sidewalk on their machines. One of the policemen waved back. The other turned to glance at the truck, then went back to waving his arms, as if he'd been interrupted in the middle of a particularly good story.

They entered another narrow street, and Hikmal breathed a sigh of relief. "It's hard to appear nervous without looking too nervous, and confident without looking too bold. Either way you might get some attention you'd rather not have."

"Do you get into Kabul often?" Bolan was asking more to change the subject than anything else, but Hikmal seemed glad of the opportunity to talk.

"Once or twice a month, except when I'm out of the country. Sometimes I have to go to Paris. I can't go directly, so I have to go to Pakistan and then fly to France from Karachi. It takes too much of my time, but I have to go where the help is. Since the Americans are so stingy with me, I have no choice but to travel from door to door like a peddler or a beggar. It's demeaning." He shrugged. "But we all must make sacrifices. I'm no different."

"Why haven't you been getting more help from the CIA?"

"They only help certain people. I think they're afraid of another Ayatollah. They dislike those who aren't Western enough to suit them. And those who are too independent. I'm not a mullah, so I guess I fall into the second class. And I had an argument with your Mr. Rucker four years ago, just after he got to Pakistan. Since then I've been hard-pressed to get anything from anyone. I think maybe he has something to do with that, but I can't prove it. It seems like too much of a coincidence, though, to be anything else."

"You don't like him much, do you?"

"Do you?"

"Not particularly."

"I learned a long time ago that every man has his own agenda. Sometimes he's man enough to put it aside and do what he thinks is right. Sometimes not. Who knows? Perhaps Allah has a purpose for all this suffering, but I don't know what it might be."

"Who do you think planted the radio beacon, Hikmal?"

"I don't know. If I had any idea, I... Well, it doesn't matter. Now it's in the middle of the desert in the Russian's pocket. It would be interesting to know what kind of flies it draws, Russian or American, or perhaps even one of my own people.

We have a habit of fighting among ourselves, too. There aren't enough enemies to go around, so we have to find new ones all the time.''

They were entering the old part of the city, and Hikmal pointed through the windshield. "This is what we're fighting against, too. A thousand, two thousand years of tradition, backward ways so old they seem like the only ways. This war isn't just about who runs Afghanistan. It's also about what Afghanistan is going to be in ten or twenty years.'' He lapsed into silence, and his face looked like that of a man twice his age. The reality of war weighed heavily on him.

Bolan wanted to say something to encourage him, but there was nothing to say. It wasn't his country, and no matter what happened with Sharkov, he would go home. In a box if he failed, but home no matter what. Hikmal's war had nothing to do with him, and it would be arrogant to pretend otherwise.

"We're almost there," the Afghan said.

The truck was nearly as tall as the buildings now, and they had a decidedly ancient look about them. He'd seen neighborhoods like this before—in the slums of Rio, Mexico City and the South Bronx. It was a world so thoroughly and permanently gray that it made one wonder whether the sun ever shone on these dingy blocks.

The truck slowed, and Hikmal wrestled with the wheel to negotiate a tight turn into a narrow alley. The sound of the truck's engine slapped back at them, bouncing off the mud-and-stone walls almost as soon as it came out from under the hood. It was nearly midnight, and the sound was loud enough to wake the dead.

"Not far now," Hikmal muttered. The truck slowed still more, and Bolan wondered whether it could possibly make it through the remaining stretch of the narrow alley. As it was, he didn't think he'd be able to open his door far enough to get out of the truck if it should stop where it was.

Then Hikmal braked. A horrible squeal like that of a dying pig echoed off the walls, then disappeared as the truck rolled past the last building on Bolan's side. A courtyard, littered with papers and piles of wood, occupied the space of three buildings. Hikmal pulled the truck in and nosed up close to a wall, then opened the door. He left the engine running and waved to Bolan to join him on the ground.

Walking to a scarred wooden door, Hikmal rapped on it softly, then leaned close to listen for any sound. He was about to knock again, when the door swung open on noisy hinges.

The Afghan ducked through the empty doorway and pulled Bolan in after him. The door closed, and the Executioner's eyes swept the dimly lit room. An old man, little more than five feet tall, looked up at him, his yellowed beard and white hair tangled like a rat's nest.

"Hakim," Hikmal said, "this man must stay here tonight. I'll be back tomorrow—early. See that he has a place to sleep."

In faultless, British-accented English, Hakim replied, "Just this one night, Arbak. No more. It's too dangerous."

"Not now, Hakim. We'll talk about it later."

The old man nodded. He raised one clawlike hand and waved to Bolan to follow him as the rebel leader slipped back out the door. The engine rumbled more loudly as Bolan stepped through a beaded curtain and into a dark room beyond. The old man struck a match, lit a small kerosene lantern and waved Bolan into another room. He opened a door and led the way down into a musty basement.

Setting the lantern down carefully, the old man reached for a carton against the wall. Bolan made as if to help him with it, but the old man waved him away. He pulled, and a whole wall of cartons swung out with a grating noise. Pointing to a straw mattress and several blankets neatly folded on top of it, he said, "Don't use the electric lights. I'll bring breakfast in the morning." Then, pointing at a small window high on the wall, he said, "If anyone comes, that window leads into a small garden.

It's blacked out, but keep the lantern low. You can get out that way if you have to. If they come for you, I won't try to stop them. I'm much too feeble for that sort of thing."

Bolan nodded. "Thank you."

"It's not for you. It's for Arbak. Let him thank me."

The old man turned and moved toward the staircase. Over his shoulder he said, "I'll leave the lantern." Bolan walked to the doorway and watched him climb up and out of sight, then heard the door close at the head of the stairway. The warrior pulled the carton wall back into place by its greasy rope handle and wondered how many men had come there under similar circumstances.

He walked to the mattress and sat down, leaning against the pile of blankets and closing his eyes. He took a deep breath and wondered just how long the odds were against finding Viktor Sharkov. He hated feeling hostage to Hikmal's whims, but there was no other way.

Opening his eyes again, he reached for the lantern and pulled it closer. Leaning the AK-47 against the wall, he fished matches out of his pocket, placed them beside the lantern, then turned the wick down until the flame went out. He was asleep almost before he knew it.

Bolan tossed and turned, waking up several times with a start. Each time he would listen in the dark, his hands reaching for the rifle. When his finger closed over the trigger, he would wait for whatever it was, the sound, or the silence, to tell him something. Each time nothing happened, and he tried again to drift off to sleep. Finally, checking his watch, its green face glowing softly in the pitch-black basement room, he sat up and leaned against the wall.

It was 3:00 a.m. He waited patiently for the sun.

As soon after daybreak as he could, he wanted to leave the safety of Hakim's cellar. If he could prevail on the old man for assistance, so much the better. The specter of Viktor Sharkov, and the smell of betrayal, made him uneasy. He couldn't shake the feeling that he was a sitting duck in the basement.

It was almost three-thirty when he heard the noise upstairs. Something bumped the floor, landing hard and heavily. Straining his ears, he heard footsteps. He grabbed the Kalashnikov. A moment later he heard the creak of a door. He couldn't tell if it was the door leading to the basement, but he knew it was being opened with deliberate quiet.

A board creaked, then a second. Someone was descending the stairs. He held the rifle, then realized he couldn't afford to use it. Gunshots would attract the army patrols.

He pushed against the carton wall just an inch or so, enough to open a narrow crack into the basement. A beam of light swept past, then back again. A third step creaked, and the light grew a little brighter. It seemed focused on the flimsy partition in front of him, as if the man with the light already knew it was a sham.

Bolan stepped back away from the door, flattening himself against the wall and holding his breath. Footsteps approached the partition, then stopped. The light went out, and he heard the rustle of a hand on cardboard as the partition began to move. The warrior ducked into a crouch and drew his Beretta.

He felt a slight draft as the partition opened, then something clicked and the room was full of light. A man darted in, a silenced Uzi in his hands, and ripped a short burst at the mattress as Bolan charged, catching him with a shoulder. The man went down and the Uzi skittered away. Bolan grabbed for the assassin's throat, but the man was strong and wiry. He managed to break free and scrambled for the gun as Bolan dived after him, catching him around the ankles and bringing him down hard.

Getting his weight into it, the Executioner crawled over the squirming hit man and pinned him to the damp floor. He brought the Beretta up under the gunman's chin and shoved the barrel into the soft flesh. "We have to talk."

CHAPTER THIRTY-THREE

Sharkov paced angrily. The sun rising over the city did nothing to calm his nerves. "Where's Rostov? He should have been back by now."

Chebrikov shrugged. "I don't know. Maybe he was delayed. It happens."

"And maybe he made a mistake. Maybe the American wasn't such an easy target after all, eh?"

"Don't panic, Viktor. You always jump to conclusions."

"I don't have time not to jump. The Turk will be back soon with the next shipment. And right now Hikmal is at the rendezvous point. He's early, and I don't know why."

"How do you know that?"

"Never mind. I know, that's all."

"What are you worried about? Even if Rostov failed, the American can't get away. And even if he does, what harm can he possibly do? He has no support. He doesn't know the language. He doesn't have contacts here."

"Then how did he get this far, Vasily?"

"The Afghan probably. How else?"

"Precisely my point. The Afghan has turned on me, Vasily. I can't allow that."

"Then do something about it."

"No, *you* do something about it. Now."

"What do you want me to do?"

"I want you to kill the treacherous bastard. Take two helicopters and go to the camp in the mountains. Take as many men as you need. And don't make a mistake. I won't allow any more mistakes. Do you understand me?"

"Am I a whipping boy, Viktor? Is that what I am? I told you before you shouldn't have cut me out of all the planning. But you did, and now, when it looks like you made a mistake, you want me to clean up after you."

"Or else, yes. Clean up, or else."

"Don't threaten me, Viktor."

"I do what I want, Vasily. And if you know what's good for you, you'll do what I want, too."

"I think we should talk about this."

"We'll talk after you've killed the Afghan, not before. And if you don't take care of this, there'll be nothing to talk about. Am I making myself clear? You better leave now while he's still there."

Chebrikov slammed the door behind him. Sharkov could hear his lieutenant stomping down the stairs. The balance was so critical, and it was so close to coming undone. Such a beautiful scheme.

It should have worked without a hitch, but it hadn't. Someone had betrayed him, but who?

Not Vasily. The man didn't have the spine to betray him. It took all his nerve just to argue. Hikmal, certainly, but why? All the pieces had come together. All that needed to be done was to work out a few bugs, find the little glitches that any new system had. But things had gone too far wrong to be explained away as glitches. No, someone had done this deliberately. And whoever it was had to be found before he could do any more harm.

Maybe the American. Maybe that was it. Maybe... but, no, it had to be someone else. The other American, Belasko, was just a soldier, a hired gun. It had to be someone higher than that.

And then it hit him. "Of course," he whispered. "Of course."

Sharkov pulled the curtain aside and stared down into the street. He saw his second-in-command come out of the building and look up at the window.

CHEBRIKOV WAVED and Sharkov, taken by surprise, waved back. Chebrikov turned then and disappeared into the alley. He walked to the jeep and climbed in. He stuck the key in the ignition, then, on a hunch, climbed back out and opened the hood. He looked the engine over, then dropped to his knees to look up at the engine block from underneath.

The red light of the early sun spilled through the hood and down through the tangled wires and hoses. Satisfied, Chebrikov closed the hood, brushed off his pants and clapped his hands together to rid them of the last particles of sand before climbing back into the jeep.

He hesitated for a split second before turning the key, then, with a shrug, cranked up the engine. If he suspected Sharkov of going that far, maybe he should get out now while he still had the chance. But then the big payoff was still in the future. And Sharkov needed him as much as he needed Sharkov. Once they made the money, then he could walk away. Sharkov wouldn't care then. He would let him go, maybe even be glad to see him leave.

Checking in his coat pocket for the forged papers just in case, he backed out of the narrow alley and looked up at the window once more. This time it was vacant. Settling into the sparse early-morning traffic, he mulled things over in his head the way he had a thousand times in the past year.

He still didn't know who had been in the American helicopter that had paid Sharkov a midnight visit. He knew his superior well enough to know that he had lines out in every direction, a finger on every pulse. That someone among the Americans was cooperating with him, perhaps even a partner in the venture, seemed indisputable.

But the other American, the big one, the one who had probably killed Rostov—although he didn't want to admit that to Sharkov yet—was another matter. And at the center of the whirlwind was the figure of Arbak Hikmal. What was his story? Whose side was he on, besides his own?

And in asking the question, Chebrikov had already answered it. Hikmal was on no side *but* his own. But it didn't really matter. In a few short hours there would be no Arbak Hikmal. They would have to find a replacement for him, but that would be easy enough. Sharkov could get enough money, or enough guns, to solve that problem easily.

But something had changed. And there was no way to deny it. He and Sharkov were heading toward a confrontation, and it would be up to him to prevent it. Sharkov was getting desperate, and he was dangerous to begin with.

The hangar, tucked away in the foothills, was just a few kilometers away, and he turned his attention to the next step. The choppers were always ready to fly, the crews on permanent alert. It would take only a couple of hours to fly to the ruined village. He would take care of Hikmal and his friends and wipe the slate clean.

Then he could decide how to handle Sharkov over the next couple of months. As he approached the hangar, he saw that the door was already open. Sharkov must have told them he was coming. He gunned the engine, enjoying the rumble of the floorboards under his feet as the jeep sped over the rough ground toward the open hangar.

Once inside the structure he raced the jeep nearly to the back wall, laughing as the lounging soldiers scattered in fright. It was one of the perks of working with Sharkov to have access to a special detachment of the Afghan army. With corruption a way of life, it hadn't been difficult for the Russian to buy his own unit. It just took a few percentage points and a little front money. The commander was more than willing to turn a blind eye to Sharkov's use of his men.

Now, shouting orders before the jeep engine had even died, Chebrikov sent the men scurrying for their weapons. He waited until the pilots and three soldiers had boarded each craft, then grabbed a helmet and a rifle for himself and climbed into the nearest modified Hind.

He put on a headset, got both pilots up on tactical and gave them their orders. The choppers, like squat grasshoppers, lifted off the floor of the hangar and seemed to slide toward the door. Out in the open they climbed rapidly to five thousand feet.

Chebrikov watched the other Hind from the open door of his own. So ugly it was beautiful, the machine was the perfect war vehicle. Hikmal would never know what hit him, and Chebrikov smiled at the thought. The Afghan was too arrogant by half. They all were, really, and this would be a nice reminder of just where the power in Central Asia really lay.

It was important to come in fast and hit them hard, because Hikmal had gotten his hands on some American weapons somehow. It had already cost them two choppers and nine men. Losses at that level might be hard to explain away, even for Sharkov's friends, and Chebrikov crossed his fingers, hoping he had better luck than the previous assault team.

It still ate away at Chebrikov that he didn't know how Sharkov got his information. He had dispatched the previous team over Chebrikov's own objections. He refused to say why he was so sure Hikmal's band was where he claimed it was. But it had been. That Sharkov was plugged into some circuits Chebrikov didn't know about was something he took for granted. But it bothered him all the same. It made him feel insecure somehow, and that was the first step on a long downhill slide. He had to be extremely careful, and he didn't like feeling so vulnerable.

He watched the ground slide by, almost mesmerized by the rippling effect of the rolling foothills. On the horizon he spotted the ruined village. It looked deserted, and he yanked a pair of binoculars off the cabin wall. Trying to keep his hands steady, he wheeled the focus and zeroed in on the hilltop.

The buildings were still there, as always, but there was no sign of any humans. If Hikmal had come, even alone, there would have been a horse or a jeep. He certainly wouldn't have walked. And he didn't have access to any other means of transportation.

Or did he?

Chebrikov wanted to raise Sharkov on the radio, but that was an emergency procedure only. This wasn't an emergency. Not yet.

He got back on the tactical radio and sent the first Hind in for a closer look. If this was some kind of setup, maybe a dozen rebels hiding in the ruins with SAMs, as unlikely as it seemed, he wanted someone else to take the risk. That was how Sharkov worked, and it was a lesson Chebrikov had learned quickly and well.

But as he thought about it, he realized a trap would mean that either Hikmal and Sharkov were working together, after all, or that Hikmal had somehow guessed that Sharkov would know he was there. But how could he know that?

Chebrikov watched as the Hind made its first pass, circling around the hilltop at three thousand feet. On the radio the pilot informed him that there was no sign of life.

"Go lower," Chebrikov ordered. "Look again."

He watched while the Hind, like a gargantuan wasp, descended over the village, its noise angled down and, no doubt, the pilot's finger on the trigger.

"Still nothing," the pilot reported.

"Strafe a couple of the buildings."

"Why?"

"You heard me. Just do it!"

The pilot did as he was told. The nose cannons flashed in the sunlight, and small gouts of stone and mortar flew off a pair of already ruined buildings.

There was still no evidence of anyone in the camp. "All right," Chebrikov barked, "forget it."

He chewed on his lip while he wondered what he should do. Suddenly, having to make a decision, he was frightened. After a long silence he decided to send the lead chopper home. Before he could frame the command, his own pilot spoke through the tactical radio. "What do we do now?"

"We're going to land and have a look around."

"Why?"

He knew the answer, and it felt good just to form it in his mind and listen to it quietly first, where only he could hear it. Then, almost smiling, he said out loud, "Because I said so."

CHAPTER THIRTY-FOUR

Bolan climbed the stairs cautiously, prodding the frightened gunman with the muzzle of the Uzi. The man stumbled once, almost losing his balance, and caught himself against the wall with one hand. He glared at Bolan for an instant, as if in losing his balance he had almost lost his composure, as well.

At the top of the stairs Bolan signaled for the man to wait. The door was open, but he couldn't hear anything from the darkness beyond. The gunman watched the Executioner warily, half afraid the man might change his mind and blow him away. Bolan gestured for the gunman to turn around, then rapped him sharply across the base of the skull. The man teetered backward, and Bolan caught him, using one shoulder to hold the man erect while he stepped close to the open door.

He couldn't risk using the flashlight until he was certain there was no one else waiting on the first floor. Shoving the door open still wider, he edged through, dragging the limp gunman along and shielding his body with the unconscious man.

He found an old light switch and held his breath. On three he twisted the knob, filling the room with dim light. It took his eyes a second to adjust, and he crouched behind the unconscious man until he felt certain that he was alone.

The room was empty, and he noticed a dull glow in the room beyond. Letting the gunman slide to the floor, he hefted the Uzi and moved to the doorway. As he drew closer, he realized the glow wasn't electric, but sunlight seeping in around heavy curtains. He glanced at his watch. It was nearly six-thirty, and Hikmal was due any minute. If he planned on coming back at all.

Easing up to the doorway, Bolan stared into the other room, looking for the slightest sign of trouble. He wondered where Hakim was. The old man should have said something by now if he was there. Finally, as sure as he could be that the next room was uninhabited, he slid one hand along the wall and groped for the light switch. He couldn't find one on that wall and dropped low enough to slip into the room at minimum risk.

Crawling as quietly as he could on hands and knees, Bolan moved into the middle of the room, trying to decide where the light switch would be. Concluding it must be on the wall by the front door, he changed directions. His hand felt sticky, and he rubbed the fingertips together. He knew, without benefit of light, what it was. Reaching out blindly, he brushed against cloth, then wrinkled skin. Hakim.

Under the old man's chin there was more sticky fluid. He dashed for the doorway and slapped at the wall, finding the switch and turning it on. At the same instant he whirled, sweeping the room with the muzzle of the Uzi.

But only Hakim was there. And he wasn't going to be any trouble for anyone ever again.

A series of ugly holes in the light beige cloth of Hakim's shirt showed where the Uzi had done its bloody work. The old man lay on his back, his eyes wide open in astonishment. Behind his beard his mouth was still shaped in the sudden pain of the assault.

Bolan had two options, and neither one was pleasant. He could go back to the basement, rouse the gunman and try to force him to say who had sent him and why. He didn't know what the chances were that the gunman would know even that much. When bread was scarce, it was possible to buy a life rather cheaply, no questions asked. And that assumed the gunman and he shared a language, which was far from a certainty.

Or he could leave the house and take his chances on his own, try to find Sharkov without a clue where to look and with no way out of the city even if he succeeded. Either way the odds were long.

Bolan rubbed his cheek with the squat suppressor of the Uzi, wondering which knife he should use to cut his throat. It seemed that would be the end

result no matter which choice he made. He walked
into the next room and yanked the gunman off the
floor by the shirtfront, then dragged him to the
basement.

Once he had the man downstairs he walked back
up, jerked the door closed and returned to the
basement. He sat on a broken chair, his eyes fixed
on the gunman's face under the beam of the flashlight. The man looked Slavic. He was definitely not
Afghan.

Okay, that was one link maybe. Perhaps the guy
was in Sharkov's employ. Had Hikmal sold him
out?

He didn't want to think so, but he had no better
guess. Bolan looked around the basement for a
source of water, even a cold water tap, anything he
could use to hasten the gunman's return to consciousness. But there was nothing he could use. He
got up and walked to the man, knelt beside him and
tried slapping his cheeks.

The man groaned, turning his face away from
Bolan's palms, but the eyelids never moved.

Bolan heard a thud upstairs. He stood and
backed away from the stairs, pressing himself into
a corner that would leave him behind anyone
reaching the bottom of the stairs. Then he doused
the flashlight and waited.

He heard a muffled voice and a shout. Then
footsteps rapped on the ancient floor above his

head. Finally he heard a voice ask, "Hakim, who did this to you?"

After a few moments of silence, the footsteps proceeded downstairs to the basement.

"Hold it right there, Hikmal," Bolan ordered.

The Afghan jerked his head around. He seemed stunned to see Bolan holding a gun on him. "What's this? What did you do to Hakim?"

"I didn't do anything." Nodding his head at the prostrate gunman, Bolan said, "He did."

Hikmal yelled and threw himself at the unconscious assassin. Straddling the limp body, he locked his hands around the man's throat and leaned into it with all his weight.

Bolan leaped toward the Afghan as he raised a gleaming knife in a white-knuckled fist. Lashing out with his foot, Bolan kicked Hikmal in the ribs, knocking the air from his lungs and doubling him over. The knife flew from his grasp and rattled into a corner.

Hikmal got to his feet, still clutching his ribs. "You bastard. Why did you stop me?"

"It should be obvious."

"Then I'm thick. Explain, please."

"He was after me, not Hakim. If you sent him, the last thing in the world you'd want is for him to tell me so."

"If *I* sent him? Are you insane? Why would I send scum like him after you? And why would I tell him to kill my uncle in the process?"

"Your uncle?"

"Hakim, yes. My father's brother."

"I see."

"No, you don't see. That old man sent me to university when I couldn't pay on my own. He worked until he couldn't keep his eyes open, supporting his own family and mine, after my father and mother were killed. This man killed my uncle, and he'll pay for it with his own life. Besides, you don't have to wonder about who sent him. I know who sent him. His name is Rostov, and he works for Viktor Sharkov."

"So you say."

"Fine, very well. Wake him up and ask him. But I'll kill him whether you try to stop me or not."

"No, you won't. Not an unarmed man."

"There's no such thing in Afghanistan. This man is armed with all of Sharkov's weaponry, all of his treachery, all of his resources."

"Take me to Sharkov," Bolan said. "Now."

"No, not yet. First you must ask Rostov your question and hear his answer. Then perhaps I'll take you."

"You *will* take me."

"Perhaps not. Perhaps I'll kill Sharkov myself. He's used me, and he's betrayed my trust."

"No, Hikmal, he didn't use you. You let him tell you what to do for money. It's not the same thing."

"To me it is."

Bolan sighed in exasperation. He knew Hikmal didn't entirely trust him, any more than he trusted Sharkov. But now he had an additional reason to mistrust the Afghan. Hikmal wanted revenge. He wanted it for himself, to taste Sharkov's blood. Provided he was telling the truth, and Bolan wasn't sure of that. Not in the least.

"If Sharkov sent him, how did he know where to find me?" Bolan asked.

The question took Hikmal by surprise. "I don't know. Maybe someone saw you come in last night."

"You know that's not true."

"Then I don't know how."

"The hell you don't. You told him. That's how he knew. How much was he going to pay you? Fifty dollars, a hundred?"

"You hold yourself that cheaply?"

"How much, then?"

Hikmal shook his head. "No, you just don't understand. You're an outsider here. You don't understand how things work."

"I understand enough. I know greed when I see it."

A groan caused both men to look at the gunman. One hand groped for his eyes, and he tried to sit up. Bolan leaned forward to push him back. When he looked back at Hikmal, he found himself staring into the barrel of a large automatic pistol.

"Please, Belasko, put down the gun. I don't want to shoot you, but I will if I have to."

Bolan lowered the Uzi to the floor. When he straightened again, Hikmal nodded toward his coat. "Now the others. Slow, please, very slow."

The Executioner did as he was told, pulling first the Beretta, then the Desert Eagle. When both pistols were on the floor, Hikmal said, "Kick them over to me one at a time. And please don't make me shoot you."

Bolan rapped the Beretta with the toe of his boot. Then the Desert Eagle skidded across to where the Afghan could reach down for it.

Tucking both pistols into his own coat, Hikmal said, "Sit down." When Bolan dropped to the floor, the Afghan said, "Your hands behind your head, please."

After Bolan had obeyed, Hikmal looked at the man on the floor. Swiftly but calmly, he flicked the pistol to one side and shot the gunman through the forehead. The explosion was horrendous in the enclosed space.

"I told you I would do that."

"What now?" Bolan asked.

"Now we wait. I have to think."

CHAPTER THIRTY-FIVE

Chebrikov chewed his lower lip. He could hear Sharkov now, the voice dripping acid, impugning his legitimacy and that of his mother and her mother before her. Damned either way, he broke the skin of his lip, then nodded as if someone were waiting for an answer.

He ordered the second chopper home. The pilot seemed surprised, almost to the point of challenging the order, but not quite. That was always how it was. When Sharkov said jump, they didn't wait long enough to ask how high. But when Chebrikov gave an order, they seemed hard-pressed to believe he could even speak, let alone issue a command.

The Hind dipped its nose and took one last loop around the hilltop, as if to give Chebrikov time to come to his senses. Then, when the radio remained silent, the aircraft veered off and started to climb. Chebrikov waited until the chopper was just a speck in the sky. When the other helicopter was finally gone, he told his own pilot to make a slow pass over the hilltop.

"Take it easy and be ready for anything," he warned.

The three men in the cabin shifted uneasily. They were trying not to look at him, and Chebrikov knew it. He glared at them, waiting for one of them to open his mouth, but the men just shuffled their feet, watching the toes of their boots.

Chebrikov raised the glasses, then turned to look at the ground. He checked out one hut after another. The few with roofs he examined even more carefully, but he didn't see a hint of anything out of place. As far as he could tell, the place hadn't been disturbed since they'd left.

In the back of his mind he kept hearing Sharkov over and over again, the certainty in his voice when he claimed that Hikmal was here. How could Sharkov have been that wrong? he wondered. It never happened. Sharkov just didn't make that kind of mistake.

Or did he?

When they had covered the hilltop thoroughly, he told the pilot to climb to two thousand. Maybe the long view would show him something he couldn't see from close in. He couldn't imagine what, but he knew he'd better be damn sure before he told Sharkov the place was uninhabited.

The whole business was starting to have a sour smell to him now. It had sounded so good, so right, when Sharkov had first approached him. Sharkov was the genius, the man who never made a wrong move, who never stumbled. They had worked together for years. He had never known Sharkov to miscalculate.

But things were changing now. And that made him wonder all the more.

It was time for him to be decisive. "Take us down," he said, glancing at the three silent soldiers as he waited for the pilot's response.

"Where?"

"At the bottom of the hill, but not too close. About three hundred meters. Do you see that boulder shaped like a horse's head?"

"I see it."

"Land on the far side of it."

The pilot clicked off without an acknowledgment, and Chebrikov waited for the sinking feeling in the pit of his stomach when the chopper fell away beneath him for a split second. When it came, the three soldiers finally looked at him. He smiled, then wondered why he'd done it.

When the Hind touched down, Chebrikov jumped out and ducked under the rotor. He stood just outside the sweep of the rotor wash, squinting against the dust it kicked up, and waited for the three soldiers to join him. They paused in the door, still not certain what was happening. When he waved them out, they looked at one another, then jumped to the ground.

The pilot opened his window and leaned out. Cupping his hands, he shouted, "What now?"

"Just wait here. If anything happens, and I don't think it will, use your own judgment."

Chebrikov turned and started toward the hill. "Watch for mines," he said, not bothering to look back. He didn't know whether the men had heard him or not, and he didn't care. As soon as he reached the base of the hill, he slowed, tilted his head to one side and studied the ground. A few spots looked as if they'd been disturbed recently, but if he avoided them, he should be all right. He glanced back once and smiled when he realized the soldiers were following him in single file.

Once he cleared the inner ring to the mine field, he relaxed a little. He stopped to examine the nearest of the buildings. The place was empty. He was convinced of that. It just wasn't possible for it to be otherwise.

With a shrug he started up the hill again, sweeping his eyes from left to right and back. The hair on the back of his neck was standing straight up, and an involuntary shiver shook him as he felt a chill creep up his spine.

Chebrikov held his gun nervously. He had never liked heavy artillery. He was a pistol man. A Makarov was all he had ever needed. Behind him the soldiers whispered among themselves until he turned and held a finger to his lips. He felt foolish doing it. Anyone hiding here would have heard the chopper. But it seemed important to assert his authority, and he didn't know what else to do.

He was at the top of the hill now, and the nearest building was just fifty meters away.

Again he stopped.

"What do you want us to do?" one of the soldiers asked. Chebrikov looked at him as if he'd been asked to explain quantum mechanics. The truth was, he didn't know what he wanted them to do. And they all knew it.

"Spread out," he said, not knowing what else to say. "Search every one of these hovels."

"What are we looking for?" It was the same soldier, obviously the leader of the troika.

"You'll know when you find it."

The man nodded as if that made sense to him.

Chebrikov waited while the men fanned out, each heading toward one of the structures in the first tier. He debated whether he should join the search or just stand back and let the soldiers do it. Standing around gave him too much time to think, and he wanted to do something to quiet the nervous tremors beginning to attack his legs. His knees felt as if they might come unhinged.

He shook off the nervousness and walked toward the second tier. Most of the buildings were empty, and most were roofless, so seeing wouldn't be a problem. Some, though, housed munitions and weapons, and a few still held the pathetic wreckage left behind by uprooted families. He picked one without a roof and stepped through the shattered doorway. The building held nothing but the same broken table it had always held. The interior showed signs of having been ransacked. Litter in one corner had been kicked over. He could tell that by the moisture still showing on some of the pieces of wood.

The next one, also roofless, was just as vacant. These buildings were lifeless cells not even fit for monks. He didn't bother to search the jumbled trash against one wall.

Entering the third, he heard a shout and stopped in his tracks. He backed out of the doorway, heard another shout and ran toward the source of the sound. Entering the building, he found one of the soldiers standing over the prostrate form of a second. The man's throat had been cut, and he lay staring up at the sky.

"What happened here?" Chebrikov demanded as the third soldier ran in to join them.

"I don't know. I found him this way. I wanted a smoke and I called to him. He didn't answer. I knew he'd come in here, so—"

"You didn't see anything?" Chebrikov demanded, cutting him off. "Hear anything?"

The soldier shook his head. "Nothing..."

"So Hikmal is here, after all," Chebrikov whispered. Then, louder, he said, "Keep looking. There are only forty or fifty buildings, and he can't get off the hill. Work as a team now. One stand guard while the other goes in. Got it?"

The men nodded, but there was no enthusiasm. Chebrikov noticed but didn't comment. He didn't blame them. They wanted to be here even less than he, if such a thing was possible.

He watched the men work their way along the next ragged row. Each time one of them entered a building, Chebrikov felt his jaw tighten. The tension lasted until he saw the point man reappear and move on to the next. They came up empty and moved to the next row.

The arm snaked around his neck before he knew it. Chebrikov felt the blade press against his skin as he was dragged backward. He struggled to relieve the pressure on his windpipe, but the powerful forearm was unyielding. He felt himself starting to black out as he was hauled through a doorway to one of the buildings already searched.

The pressure relaxed for a moment, and he gasped for air. A voice hissed in his ear, "If you make a sound, Vasily, I'll cut your throat. Do you understand?"

Whoever it was knew him, but he couldn't see the man. He knew it wasn't Hikmal, because the man's Russian was flawless and untainted by an accent.

He nodded that he understood, and the pressure relaxed a little more. Then he felt the crack against his skull, and everything went black.

When he came to, he was trussed up like a pig, and a dirty rag was forced so far into his mouth that he had to struggle to keep from gagging. He lay there listening, wondering what was going to happen to him.

Chebrikov stared up at the sky, where a huge bird, its wings barely moving, soared on the wind. He wondered if it would pick his bones clean. He knew they went for the eyes first because they were soft and easy to get at. The thought made him want to gag again, and he turned on his side until the sensation passed.

He closed his eyes, trying to blot everything out, but there was no way. He heard footsteps now, and a moment later someone stood in the doorway. Through half-closed eyes, everything tinted red by the blood in his eyelids, he understood what had happened.

"You," he said. The one word summed everything up.

"Me."

CHAPTER THIRTY-SIX

Hikmal seemed nervous. He kept looking away from Bolan, as if he were ashamed of himself. The warrior tried to get him to talk, but the Afghan just kept looking away whenever Bolan opened his mouth.

Finally, after the fifth or sixth attempt, Hikmal spoke. "I'm sorry about this, Belasko."

"Sorry about what?"

"I don't like holding a gun on you."

"Then don't."

Hikmal laughed. "It sounds so easy."

"Why shouldn't it be? I'm no threat to you."

"No, but you're valuable to me—and to others."

"Not really."

"You're too modest."

Bolan didn't answer right away. He wanted to let Hikmal's nerves ratchet another notch or two tighter. If the rebel leader was nervous enough, he just might say more than he intended. Right now Bolan was completely in the dark. He didn't know why Hikmal was holding him captive, though he could guess. And he didn't like what he was thinking. If Hikmal really was sorry, then maybe his conscience would eat at him a bit, maybe even enough to turn him around.

But Bolan didn't know if he had enough time to play that sort of waiting game. Hikmal seemed to be waiting for a specific time to arrive, or for a visitor to do the same. Either way the clock was ticking, and Hikmal was the only one who could read it.

"I suppose you think you'll get quite a lot of money for me," Bolan finally said.

Hikmal actually laughed out loud. "Oh, you Americans. Everywhere is Beirut to you, isn't it? You think I'm holding you for ransom?"

"Aren't you?"

"Of course not. What do you take me for—some sort of terrorist?"

"What's in a name?" Bolan asked.

"I suppose I should be insulted by that."

Bolan studied the Afghan. "You're waiting for Sharkov, aren't you?"

The Afghan didn't answer.

Bolan tried again. "Do you trust Sharkov?"

"No, of course not." Hikmal looked at Bolan as if he were insane.

"But that's who we're waiting for, isn't it? Sharkov or one of his people?"

"It makes no difference. It's already too late for me to do anything about it."

Bolan tried another tack. "Why not shoot me now if that's what Sharkov wants?"

"Maybe he wants you alive."

"Why?"

"Perhaps he thinks you're worth something to certain people."

"If that's what he told you, you've been had, Hikmal. Sharkov doesn't know who I am. In fact, neither do you. Not really."

"Sharkov may not know who you really are, Belasko, but he does know you're somebody. You might say he has the eyes and ears of someone on your side who's in a position to know such things."

Bolan was really interested now. "What difference does it make who I am? Sharkov's a rogue agent. His own boys want him dead."

"I don't care why he wants you, Belasko. I only know that he does."

"So you are holding me for ransom. What's in it for you?"

"Surely you can see that Afghanistan is fighting for her survival. Alongside that, all else is insignificant. It was the Russians who almost destroyed my country. It seems only fitting that one of their own should help pay for its continued survival. Poetic justice, no?"

Bolan looked at the Afghan sadly. "Sharkov doesn't give a damn about your country. As soon as he gets what he wants, he'll walk away."

"I never expected otherwise, but I can make enough money to buy weapons and ammunition for two or three years. That's more than anyone else has offered me. What do I care what happens to America? Your government turned its back on me and my country."

Bolan realized there wasn't much he could say to counter that.

"You must turn around now," Hikmal said. "I have to go soon."

Bolan started to argue, but the Afghan waved the gun menacingly, so he did as he was told. He heard the whistle of air as the heavy gun descended, and ducked to one side, but not quickly enough. The blow caught him high on the back of the head. He went down hard, but he was still conscious.

He felt the rope snake around his wrists and lay still, hoping Hikmal didn't discover he was still conscious. It was all he could do to let his muscles go limp so that the Afghan wouldn't detect any resistance. Hikmal was in a hurry, and he seemed distracted. With any luck he wouldn't be too careful.

When the Afghan was gone, Bolan lay motionless for a while, listening. His head throbbed, but he could live with it. He could hear someone moving around upstairs, then it got very quiet. Bolan worked at the ropes until they scraped his wrists raw, but Hikmal had done his work well.

A distant rapping, possibly someone at the door upstairs, made him lie still. He heard voices, but they were muffled so thoroughly that he wasn't sure they were in the same building. Working at the ropes again, this time more deliberately, he felt them loosen a little, but not enough to do him any good.

He was panting from the exertion, and he had to stop frequently so he could cock an ear toward the upper floor. Back at the ropes again, he felt them give a little more. He stopped to rest, resolving to give it one more all-out effort. Just as he was ready, he heard steps directly overhead. Voices again, this time louder. Some sort of argument, but he couldn't tell for certain.

Then the door at the head of the cellar stairs was thrown back. It slammed into the wall, and the whole staircase seemed to creak a little, as if the house were ready to fall apart at the least strain. Voices argued again, this time in Russian. They were fighting about him, but he wasn't quite sure why.

Light flooded the cellar suddenly, and a pair of boots topped by beige fatigue pants seemed to float down, dragging a body behind them. Bolan's eyes hurt and he blinked, then shut them to accustom himself to the sudden brilliance. When he opened his eyes again, he saw two men. Hikmal stood in the background. In front of him stood a man he'd never seen.

But he knew who it was.

"I'm surprised you'd come such a long way to catch such a small fish, Mr. Belasko."

"Not so small, Sharkov," Bolan said.

"Oh, but I really am."

"Right now maybe, but it won't stop there."

"You seem so sure."

"I know your type, Sharkov."

The Russian nodded. "It seems this is a season of betrayal, Mr. Belasko. Perhaps if you Americans hadn't been so particular in parceling out your aid, our friend Arbak here might not have been so ready to make a deal with me."

Bolan glanced at the Afghan, who looked away. "Nobody's going to pay to get me back, you know."

"I wouldn't be so sure about that. I'm told you know all sorts of interesting things. Many of your own people would like to see you eliminated."

"How much are they paying you?"

"That remains to be negotiated. Actually they just wanted you dead. But that didn't work out as well as I'd hoped. Then it occurred to me. Why should I do for free what someone would be willing to pay to have done? It was an interesting question. I thought about it, and the longer you managed to stay alive, the more interesting the question became. Now I think I have the perfect solution—to my own problem, and to that of your friends.''

''They betrayed me. What makes you think they won't betray you?''

''A simple matter of value. I'm new at this capitalism business, but I've always learned quickly. This is no exception. It seems to me that you're a liability to them, whereas I'm a business partner, an asset, if you will.''

''So where do we go from here?''

''I have someplace in mind, quite secure, even comfortable, actually. We'll have to wait until dark, but it won't take long. And I wouldn't get my hopes up if I were you. It won't be so easy to escape from me this time. Now that I know just what caliber of man I'm dealing with, I'll take all necessary precautions, something I'm very good at.''

Bolan looked at Hikmal again. ''I hope you're getting a good price. And if I were you, I'd demand payment immediately. Something tells me an IOU from Comrade Sharkov might not be so valuable.''

''Oh, I always pay my debts, Belasko,'' the Russian said. ''Especially when there's the possibility of even greater profit.''

CHAPTER THIRTY-SEVEN

Chebrikov stumbled down the hill, with Goncharov dragging him by the arm. Fearful of the mines, the smaller man kept dragging his feet. But Goncharov was in no mood to tolerate the obstruction. He squeezed harder, and Chebrikov winced. Goncharov jerked him around and leaned toward him. "Listen to me, Vasily. Don't give me any more trouble. You understand? I don't want to hurt you, but I will if you force me to. I don't give a damn about you. It's Sharkov I want."

Chebrikov swallowed hard. "I don't know where he is. I swear it."

"You never were a good liar, Vasily. That's why you were never promoted. A yes-man—that's what you are. And you always think Sharkov can save you. But that's over. Sharkov's a dead man. If you want to join him, it can be arranged. But it's not necessary. Do you understand?"

"You think I'm Viktor's stooge, don't you?"

"That's right, Vasily. What's more, so do you. So does everyone who knows the two of you."

"You bastard. It was Grebnov who made you. Everybody knows that. You're nothing without him. And look at you now, doing his dirty work again. Where's Peter, Maxim? Tell me that. Where is he while you're out here in the middle of this wasteland, risking your neck for nothing?"

"That doesn't matter. I'm a soldier. I do what I'm supposed to do. That was always the difference between you and me, Vasily. I understood what my obligations were. All you were interested in was currying favor."

"Sucking up to Grebnov—is that what your obligation was? Because that's what you did. Viktor and I, we got tired of it. We realized we were being used. We decided to do something for ourselves for a change."

"At whose expense, Vasily?"

"What difference does it make?"

"Children. American children for now. But children everywhere, eventually. And do you think Sharkov will stop at that? Do you think he cares who uses that poison? Now that he's got a taste of the profit, do you think he'll walk away from it? Can you walk away from it, Vasily?"

Chebrikov shook his head. "No, I suppose not."

Goncharov nodded. "So you see how it is?"

Chebrikov took a deep breath. "Go ahead and shoot me, then."

"Only if I have to, Vasily. I'm not interested in pointless bloodshed. Sharkov's the problem, not you."

"You mean I'm useless without him, don't you?"

Goncharov sighed. He'd never been fond of Chebrikov, but it was never easy to tell a painful truth. "Yes, that's what I mean."

Chebrikov turned away, still held by the arm, and started to walk. Goncharov let go. He knew he no longer needed to hold on to the little man ahead of him.

The chopper was now three hundred meters away. "How many men are with the helicopter?" Goncharov asked.

"Just the pilot."

"If you're lying to me, I'll kill you first. You know that, don't you?"

Chebrikov cleared his throat. Even so his voice broke. "Yes, I know that."

They walked the rest of the way in silence. When they reached the chopper, the pilot was standing by the open cabin door. "What happened? Where are the others?"

"They're staying," Chebrikov said.

"Staying? Here?"

Chebrikov nodded. "Captain Goncharov is coming back with us."

The pilot eyed the big Russian warily. "What's going on?" He asked the question as if he already knew the answer. "I don't like this."

Goncharov stood casually, his hands stuffed into his coat pockets. The assault rifle draped over his shoulder didn't seem to be a threat, but the pilot was suspicious.

He reached for his sidearm, but Goncharov was ready for him. The KGB agent fired once through the coat. The bullet slammed into the hard dirt between the pilot's feet. He raised his hands and backed toward the chopper until he slammed into the floor of the cabin.

"I don't want to hurt you," Goncharov said. "Just drop your pistol carefully and kick it toward me."

Gingerly one hand came down, the fingers groping for the flap over his holster. The pilot found the snap, popped it open, then took the pistol grip between his thumb and one finger. It slipped out of his grasp before clearing the holster and fell to the ground. "Sorry."

"Kick it over to me quickly."

The pilot did as he was told.

Goncharov bent to retrieve the pistol. He tucked it safely into his pocket, then motioned for both men to get into the chopper. The pilot looked surprised, but Goncharov waved his Makarov and the bewildered airman climbed in. Chebrikov followed him. Goncharov stood on the ground, leaning into the Hind. It took him a moment to find what he wanted. Spotting a coil of nylon rope in one corner, he gestured to it. To the pilot he said, "Tie up Comrade Chebrikov. Do it well. Both of your lives depend on it."

The pilot grabbed the rope and tied up the little KGB man. Then he leaned Chebrikov against the wall, but he couldn't bend his legs enough for the Russian to sit.

"Put him on the floor. Carefully." When the pilot was finished, Goncharov pointed at the cockpit. "Get in and start the engines."

"Where are we going?"

"Where do you think?"

Chebrikov laughed. "You're out of your mind, Maxim. Viktor will never let you get away with this."

"It's not up to Sharkov, Vasily. It's up to me."

"We'll see about that."

"No more talking, Vasily. I don't want to have to gag you, but I will unless you keep quiet."

"Quiet won't change the facts, Maxim."

"You wouldn't know a fact if it bit you on the ankle, Vasily." Goncharov grabbed a dirty rag from the floor and wrapped it around Chebrikov's mouth. "I warned you."

Chebrikov mumbled something that sounded vaguely like a threat, but the words were unintelligible. The Hind started to shudder as the pilot kicked the engines over. The floor of the cabin vibrated, and the noise of the engine settled into a steady growl.

"Where to?" the pilot shouted.

"Back to your hangar, Lieutenant. And do as I say if you want to live through this."

"Yes, sir."

The pilot opened the throttle, and the engine started to whine. The big chopper trembled for a few seconds, then lifted straight off the ground. As they climbed, Goncharov looked at the ground falling away beneath him.

It was a long way to fall.

Goncharov slipped on the headset and raised the pilot. "I want you to tell me everything you can about the hangar. I already know something, but I want to know it all."

"Yes, sir," the pilot responded.

Goncharov was lying. He didn't know the first thing about the hangar, but as long as the pilot wasn't sure, Goncharov was banking on being told the truth. He'd spent several years in and around Kabul, and he knew his way around the city and the surrounding country. But this particular installation might not have been there during his tours. Even if it was, things were certain to have changed.

As soon as the pilot started talking, he recognized the base. It was small, once used by the Spetznaz troops during the height of the war against the mujahadeen. He'd been attached to the base on his first tour. Now it looked deserted.

According to the pilot, it housed one chopper squadron, consisting of four modified Hinds like the one he sat in, hybrid units that could transport a small squad of shock troops and still function as full-fledged assault choppers. Also at the base were a few commandos and their officers.

The Spetznaz, of course, were long gone. But it was still going to be rough. And despite his threat to Chebrikov, he needed the little man to guide him to Sharkov's headquarters. He knew he could find the colonel, given enough time, but that was a luxury he didn't have. And he was determined to get to Sharkov before Belasko did.

Goncharov walked over to kneel beside Chebrikov. He had to shout to make himself understood. "I'm going to take the gag off now."

Chebrikov coughed when the rag was loosened, then turned his face away to throw up. A foul smell filled the cabin for a few moments, then was ripped away by the wind coming through the open door.

"Listen to me, Vasily," Goncharov said. "When we land, I don't want any trouble from you. You're going to take me to Sharkov, or I'm going to shoot

you in the head. Whatever else happens, I *will* do
that. Clear enough?''

Chebrikov nodded. "I don't care anymore. I'll
do whatever you want."

"Good. For your sake, I hope so."

CHAPTER THIRTY-EIGHT

Using Chebrikov, Goncharov had had no trouble getting the chopper refueled at the old Spetznaz base so that they could fly over to Sharkov's hideaway in the hills near Kabul. The chopper, with Chebrikov and the pilot safely tied up, was hidden in a nearby canyon.

Under cover of darkness, Goncharov had been casing Sharkov's hideaway for some time now and had discovered the room where the American was being held prisoner. Finding out that the Afghan was in league with the rogue KGB agent had dismayed Goncharov more than he'd have thought possible. After all, they had been partners, of a sort.

At the sound of approaching helicopters, Sharkov had bolted from the house and disappeared. Now was the time to spring Belasko, Goncharov thought. He was alone in the room with Hikmal, who had inexplicably released the American from his bonds.

Goncharov didn't know what that meant. The Afghan kept switching sides so much it made him dizzy. Still, if Hikmal made the slightest hostile move, he'd have to be taken out. Period.

Bracing himself, the KGB man crashed through the open window, rolled and came up brandishing his AK-74. With lightning-fast reflexes, he tossed Bolan a second assault rifle. Always combat ready, the warrior caught the weapon on the fly and swung it in the direction of Hikmal. The Afghan looked as if he were welded to the floor, his hand wavering over the pistol stuck in his belt.

"What took you so long?" Bolan asked. Then he charged through the doorway into the next room. It was still empty. Holding up a hand, he stopped Goncharov from rushing out into the open. "Wait, those choppers belong to Rucker. He's the guy Sharkov's been waiting for."

Goncharov shook his head. "Not Rucker."

Bolan raised his eyebrows. "What?"

"Rucker's on our side," the Russian said. "He has been all along. He and my superior, Peter Grebnov, have been coordinating this thing together from the start."

"Then who is Sharkov waiting for? I know it's someone in the CIA."

"Your guess is as good as mine. But we've got more important things to worry about now. Like finding Sharkov." The Russian turned to look at Hikmal, who was still frozen in place. "What about him? What's his story?"

Bolan frowned at the Afghan. "Seems Arbak is a mite indecisive, but I think he's beginning to come around. He was about to let me go."

"Maybe I can convince him," Goncharov said. He turned to the Afghan. "You know our ploy to smoke out Sharkov with the radio beacon? Well, it didn't work. But I did catch a snake—Chebrikov, Sharkov's flunky. Seems Sharkov ordered him to wipe you out, Hikmal. Only you weren't where he thought you'd be."

The Afghan frowned, then finally spoke. "I won't interfere with your mission anymore."

"But you won't join us, either," Goncharov said. "Is that it? Well, in that case give me your pistol. You might change your mind again."

Hikmal handed over his weapon.

"Armageddon time," Bolan said, putting his AK on full-auto.

"Let's hit the barn on the other side of the field first," Goncharov suggested. "Sharkov's got at least eight men in there. And we'd better take them out before those choppers land with reinforcements."

"Let's go."

They moved into the field, which they scanned for any sign of Sharkov, but the man was nowhere to be seen. Lights went on in the barn, and Bolan spotted a handful of figures spilling out of the back of the building. Then the lights went out again, and the warrior could barely discern several more figures moving in a group out of the barn.

"How many?" Goncharov asked.

"Ten or twelve at least," Bolan replied.

The choppers were getting closer, and he turned to see a spear of light dart out of the lead helicopter, dance uncertainly across the hillside beyond the house, then wink out.

"Come on."

Bolan got to his feet and broke into a sprint. He heard Goncharov's footsteps pounding along behind him. They hit the wall of the barn almost simultaneously. Using hand signals, he told Goncharov to move along the building and check the right-hand corner while he took the left.

As soon as the Russian nodded, Bolan took off. He sprinted the length of the barn, halting just before the left-hand corner. He pressed his back against the wall, the AK held at chest level, and watched as Goncharov reached the opposite corner. He saw the Russian drop to his knees and lean forward to peer around the edge of the building.

Nothing happened.

Goncharov turned and waved a hand high over his head. It was Bolan's turn.

Leaning forward, the Executioner listened intently for several seconds. He heard nothing. Leaning a little closer to the splintered corner, he pressed his cheek against the rough boards, peeking out just enough to sight along the flat end of the building. A pair of tall doors yawned open, and dim light spilled out onto the dry ground, highlighting patches of strawlike grass. It was perfectly still. He waved for Goncharov to join him, then ducked back to wait.

The Russian moved quickly down the length of the building. He looked quizzically at Bolan, who shrugged his shoulders. "Nothing," he whispered.

"Where did they go?"

"That's not what worries me as much as why."

The first chopper was hovering over the ground at the edge of the house now, wobbling a little, as if the pilot were unfamiliar with the terrain, the machine or both. Bolan watched as it descended to the ground. Two men got out and ducked under the rotors. The engine died, and the rotors slowly spun to a standstill.

"I don't understand what's happening," Goncharov said. "What spooked Sharkov?"

"I told you," Bolan whispered. "He was waiting for his American contact. But I don't think he expected two helicopters. Probably one, maybe just a jeep. He's ready to go over the edge, anyway, and the two choppers may have given him the push he needed. It wouldn't have taken much."

"But we're so close. We can't let him get away, not when we've come so far."

"Don't worry," Bolan said. "He's not going anywhere."

As he spoke, the second chopper dropped out of sight behind the house. He could still hear the engine and the thump of the rotor. This one was ready to lift off at a moment's notice.

"Let's go welcome the new arrivals," Bolan suggested.

"You go. I'll stay here and see what I can find."

The Executioner nodded and started across the field. He kept low and zigzagged. Not knowing where Sharkov's men had gone made him uneasy. He was halfway across when the chopper blew. There was a bright flash of orange, a tremendous boom, like thunder, and then a huge fist slammed him in the chest and knocked him down as the concussion wave roared past.

He scrambled to his feet. The two men from the chopper were outlined in the brilliant light from the burning aircraft. Bolan saw them in the doorway to the house. He sprinted toward them, giving the ruined chopper a wide berth in case any of its munitions blew.

As he approached the porch, he recognized Tim Rucker. The other man looked familiar. He knew he'd seen him somewhere before but couldn't place him. Then the chubby man turned sideways and he recognized Charles Royce.

Rucker saw him and waved, then moved to the edge of the porch, dragging Royce by the arm. Rucker stepped down and Bolan waved, shouting for him to get inside. The CIA man froze, then, when the warrior's words sank in, he hauled Royce backward and jerked him through the doorway. Through the door, outlined by the lights inside the house, he saw Hikmal standing motionless.

Bolan sprinted for the porch. A burst of gunfire behind him jerked his head around, and he dived for the ground as bullets whizzed past. He crawled the rest of the way to the porch and scrambled up the steps and through the doorway.

Another burst ripped at the door frame as he tumbled through, scattering hunks of wood in every direction. "Get the lights!" he barked.

The command seemed to galvanize Hikmal. He reached for the wall switch, swept his palm across it and plunged the house into darkness. Bolan could hear the steady throb of the chopper behind the house, and beneath it another rumble. He figured someone had blown the gasoline generator that provided power to the house, and maybe to the barn, as well.

With the lights out he was able to crawl closer to the doorway. Peering out into the night, he covered the field from edge to edge. There was no sign of Goncharov. Or Sharkov.

Rucker dropped to the floor and crawled alongside him. "I guess you're surprised to see me."

Bolan grunted. "Nothing surprises me anymore."

"What are we up against?"

"I'm not sure. Goncharov's out there somewhere. So's Sharkov."

"We have another chopper. I can have the barn taken out."

"No!" Bolan snapped. "Not until I'm sure Goncharov is clear." He heard fumbling in the dark, then a thud. "What was that? Hikmal, you there?"

"I'm here."

"Royce?"

No answer.

This time Bolan yelled louder. "Royce?"

Still no answer.

"Find him," Bolan ordered.

As if in response, a machine gun opened up from the slope beyond the barn. It was a good five hundred yards, and accuracy was minimal, but the slugs ripped through the flimsy walls of the house, and Bolan flattened himself on the floor.

"Jeez, that was close," Rucker said. Bolan noticed that his voice was steady. Apparently Rucker had been under the gun before.

"You all right?" Bolan asked.

"Yeah."

"What's Royce doing here?"

"He's our bad guy. Something I should have figured out a long time ago. He used to have my job, you know."

"So I've heard."

"Damn fool tried to take out Mahoney all by himself in Islamabad."

"Brian okay?" Bolan asked, a worried look on his face.

"Yeah, sure. He even gift-wrapped Royce for us. The kid wanted to come with me, but he's still pretty weak from that wound. I made him stay home."

"Thanks, Rucker."

"Don't mention it." He grinned. "Anyway, ol' Charlie's been singing up a storm. Appears Tony Salvato, Mahoney's partner, was on the take. Mahoney was the one who was supposed to get whacked in the desert back in the States. Guess they didn't figure on you, Belasko."

Bolan got to his feet.

"What the hell are you going to do?" Rucker rasped.

"Go find Sharkov. You take Hikmal and find Royce."

Bolan dashed out the door and dived off the porch, avoiding a burst of lethal lead. He had a rough fix on the machine gun and worked his way into some sparse woods and toward the distant hill.

Before he was halfway there an engine turned over, then a second and a third. Headlights exploded past the trees and three jeeps, each carrying four men, burst into the open. The vehicles lurched over some rough ground, then started toward the house.

Bolan ripped an arc across their path. Taken by surprise, the lead driver swerved, and the Executioner took out two tires with a second burst. Sprinting through the trees, he came up broadside, fired again and nodded with satisfaction when the fuel tank blew, sending pieces of the jeep and its occupants cartwheeling ahead of the ballooning fireball.

The remaining pair split, passed the wreckage on either side and continued on toward the house. Someone inside the house opened up, and Bolan saw the windshield of one jeep go as two men jumped out. The driver slumped over the wheel and the jeep continued toward the house, where it slammed into the porch. The driver and the man in the front seat tumbled over the shattered hood and sprawled motionless on the porch.

The third jeep skidded into a wild curve and roared back toward the barn. As it rushed past the far corner, someone, probably Goncharov, opened fire. The jeep swerved, its front wheels locked, and it fell over onto its side. A second burst from the corner of the barn finished it. Then its fuel tank ignited, sending a long tongue of flame licking toward the barn.

Bolan saw the gunman sprint along the edge of the building, then duck around the corner and into the shadows. Meanwhile, the machine gun on the hill poured a hail of lead and tracers into the house. This time no one returned fire.

Bolan wondered if Rucker and Hikmal had bought it.

CHAPTER THIRTY-NINE

Bolan sprinted for the barn. Goncharov saw him coming and raced along the wall, a shadow against the gray wood, and met him at the corner of the building.

"No luck," the Russian said. "You?"

"Nothing."

"What about that machine gun?"

Before he could answer, a tremendous roar thundered across the open field. He looked toward the house, half expecting to see it blown to pieces. Instead, he saw the chopper hovering like a deadly wasp just over the roofline. As he watched, a bright flash, then another, winked from the undercarriage of the aircraft. Even before Bolan realized what was happening he heard the blast behind him. He snapped his head around in time to see the second rocket slam into the hillside beyond the barn. A bright greenish-yellow ball seemed to expand, then roll up and over the crest of the hill.

The machine gun was no longer a problem.

"Into the barn!" Bolan shouted. He dashed for the door without waiting to see if Goncharov followed him. Once inside he groped for obstacles with one hand, sweeping the AK-74 in front of him with the other. Something caught his eye near the far wall. It looked almost like a window, but it lay on the floor. He moved toward it cautiously.

Bolan scraped his shin on something, stopped and bent down to feel with one hand. It was the steel frame of a cot. The barn must have been used as a barracks of some sort. Using his right foot now, he stepped tentatively, moving forward only when his shin no longer felt the pressure of the metal bar against it.

He found an aisle and stepped carefully between rows of cots, always keeping one eye on the strange light. When he was no more than twenty feet away, he realized it was a trapdoor of some kind set in the floor of the barn. Whoever had used it had left it open. The light was coming up from below. For the first time he noticed the pale rectangle among the rafters.

"This way," he whispered, waiting for an acknowledgment from Goncharov. When he got it, he moved more quickly toward the hole in the floor. He could see the outline of a hatch cover, tilted back against the barn wall. Peering over the lip of the hatch, he saw a wooden ladder made of two-by-fours nailed into a pair of two-by-eights. It ran down as far as he could see. Dropping onto his stomach, he peered into the shaft. A burst of gunfire chipped the edge of the hatch away, several slugs slamming into the roof over his head.

"Where does it lead?" Goncharov asked.

"I don't know. I can't even see the bottom, but I'll bet it leads back to the house. I wish I had some tear gas."

"Get back," the Russian whispered.

Bolan heard a click, then Goncharov flipped something over his head. As it arced past, the warrior realized it was a grenade. The device landed with a thud. Someone far below shouted, then the grenade went off with a dull crump. For a second it looked as if the shaft had caught fire, then the glow was suddenly gone.

The Executioner groped on the floor for something he could use to draw fire, found a board and set it against the edge of the hatch. He counted to three, then shoved it back and forth.

Nothing happened. He tried again and still failed to draw a single shot.

"Let's go," he whispered.

"I'll go first," Goncharov said.

"Wait a minute. You can't—"

"Sharkov is a product of my system. We made him and we should unmake him. You want him out of the way, don't you?"

"Yes."

"Then what difference does it make how?"

"None, I guess."

"Cover me, then."

Before Bolan could answer, Goncharov scrambled to the edge of the hatch and started down. The Executioner kept watch over the Russian's broad shoulders. If anyone below had a notion to check the shaft again, assuming anyone had survived the grenade, Goncharov was in big trouble.

The Russian was halfway down when something stirred below him. He flattened against the ladder, and Bolan saw the movement. He cut loose, holding the AK in one hand.

Someone below groaned, then plunged to the bottom of the shaft. Goncharov looked up, made a circle with thumb and index finger, then dropped another few rungs.

Bolan held his breath as he watched the Russian push off and drop several feet to the ground. He landed on the dead man at the bottom, nearly fell, and staggered back against the wall. He never took his eyes off the opening. When he regained his balance, he glanced up, waved once, then moved aside, waiting for Bolan to descend.

Twenty feet down the ladder the warrior realized why the Russian had jumped. The grenade had sheared off the last several feet of the wooden ladder, leaving splintered ends, rungless and dangling in space nearly twelve feet off the floor of the tunnel. Bolan let go, landed heavily on damp earth and looked at Goncharov.

The Russian shrugged. "Nothing."

Bolan nodded, then ducked into the opening and advanced ten yards when the light went out. Plunged into total darkness, the warrior came to a sudden halt. Goncharov nearly slammed into him and stumbled when he sidestepped to avoid the collision. Gunfire exploded far ahead of them.

Goncharov had a flashlight but didn't want to use it. There was no point in providing a target. Slowly they moved forward a few feet at a time. The gunfire died away after a second sharp burst. Bolan listened for footsteps, voices, anything at all to tell him he was getting close. But there was nothing.

Feeling along the wall with his left hand, the Executioner scraped his fingertips over the damp earth. Every few feet a thick wooden beam shot up, its surface wet with seepage. The musty smell of the tunnel was unrelieved by any draft.

The barn was three or four hundred yards from the house. So far they had gone about a quarter of the distance. Working on the assumption that the tunnel led straight to the house explained where Royce had gone. But where was he now?

And where was Sharkov?

A sudden flicker momentarily filled the tunnel with dim light. Bolan sprinted ahead, taking advantage of the illumination. He advanced fifty or sixty yards, then had to stop again as the light disappeared.

More gunshots sounded, this time isolated single shots and two or three short bursts. Then someone shouted.

Footsteps pounded toward Bolan, and he pressed back against the wall. Goncharov hit the wall beside him. The footsteps stopped as someone, probably the runner, fired what had to be a full magazine. Bolan heard the click of an empty clip being removed, then a second noise as a full one was rammed home.

The runner came toward them, this time haltingly, while up ahead the round beam of a flashlight played on the wall. There was a side tunnel. The runner turned the corner, and the light stabbed down the tunnel toward them. Bolan hit the deck a second before another burst, this one aimed their way, flashed toward them.

The slugs slapped into the wet earth, and Bolan heard a groan. "Maxim, you hit?"

"Nothing much. Just a graze."

"You sure?"

"I'm sure."

"You wait here."

"No, I'm coming."

Again the runner fired, this time hitting nothing as the bullets whistled down the tunnel. Bolan was reluctant to shoot, not knowing who the gunman was. He flattened himself against the dampness and held his fire. The light played back and forth, its beam sometimes a smeared expanse on the wall, sometimes a tube of light boring through the darkness without finding any place to land.

Then it flashed past the Executioner, stopped and came back. The gunman fired a short burst that narrowly missed Bolan. The warrior fired back. He had no choice.

The light fell, then went out. The gun stopped firing. Bolan heard a thud and scrambled to his feet. Goncharov clicked on the flashlight and found the gunman lying on his side, his weapon a few inches from his outstretched hand.

Bolan knelt for a second, turned the man over and sighed.

It wasn't Hikmal.

Or Rucker.

But it wasn't Royce or Sharkov, either. One more nameless soldier had bought the farm.

The Executioner used the light and raced to the right angle in the tunnel, Goncharov limping along behind him. There was another ladder ahead. At the intersection Bolan stopped, shone the light back on the Russian and noticed the blood-soaked fatigue pants. It was a thigh wound, not a scratch.

He clicked the light off as Goncharov caught up with him. "Maybe you better stay off that leg, Maxim."

"It hurts, but I can make it. You can't go ahead by yourself."

"I've done it before."

"Not this time," the Russian vowed.

CHAPTER FORTY

Bolan went up the ladder first. The block of light high on the wall was so faint that he didn't see it at first. As he got closer, it seemed to brighten. He heard Goncharov on the ladder behind him, but the Russian's leg was bothering him, and he was having trouble with the wide spacing of the wooden rungs.

The Executioner heard voices, but they were muffled, and he couldn't recognize any of them. And from somewhere high above he heard a steady throbbing. He could feel it through the rough wood as his fingers grabbed one rung after another. Then it hit him.

It was the chopper. Its powerful engine was pulsing as it idled. They were near the hill, maybe even under it, somewhere past the house. The voices grew louder, and he stopped about ten feet below the opening.

Rucker.

And Sharkov!

The Russian rogue agent was talking. "You think," he said, "that I care what happens? I'm a businessman now. All I care about are profits. My profits. Spy games bore me. I'm a businessman, plain and simple."

"Not in my book," Rucker said.

"There's no difference between my business and that of any of your corporations."

"Your business kills people, Sharkov. That's the difference."

"You remember Bhopal? Three Mile Island? What's the difference? I don't see it."

"You're grasping at straws. You're trying to justify murder, and it won't wash."

"It always washes, Rucker. You, of all people, should know that. Your career was just like mine once. People died. We had our reasons and they were good enough. Now I have a new reason—money. That's the only thing that's changed—the reason."

Bolan hung suspended in space, listening, trying to get an idea where Sharkov was. His voice was louder than Rucker's. He might be facing the opening, or he might be closer.

Goncharov caught up to him and tapped Bolan's leg to let him know he was there. The warrior looked down just as a tremendous tremor shook the ground. The lights flickered for a second and the shaft went dark. In the sudden blackness the light above seemed much brighter.

Bolan moved carefully, one rung, then a second. The men had stopped talking, and he wondered whether they were still there. At the next rung someone coughed. At least one of them was still in the chamber above.

He could see its roof now, just a sliver of rough boards. At the next rung he saw a wooden beam. The rude chamber had been carved out of the ground, and timbers had been used to support the weight of the earth above it. He wasn't quite sure where he was, so he couldn't guess how far below ground level the room was. Not too far, though, he thought, because the chopper's engine was clearly discernible. He wondered whether the tunnel connected to the house, or if there was another way out.

Then a pistol was cocked.

"I suppose you think killing me solves your problem," Rucker said.

"It's a start. Royce will have to go, too, of course. He's a liability now. But he's not the only monkey in the jungle. I can find another, and he can find another Salvato for me. That's the amazing thing about capitalism. If you have enough money, you can always get your work done. Belief doesn't enter into it. I like that."

Bolan made his move. He took the last two rungs and vaulted into the chamber, rolling over on the hard ground. Sharkov heard the noise and turned, taking his eye off Rucker for a second and letting the muzzle of his pistol wander.

Finding himself staring into the barrel of Bolan's AK, the Russian didn't blink. The pistol went off as the warrior scrambled away. The AK slipped from his grasp, and he saw it heading for the shaft. He reached out, but his momentum carried him past and the gun went over and down. Sharkov fired again as the rifle clattered into the shaft and hit bottom with a thud. The bullet passed harmlessly overhead. Bolan had nowhere to go.

"Well, well," Sharkov said. "Mr. Belasko, how nice of you to join us."

Bolan got to his knees. He resisted the temptation to glance at the shaft opening. If Sharkov didn't know there was someone else down there, so much the better. To take Sharkov's mind off the possibility, the warrior stood and took a step or two toward him.

"Not too close, Belasko."

"Give it up, Sharkov. You can't win."

"I haven't lost yet."

"Your cover's been blown sky-high. Your friend Royce is blown. Salvato and Chebrikov are gone. Your men are all dead."

"Not all of them," another voice said.

Bolan turned just in time to see Hikmal stumble through a doorway at the far end of the chamber. Behind him stood Charles Royce. He had an Uzi pressed against the Afghan's spine.

"Well, that seems to complete our little gathering, doesn't it?" Sharkov said. The Russian started to edge toward the shaft, letting his gaze wander. If he saw Goncharov on the ladder, their last hope would go down in flames.

Bolan tried to distract him. "Sharkov, don't you think Rucker delivered the intel on your operation to the right people? And then there's Mahoney."

"It hardly matters," Sharkov replied, halting. He seemed amused. "I made my living by staying out of sight. I know how to use people, how to cover my tracks. Nothing Rucker's done or Mahoney can do is of the slightest concern to me." He started toward the shaft again, smiling a little. "You don't seem to want me to look down there," he said, nodding toward the shaft. "I wonder why?"

Hikmal made the first move, falling backward and slamming into Royce just above the knees. The fat little man fell backward, inadvertently squeezing the trigger for a second. The explosion of the machine pistol stopped as suddenly as it had begun, and the Uzi spun away, slammed into the wall and dropped to the ground.

Bolan reached out and wrestled Sharkov's wavering pistol out of his hand. He fired the weapon once, narrowly missing Sharkov as Goncharov flew up the ladder. Sharkov pulled another gun and fired at his charging countryman. Goncharov dropped below the edge of the hatch, while Royce crawled on his hands and knees, trying to get to the Uzi. Hikmal, tangled in Royce's stubby limbs, got there first. But Sharkov saw him and fired again, momentarily freezing the Afghan.

Each gunshot exploded in the confined space like a small bomb. Bolan's ears were ringing as he swung his captured Makarov toward Sharkov. Royce got his hands on the Uzi and cracked it against Hikmal's skull. The Afghan groaned, and Royce shot him in the back.

Rucker hurled himself onto his roly-poly colleague, struggling for control of the machine pistol. It burped once, then again, and the 9 mm slugs ripped through the boards overhead.

Bolan charged toward Sharkov, who backed away, trying to bring his gun to bear. The warrior hit him with a shoulder, and the Russian went over backward, slamming into the wall just beside the hatch.

His gun skittered away and landed with its barrel out over the edge of the shaft. Sharkov scrambled for it but fingers closed over the barrel from below, and the rogue agent cursed as the gun slipped into the shaft.

Bolan grabbed Sharkov by the ankles. He wanted him alive if possible. But something hit him high on the right shoulder. He dropped the Makarov as another wild burst from the Uzi ripped past him, chewing one of the beams into a thousand splinters. A slug slammed into his shoulder.

He lashed out with one foot as Sharkov grabbed for the Makarov, just out of Bolan's reach. The Executioner's shoulder hurt like hell, but he ignored the pain and kicked again, this time catching Sharkov in the ribs.

Getting to his knees, the warrior threw himself at the Russian, who was also trying to stand. Goncharov was in the hatchway now, starting to climb into the chamber, but another stray burst from the Uzi punched him down the shaft. Bolan, for a split second, saw the surprised look in the Russian's eyes as three dark holes appeared in his chest, splattering his jacket with blood.

Grabbing Sharkov by the legs, Bolan hauled him down and closed his fingers over the Makarov. The gun went off, the bullet narrowly missing the warrior's head. Sharkov pounded on Bolan's wounded shoulder with a fist, which almost caused him to lose consciousness for a second. Sharkov got free.

The Executioner snatched up the Makarov and fired once, then again. He saw the second slug hit Sharkov in the temple, spewing gore all over the dirt wall behind him. The Russian's eyes rolled, then went glassy as he staggered and fell, his arms and legs twitching spasmodically for a moment.

Bolan turned toward Rucker, who was straddling Royce and was squeezing the fat little man's throat. "That's enough, Rucker. We need him."

The CIA man froze for an instant, then looked at Bolan. His eyes were wild, and a strand of saliva dangled from his lower lip. "The bastard..." He staggered to his feet and backed away from the unconscious Royce, whose lips had turned purple.

"Go see about Goncharov," Bolan said.

Rucker nodded and walked toward the shaft entrance.

Bolan knelt beside Hikmal. The Afghan was still conscious, but he was bleeding heavily. His breath whistled through the holes in his chest where the bullets had passed clean through. Blood bubbled around the fingers he pressed against his wounds.

The Afghan grinned weakly. "Too many sides, eh, my friend?"

Bolan nodded. "But you chose the right one in the end."

Hikmal couldn't hear him anymore, though. The warrior sat back on his heels and stared at the ceiling until he heard the scrape of Rucker's feet on the ladder. "How's Goncharov?" he asked when the CIA man's face bobbed into view.

Rucker shook his head. "Come on, Belasko, let's go. We're finished here."

Bolan looked at Hikmal's body once more. "Yeah, you could say that."

Raw determination in
a stillborn land...

JAMES AXLER
DEATH LANDS
Seedling

As Ryan Cawdor and his roaming band of survivors desperately seek to escape their nuclear hell, they emerge from a gateway into the ruins of Manhattan.

Under this urban wasteland lives the King of the Underground, presiding over his subterranean fortress filled with pre-nuke memorabilia. And here, in this once-great metropolis, lives Ryan Cawdor's son....

The children shall inherit the earth.

On the savage frontier of tomorrow,
survival is a brand-new game.

SURVIVAL 2000

FROZEN FIRE
James McPhee

David Rand faces his final test—in the third book of Gold Eagle's
SURVIVAL 2000 series.

In the cruel new world created by the devastation of asteroid impacts,
Rand's family is held captive by a murderous gang of army deserters.

With a fortress established in a crumbling mall, the enemy will always
hold the high ground unless Rand can pass the test in a world where
winners die hard . . . and losers live to tell the tale.